THE OCEAN IN THE CLOSET

The Ocean in the Closet

A NOVEL

YUKO TANIGUCHI

COFFEE HOUSE PRESS
MINNEAPOLIS
2007

COFFEE HOUSE PRESS books are available to the trade through our primary distributor, Consortium Book Sales & Distribution, 1045 Westgate Drive, Saint Paul, MN 55114. For personal orders, catalogs, or other information, write to: Coffee House Press, 27 North Fourth Street, Suite 400, Minneapolis, MN 55401.

Coffee House Press is a nonprofit literary publishing house. Support from private foundations, corporate giving programs, government programs, and generous individuals helps make the publication of our books possible. We gratefully acknowledge their support in detail in the back of this book.

To you and our many readers around the world, we send our thanks for your continuing support.

LIBRARY OF CONGRESS CIP INFORMATION
Library of Congress Cataloging-in-Publication Data

Taniguchi, Yuko, 1975–
The ocean in the closet : a novel / by Yuko Taniguchi.
p. cm.
ISBN-13: 978-1-56689-194-3 (alk. paper)
ISBN-10: 1-56689-194-9 (alk. paper)
I. Title.

PS3620.A685O34 2007
813'.6--dc22

FIRST EDITION | FIRST PRINTING
1 3 5 7 9 8 6 4 2
PRINTED IN CANADA

For my mother and father

AUTHOR'S NOTE

The Ocean in the Closet is a work of fiction based on the real stories of the children born between Japanese women and foreign soldiers in Japan post–World War II. While the novel explores the reality of these children's struggle during the occupational period in Japan and later on in the United States through international adoptions, all the characters and events are fictional. When one moves to a foreign land, even if he or she may be successful and happy there, living away from home is heartbreaking. This novel was inspired by those who have crossed the ocean and established new lives while they carried the old memories close to their hearts and touched the native land in their dreams.

TREE SONG

After TreeSong by John Williams

Who crossed the ocean, carrying my seeds?
With such a force,
as if I were lonely,
I have coiled my roots .
into the earth and grown
layer after layer.
Follow my circles inside—
first and always, birds have
found me; rain and night
have filled me in darkness all
the way to the core,
which is a small ocean, my oldest
memory that comes and goes
like the waves.

AIRMAIL

Among all the brown envelopes of bills and business letters, the airmail envelope with red and blue edges stands out inside the dark mailbox. Eight American stamps cover half the envelope, and large capital letters list my address in one long line as if the sender had copied my address one letter at a time. The returning address is Helen Johnson in Tiburon, California. My heart beats faster, and the sound of busy traffic disappears from my mind. I carefully open the envelope and pull out the thin white paper.

November 15, 1975
Dear Mr. Hideo Takagawa,
   Hello. My name is Helen Johnson. I am 9 years old. I go to St. Mary's Catholic school. My little brother's name is Ken Johnson. He is 6 years old. He goes to my school, too. I think you are my mom's uncle. My mom's name is Anna Johnson. Do you remember her? Mom is sick. She breaks and gets nervous all the time. I want to help Mom. I want to visit you in Japan. Uncle Steve will take me to your house. Please tell him that I can come and visit you. His name is Steve Johnson.
   Love,
   Helen

Even after reading each sentence several times, I don't fully comprehend the letter. Anna. How strange to think of her as a grown woman, with a daughter named Helen. In my mind, she has remained a little girl all these years.

She breaks and gets nervous all the time. What does this mean? I sit down on the stairs against the front door. I feel the door vibrate from the deep sound of the double bass that Chiyo is practicing inside the house, going up and down the scales. The instrument's dark, heavy voice stirs me in a distracting way; I want all the movements around me to stop completely. Over and over I read Helen's letter, composed of many large capitals as if each letter were a picture of a snake. I get up slowly and walk into the house, and I don't tell Chiyo about the letter. My feet carry me to my office upstairs and I close the door.

I think you are my mom's uncle. Do you remember her? Remembering feels like touching the smoothness of scarred skin, and a queasy sensation grows in my stomach, but I could never forget Ume. I sit down to write back to Helen and Steve Johnson. My hands are shivering, but I hold the pen tightly and tell myself to write before this queasiness overtakes me; before I change my mind.

MAY 1975

Mom put us in the closet again. We used to get scared of its black air, until we came up with the idea to think about something fun, like a big big strawberry ice cream mountain in a bowl with whipped cream and chocolate sauce running down from the top. Then we weren't scared of the closet anymore, but it still felt like forever. The closet was busy with hangers, Dad's winter coats and baseball hats, gloves, bats, plastic containers, and Tupperware. My spot was right under Dad's coats because it had a little more space. Mom put ropes around the doorknobs so that the door wouldn't pop open. Sometimes, if I had to go to the bathroom, I kicked the door, but all I would get was the small light from a crack in the door. Mom sometimes forgot that we were in the closet, so we had to wait until Dad came home to let us out in the evening. He never came home soon enough though. At dinner, Dad was always so nice to Mom, holding her hand and telling us that we had to do what Mom said. His voice was so deep that I always thought it came from the bottom of the ocean.

I felt bad that Ken was in the closet with me this time. He didn't do anything, but Mom locked us both up. When she was upset, she wouldn't listen to anyone. Her body would shake hard like she was cold, and she just wanted us away from her. I didn't mean to upset her. I was just chewing the gum Lisa gave me after school. I knew I wasn't supposed to eat sweets. Mom said that sugar was poison, that it numbed our tongues to make us feel happy. That wasn't true happiness. Never, never eat sugar. It is dangerous. But everyone at school ate candy all the time, and I wanted to bring normal lunch food like a chocolate bar. Lisa said we were going to just chew the gum, not eat it. So I thought it was O.K. to put it in my mouth. The thin pink gum smelled like a strawberry. I chewed and swallowed the sweet juice. After spitting out the gum on the street, I swallowed the saliva again and again to get rid of the sweet taste in my mouth. But Mom knew about the gum when I came home. She has a dog's nose and uses it for everything. When she washed everyone's pajamas, she always made sure that no one's smell stayed on the wet cotton. But her pajamas smelled like her soft skin and spring air. I loved holding them. Dad's pajamas usually smelled like the green water he used every morning to make his hair sticky and glittering. Mine didn't smell like anything.

When I walked in the house, Mom pressed her nose on my head, face, and chest; she smelled my strawberry gum. I told her that I was just chewing it, not eating it.

"But it was in your mouth." Her nose moved again.

"I had to. Lisa gave it to me." I never lie to Mom because Mom said that a liar would drown in the ocean. Our house was up on the hill in San Francisco, so we could see the ocean from here. If I didn't live so close to the ocean, I'd eat chocolate every day and never tell Mom about it.

"You didn't get that gum from Lisa. You stole it from Polovick's store, didn't you?" Mom's face in mine.

"No, I didn't even go to the store today." I shook my head, but Mom had already grabbed her purse and said that she was going to take me to the store so that I could say sorry to Mr. Polovick for stealing the gum. All the way down to Polovick's, I told her that I didn't steal it, that she could even ask Lisa, but she wouldn't hear me. She walked fast, pulling me and Ken. Ken had been watching TV in the living room, but Mom made him come, too. I watched her pale neck turn pink all the way to the store.

The store was busy. I saw our neighbor Mrs. Hogan standing in the apple section. Mrs. Hogan liked collecting garbage like plastic spoons and plates to give to me and Ken. She said that throwing things away made her sad. I don't know why it made her sad. Mom said that Mrs. Hogan was a very nice lady, so we had to be nice to her, but I'd never seen her with any friends except for Mom. She always looked like she was about to start crying because of her narrow eyes. She always had a cigarette, and her breath smelled like smoke. Mom walked up to Mrs. Hogan and whispered that I stole candy.

"Oh, dear, you might get a stomachache tonight from eating too much candy." Mrs. Hogan came close to me and smiled. Her teeth were yellow. I thought brown air came out of her mouth. I put my hands on my nose and tried not to breathe.

"She lies to me. She keeps saying she didn't do it." Mom's voice was getting loud. I could see some people in the store staring at us.

"But I didn't do it." I glared at her face.

Mrs. Hogan patted my head. "You shouldn't upset your mother."

Mom pulled my hand until she found Mr. Polovick in the soap section, and she pushed me in front of him. He opened his eyes wide and stepped back from her.

"She stole a gum from your store this afternoon. We'll pay for it and she'll apologize to you." Mom glared at him like he did something bad. My chest was getting hot. I wanted to run away.

"I don't remember seeing your daughter in the store this afternoon. I always keep my eye on people. She wasn't here today." Mr. Polovick shrugged his shoulders, but Mom pushed me toward him.

"Go ahead, apologize to Mr. Polovick!"

"I didn't do it." My eyes were watery.

"Mrs. Johnson, your daughter wasn't here today." Mr. Polovick stood in front of Mom.

"But I know what you really think. You think my daughter would take something from your store. You're always watching us." Mom looked hard at him. His mouth opened, but he didn't say anything. I wanted to hide. Mom sometimes imagined that things happened. She went to a different world when she was mad, where she wouldn't listen to anyone and thought that everyone was watching her. People gave her funny looks because she was half Japanese, she said. But it was Mom who watched people. She was watching being watched, and even when some people just looked in her direction, she thought she was being watched.

Mr. Polovick knew I didn't steal the gum, but Mom put a nickel in his hand and walked us out of the store. On the way home, she was so mad that her hands shook. She said I didn't understand anything, that I had to be careful because people were watching us and sugar would make us do bad things and if I didn't listen to her, she couldn't protect us. But I didn't steal anything.

As soon as we got home, she said I was going into the closet. Mom pushed me into my usual spot, then pushed Ken on top of me and closed the door. She tied the doorknobs with a rope. Ken cried. I wanted to cry, too. I tried thinking about ice cream with chocolate sauce, but I was too angry. Ken and I kicked the door and called for Mom.

"Don't!" She pushed the door back.

"I'm not scared to be in the closet anymore!" I shouted as hard as I could.

"Just wait until you meet Shizuka." Mom pushed back the doors again.

"Shizuka?"

"The ghost of Shizuka lives in the closet." Mom was putting the second rope around the doorknobs. "She died hundreds of years ago in your grandma's hometown. Grandma always said the ghost of Shizuka lives in the closet." Mom told me once how

Grandma was Japanese and her name was Ume, which meant plums. How strange to use a fruit for a girl's name! I wouldn't want a name like Apple or Melon. Ume is my middle name. Helen Ume Johnson. I never liked *Ume*. It sounds like choking. Mom said she didn't remember a lot about Grandma because she died when Mom was little. So how could she remember what Grandma said?

"Shizuka took her own life when her husband died in battle." I could feel Mom standing right behind the door, but her voice seemed far away.

"Why?"

"It was disgraceful to live alone without a husband. She was a soldier's wife. She jumped in the ocean and drowned herself."

"But why is she in *this* closet?"

"Because the closet is very close to the ocean. Ghosts live behind the wall, and they want to pull us into their world," she said, then walked away.

Thinking that Shizuka would jump out from behind the wall and pull me back into her world, I was too scared to think about ice cream. Was the ocean really behind the wall? Though the black air was boiling hot in the closet, and my skin was sticky with sweat, I covered myself with an old blanket to protect myself from Shizuka.

"A ghost lives inside the walls?" Ken started to cry and kick the door again. He was only five.

"Stop it!" I yelled.

"Let me out!"

"The door won't open." I put the blanket on him.

"I don't want Shizuka to eat me!"

"Hide under the blanket."

Ken hugged me under the blanket. Our skin got sticky. Through a crack in the door, I could see Mom standing in front of the mirror, touching her face. She'd already forgotten about us in the closet. She stood there until Dad came home and let us out.

Lisa wanted me to stay overnight at her house, but Dad wouldn't let me. He asked where Lisa's family lived, and I said Mountain Point. Then his voice got sharp and asked if they were hippies. I didn't know what hippies were. Dad said they were lazy and mean. I told him that Lisa's family wasn't lazy or mean, but Dad still said no. Then he got up from the couch, went to the kitchen, poured a brown drink in a glass, and went upstairs to his office. Dad was the lazy one. Lisa's Dad always took her and her sisters to do fun things like go to drive-in movies. Dad never took us anywhere.

Dad worked a lot. He worked at a bank in a tall building in downtown San Francisco. He left home early and didn't come home until eight or nine at night. When he was home, he usually watched TV in his office, alone. Mom said Dad was a soldier in Vietnam, but I couldn't picture him as a soldier. Mr. Lehman across the street was a soldier in the Korean War. Once, he showed me and Ken his uniform and some pictures. He even let us touch the scar on his shoulder. But Dad didn't have any uniforms, pictures, or a scar. He never talked about Vietnam, except for last Wednesday. When Ken and I got home from school, Dad was already home. He was watching TV in the living room with Mom, and they both looked pale.

She took our hands, and as we sat between Mom and Dad, she put her arms around me. On TV, many people were shouting. Some men were climbing the fence, and there was a long line to the helicopter on the top of the gray square building.

"What's going on?" I asked.

"The war just ended," Dad said.

"Oh!" Ken jumped up. "We won! We won the battle!" He stood straight and started marching like a soldier. Mom pulled him back down.

"Where are they going?" I asked. Everyone near the helicopter looked scared.

"All those people have to get out of Saigon. They're coming home, to America." Dad got up and went to the kitchen. He came back with his brown drink and sat with us again. We watched one helicopter take off from the building, and another one arriving to pick up more people. It looked like the line ants made when they found a dead bug to carry the food back to their home. Out of the corner of my eye, I could see Dad's chest moving up and down. His forehead was shiny with sweat.

Since that day, Dad wouldn't come home until much later, around midnight. He said he had a lot of work to do in his office, but I knew that the bank was closed at night. Mom was always worried that he wouldn't come home at all, so we all had to stay up and wait for him. Ken and I watched TV and fell asleep on the couch. Mom would sit next to me and touch my face, hair, and neck. Her hands felt cold on my skin, but I liked that. I liked sleeping next to Mom. I could smell her flower soap. She liked to tell the story of how Dad came home from the war. It was always the same. When it was midnight, and Dad wasn't home yet, Mom would wake me up and start telling the story.

"Did I ever tell you how your Dad came home from the war?"

"Yes," I mumbled without opening my eyes.

"When James arrived at the base in San Francisco, the first thing he did was call me. I heard his voice, and he heard mine. I started to cry, and he said that hearing my voice made his heart melt. That's what he said."

"O.K." I was so sleepy.

"Before he was discharged, he had to go to the warehouse to pick up a new uniform, so he had something clean to wear home. He signed his name and got paid five hundred dollars in cash for the final month. But you wouldn't believe what he did next."

But I knew what Mom was going to say.

"James saw this guy with an old motorcycle on the street and bought it from him on the spot. Then he took off his uniform and threw it on the street. He put the rest of his cash in his boxers and rode in only his boxers and T-shirt! I couldn't believe it! But I was so happy. I prayed for his safe return every day he was gone."

I couldn't picture Dad riding a motorcycle in his underwear. But Mom said Dad has changed since he returned from the war. Usually before Mom finished telling this story, I would see bright lights coming up the driveway. Dad was home, so Ken and I could go to bed. I wanted Dad to come home earlier. I knew Mom was scared that he wouldn't come home one day. But he always did.

Soon, Dad started working weekends. Even on Sundays he got up early, put on his suit, and went to work. I didn't understand why he was going to his office when the bank was closed. Mrs. Hogan started to show up at our house every Sunday evening. She always brought grocery bags full of empty milk containers, plastic spoons, week-old newspapers, toilet paper rolls, and other crafty items.

"I brought these for Helen and Ken. They can make something with them." Mrs. Hogan's voice sounded like someone was rubbing dry leaves in my ear. She carried one bag at a time from her car into our house. Mom thanked her, nodding her head, but I wanted to tell Mrs. Hogan no thank you.

Ken and I had to stay in our rooms when Mrs. Hogan came over. She wanted to talk to Mom alone. But Ken whined about it, saying he wanted to watch TV in the living room. He could watch TV in Mom and Dad's bedroom upstairs, but I knew he was being stubborn because he didn't like Mrs. Hogan. He cried out and shouted I-want-to-stay-here! Mom took him upstairs. His cry bounced all over the house. My ears hurt. Then suddenly his loud voice got softer like a blanket had fallen on it. Then I knew he was in the closet. I went upstairs, passing Mom coming down. She didn't see me.

I hated being alone upstairs at night. The house seemed alive, making all kinds of noises. A clock ticking sounded like someone's heart beating. I could hear Ken's sobbing from the closet. I wanted to let Ken out before Shizuka came and ate him alive, but Mom put the rope around the doorknob too tight. I went in my room and started reading my favorite book, *The Little Princess*. I wanted to think about princesses instead of Shizuka, but no matter how hard I tried, I couldn't forget her. Mom said there were no princesses, no magic, no God, no spirits in this world, but ghosts were real because they were once humans. Then I was scared again. If I turned around, Shizuka's white face covered by wet black hair might be right next to my neck. Her face would smell like salt, like seaweed on a rock by the beach. I was too scared to see what was behind me. I slowly stood up without turning around and walked backwards until I hit the door to the hallway. I felt the knob with my right hand and opened the door. I could see more lights in the hallway, so I turned around and walked down the stairs halfway. I saw Mom and Mrs. Hogan sitting on the couch in the living room, but they didn't see me. Mom was talking and swaying her body to the right and left, like the wind was blowing her.

"What space, dear?" Mrs. Hogan asked.

"Do you remember when you met James for the first time before we got married? You said he was different from everyone. You said he had this space in his heart to be with someone like me safely. Do you remember?"

"Yes, I do." Mrs. Hogan nodded. I had no idea that Mom and Mrs. Hogan had been friends before Mom and Dad got married.

"I think that little space in his heart is all gone now. James doesn't want to be here anymore. He wants things to be simple. Being with me isn't simple."

Mrs. Hogan didn't say anything. She just touched Mom's head like she was a little girl.

"And my children . . . I get so nervous. I don't know what to do. I just don't know what to do alone." Mom stopped swaying and sat like a stone and gazed at the space between her body and the bottom of the stairs. Why did she get nervous when she was with us? I went back upstairs to Mom's room. I could hear Ken breathing inside the closet. I stood in front of the mirror the way Mom stared at her own reflection and looked at myself. I didn't look like Mom at all. I didn't look like anyone.

JUNE 1975

The summer in California is always blue. The next morning, Mom opened all the windows downstairs and had music playing. Her favorite song is the one that a woman sang in a high tone, *Come with me this summer, California is blue, Come with me to the beach, the ocean is blue.* Since summer break started, I could sleep in. But Mom's music was so loud that it woke me up. When I slowly opened my eyes, the bright blue jumped at me from the window. For a second, I thought I was outside. The window was so clear that I was half inside and half outside. But I knew it was closed. Mom always locked the windows in my room before she went to sleep, and she checked them at least three times. I walked to the window and saw the reflection of my face.

In the window, my face looked blue. My hair looked shorter, too. I put my hand on top of my head and let it slide down my hair. My hair was gone: not all of it, but half. I couldn't grab anything at my shoulder. I had long hair when I went to sleep. I turned my head, but I didn't see anything. I stepped back from the window a little. I touched my head everywhere. My face was hot. I ran to the bathroom.

In the mirror, my black hair came down to my cheeks. I ran downstairs to the kitchen, where Mom was washing a vase.

"My hair is gone! Look, my hair is gone!" I shook her from the back.

"It's all right, Helen." She didn't turn around.

"I'm not lying! My hair is gone! Look!" I pulled her shirt.

"It's fine. Stop." She turned around and touched my hair, and the right side of my face. "You're safe." She smiled.

"What do you mean?"

"You're safe. Shizuka came last night." Mom's hand was still on my cheek; her hand felt cold from the water. Her face was so close that I could see my face in her eyes. She kissed my forehead and both cheeks, then turned around and went back to washing the vase.

"Shizuka likes girls with long black hair. She came last night and tried to take you away, so I cut your hair. It's fine now. She left." Mom rinsed her vase with cold water. It splashed on my forehead.

"You cut my hair?" I looked at Mom's long dark hair.

"I had to. Shizuka was going to take you." Mom took a white cotton cloth and dried the vase. I kept staring at her hair.

I walked to the bathroom again. My hair was everywhere in the trash can under the sink. I looked like a boy. The pair of silver scissors was in a drawer, so I threw them away. I ran back to my room and closed the door. I stood in front of the window, listening to the woman's singing repeated over and over. The needle was stuck on the record. *California is blue, Come with me, California is blue, Come with me, California is blue, Come with me.* I put both of my hands on my ears until Mom stopped the record player and called my name.

MIRROR

I woke up overwhelmed again this morning. I haven't slept well since the letter from Helen Johnson arrived. Every midmorning when the mailman stops by, I hurry down to meet him. It has only been a week since I mailed my letter, but I keep thinking that Helen or her uncle will write back to me. I have been waking up early, and my first thought has been Helen's words: *Mom is sick. She breaks and gets nervous all the time.* I try not to let myself think about it, but the hardest time is the morning when Chiyo is still asleep next to me, and I'm lying in the dark cold room with my mind wide awake.

I make myself get up, walk to the bathroom, and wash my face with cold water. I stand in front of the mirror and study my face—the tired and timorous face with wrinkles carved into my skin like rivers. The old man in the mirror is me. After I turned fifty, gray appeared in my mustache and the front part of my hair, as if I had pushed my face into the snow. Dark pores cover my brown skin, which feels oily from sweating in the restless night.

With cold water, I roughly scrub my cheeks. I stare at my wet face in the mirror again until my dead father, mother, brother, and sister all appear behind my face, gazing back at me. I have my father's chin: strong bones, pointing down to the center of earth. He used to touch his chin as he read the newspaper every morning before breakfast. My father, Shinichirou Takagawa, was like his chin, powerful and strong enough to fulfill his obligation as the first son of the Takagawa family and

the family business of silk farming, which came with generations of pressure. Our family lived by the strict order and rules
of the Takagawa tradition, and we were expected to be present
at all meals, fully dressed and ready to bow at my father's
entrance. Father greeted us as he touched his chin with a sense
of pride, confidence, and sharpness, and looked at each of his
children intently. When Father's eyes moved and stopped right
in front of me, my stomach tightened. Meals were a burden to
me during my childhood.

I bring my hand over my chin and touch it the way my
father did, though mine looks out of place against round cheeks
and a flat and smooth forehead, which is my mother's. She
always carried a white handkerchief to wipe nervous sweat
from her forehead. My mother was named Tomiko, which
means "the child of prosperity," though she wasn't as fortunate
as her name. Father's younger sister, Aunt Fuyu, used to say
that the width of the forehead reflects one's wisdom, and she
didn't understand why my mother was unwise. But it's not that
my mother was unwise; she was just weak. Her main focus was
to survive—as long as she could without making mistakes, as
long as she could serve my father and his family the right
amount, not too much or too little. Every year, her forehead
would gain wrinkles, and she called them rivers. These rivers
carved into her skin, and someday, she said, her entire face
would be rivers; *water face* is what she called herself, but she
didn't live long enough for that.

Overall, I look like my mother, which would disappoint my
brother Shinya, who told me never to become like her. We
either sympathize with or despise a weak individual, and while
my sister Ume and I sympathized with Mother, Shinya reviled
her. Every day, once Father got up at five in the morning and
went to the work houses and silkworm rooms, Mother came
and woke us up with urgency, as if there were fire outside or
an earthquake coming. Ume and I obeyed her so as to comfort

and protect her from being crushed by anxiety, but not Shinya. His eyes beamed with confidence, glaring at Mother in disgust. He wanted to watch her become lost in anxiety. Occasionally, he didn't get up in the morning on purpose. While he pretended that he was in a deep sleep or too tired to get up from under the blanket, Mother begged him to get up. Soon, Father abhorred coming home for breakfast and seeing that Shinya wasn't present at the table. Father despised laziness, looseness, and broken laws. Like his shirt of straight stripes, he demanded everything to be in order, flat, and clean. Father grabbed Mother, slapped her face, and asked where Shinya was. She fearfully apologized for her failure to impose properness. Father stormed into Shinya's room. Shinya was up, dressed, and sitting by his desk. Father slapped Shinya's face and then state that those who could not follow the rules were worthless and that the first son must set a good example. Shinya simply replied that he was sorry and that this would never happen again. He didn't care if he was hit by Father, as long as Mother was also punished for her weakness. Shinya used to say that our fragile mother, living in fear of making mistakes around Father, was embarrassing. Secretly, I knew Shinya hated Mother for being afraid of him the same way she was afraid of Father. Shinya was expected to become like Father and accepted his destiny and responsibility as the first son of the Takagawa family. But he wanted something from our mother, not necessarily strength, but more like a willingness to open her eyes all the way when she looked at him.

If Shinya were alive, he would have torn apart and burned the letter from Helen. He could make a decision without having any doubts. He always knew how to maintain an acceptable environment, a talent I didn't share. I often felt as though I were left in the middle of a large field with strong winds blowing over me. And my dear sister, Ume, was also clumsy. She and I never learned to build a fence around ourselves, letting everything come to us. During our childhood, Ume was safe, protected by Mother, who kept Ume close and didn't allow her to work for the silk farm. If Ume wasn't with Mother, she was with me. Five years younger than I was, she followed me everywhere. In May, I had to work out in the mulberry field with the children of Father's employees, and Ume would beg to come along. I tried to reason with her, but she called my name all the way down the hill: *Hideo ni chan—Big brother Hideo, I want to go with you!* Once, when she was absolutely determined to come with me, I calmed her by promising that I would take her to the silkworm room later. That night after dinner, I secretly took her there. There were thousands of white silkworms on the wooden shelves in the room, and I ran around putting mulberry leaves in each section. The room was filled with the sound of silkworms biting the leaves. I told Ume that the silkworm farmers often said the sound of the silkworms eating was like the rushing of a mountain stream. But Ume shook her head and said it was more like the ocean. *The waves are in the room,* she exclaimed.

The waves are in the room, Ume said again when she was dying in my apartment after the war. Ume's health declined at the end of her pregnancy, and after a long labor in which she lost a lot of blood, she was unable to recover from pneumonia. When the rain hit the tin roof of my apartment, the whole room was covered with the sound. While she was dying, I wished that it would keep raining so that she could be embraced by the ocean waves and the memory of the silkworm farm, our large house up on the hill, surrounded by gardens and a pond, in Kusazu, on the outskirts of Hiroshima. If we went all the way up the hill, we could see the ocean. In between the coughs and heavy breathing of her last week, she could also hear cars passing, people talking, children running, trees swaying, windows shaking. Amazed how much sound humans make in order to live, *The earth never goes to sleep,* she said. Two days before she died, all she could hear was her own rough breathing. She had difficulty inhaling; the doctor stayed for a few hours on the final night as he checked her white tongue, gave her a shot, and told me that the end was near. Her lungs were filled with fluid, though the medication he injected should make her feel a little more comfortable. But her breathing sounded like suffering to me.

Ume died on my futon on the cold morning of December 27, 1947. The landlady brought clean towels and offered to wash her body. After she was washed and dressed in a white kimono, the landlady told me to stay nearby all night to make sure that she wouldn't be lonely before the cremation. Loneliness before cremation could turn into a desire to stay in the human world. Ume's spirit might stay behind, unable to be at peace. I didn't really believe this, but I did stay awake all night, looking at Ume's white face.

Over the years, I've never had the sense of living just one life. Looking at my face brings back my dead family, which makes me wonder if the landlady was right about lost souls wandering in our world, unwilling to get to the next stage. Shinya volunteered to join the Youth Bravery Military Force at the age of eighteen and was sent to Manchuria. His troops became lost in southern China during the Japanese invasion, and his death was never confirmed, but since he never came home, we assumed. I often wonder how he died. Was it a quick death by getting shot in the middle of intense fighting, or was he left alone to suffer and slowly die? If something kept his spirit in this world, loneliness wouldn't have stopped him. It was anger that filled his heart.

Mother, on the other hand, died during the Tokyo bombing, and I always imagined that her death and cremation happened at the same time. After my father was drafted in 1941, I was accepted by Tokyo University, so my mother and Ume also moved to Tokyo to stay with her sister. But shortly after we moved, I was drafted, leaving Mother and Ume in a city that was about to be burned away. My mother was hit by one of hundreds of bombs that were dropped on the night of the Tokyo bombing, and I heard about many missing corpses due to severe burning and melting. I didn't expect my mother, of all people, to survive such a scene. I felt sorrow at my mother's death, but I expected it. While people with quickness, strength, and determination barely survived the bombing, Mother had no chance. She would be too frightened. Her body would freeze, and she wouldn't fight for her life under a sky with bombs falling like raindrops. I imagine that when the bomb hit, her body evaporated—death without dying. I don't associate her death with loneliness. She suffered loneliness while she was alive, but not in death.

But I'm certain that my father did struggle with loneliness and regret before his death. Father survived the war and returned home safely, though five years later, he died. After he returned from the war, Father didn't believe in getting medical treatment. The complete destruction and defeat of Japan caused him to be suspicious of everything, especially authority figures. Father never went to the doctor, since he believed that we must accept death the way it came—a lesson learned in war. No one knew that he was dying; his body was found up on the hill, in the family cemetery. After his death, the autopsy showed that cancer had been rotting the inside of his stomach, which must have caused intolerable pain for the last three months of his life. He had been dead for about two days when his body was found by a neighbor. He was curled up, both arms holding his stomach. His eyes and mouth were wide open as if his hoarse voice could still rise from deep in the dark hole of his mouth. Father's terrible face was hardened, and we couldn't fix his expression. I could hear his dead body shouting his last painful moment of life. A dead face reveals who we really were. We kept Father inside the dark wooden casket and didn't show his face at the funeral, before he was taken to be cremated. If the landlady's story is true, Father's bitterness and loneliness must have filled the dark casket, and his spirit never left this world.

I am almost as old as my mother when she died. My sister and brother remained young in my mind, behind the mirror in front of me. Once I told Chiyo how the dead faces of my family emerge in my reflection. She laughed and said, *A mirror is a door to the ghost world; you can greet them, but don't accept their invitation to enter.* Chiyo wasn't serious, but I often wished that the mirror was in fact a door to the ghost world. I want Ume to reach out to me from the other side of mirror and tell me what to do. My life lasted, and everything that my family left became my responsibility, though I hardly know what they wished me to do. I carry their deaths on my back, hoping that I'm carrying out those wishes.

I rub soap between my hands and wash my face hard with the bubbles to erase my oily smell. The water is cold. In Kamakura, the water comes from the Tsutsui river, but from the window in the bathroom, all I can see is the ocean. Even though Chiyo tells me to use warm water during the winter, using heated water doesn't seem right when I can see the cold ocean. Our bathroom is the only place in our house where we can hear the sound of the ocean. Standing here alone, I blankly stare at the mirror one last time and wish that I had died during the war like my brother and mother, which isn't to say that I want to die now, or that I'm not grateful for my life. Death appeared very simple to me when I was young. I don't know how death has become more frightening and complicated over the years. When it's time for me to die, I don't know if I can die well. Living feels like an expectation. I carry so many deaths on my back, and my bones have thinned over the years. But as long as I'm alive, I have to endure my family's dead faces in the mirror.

JULY 1975

In May, Lisa told me about the sleepaway camp that she went to every year. There was singing and hiking in the morning, art classes in the afternoon, and a campfire every night. Lisa wanted me to come with her this year and be her roommate. Hearing about this magical place, I got very excited and really wanted to go. I told Dad about the camp, and he was surprised that I wanted to go away for three weeks.

"This isn't a camp for hippies, is it?" Dad asked, looking at the section in the camp brochure, *Living with Nature.*

"Hippies don't send their children to summer camp." Mom rolled her eyes.

"For this price, they wouldn't." Dad pointed at the tuition on the last page. He gave the brochure to Mom.

"Is it safe?" Mom asked me.

"Lisa goes there every year, and she says it's a lot of fun. Look, they even have a big pool." I pointed at the picture of kids in a pool, splashing water. Mom didn't look down at the picture and instead she raised her voice.

"I asked you if it's safe."

I didn't know. Why wouldn't it be safe?

"It must be safe for this price." Dad pointed at the last page again. Mom stared at his face. She wanted to say something because her mouth moved, but instead, she stood up and picked up the phone. She called Lisa's mother and asked her if the camp was safe. She asked the same question at least three times and hung up the phone. Dad had already gone back to his newspaper. Dad never said very much.

"Can you be away for three weeks?" Mom looked into my face. I nodded hard.

Then Mom began filling out the form. I couldn't believe how easy it was! I was going to camp! I jumped and danced around the house, saying thank you, thank you, thank you.

When Ken found out that I was going to this magical place, he said he wanted to go, too. He was too little for camp. I said only older kids could stay at the camp. But Ken knew that Lisa's younger sister was going, too. She was in Ken's class. Ken didn't stop whining and begging to go to camp for an entire week. Mom put Ken in the closet when he followed her everywhere in the house, shouting, "I want to go to camp, too!" Even Dad thought Ken was too little to go. Then Ken said he wouldn't eat until they let him go with me. He didn't eat for a day and a half. Mom even scooped vegetable soup in a small spoon and tried to put it in his mouth, but he turned his head and shut his mouth tight. Then Mom stood up; I thought she was going to put him in the closet again, but instead, she threw her spoon on the floor and yelled, "If you want to leave, I'll send you away." She ran to her bedroom and locked the door. She didn't come out that night. I knocked on her door many times, but she didn't answer. That night, Ken and I had a bowl of cereal for dinner, and I had to help him take a shower and brush his teeth. I even put him to bed. We all knew that Ken couldn't be away for three weeks. When Ken went to his friend's house for a sleepover, he called home in the middle of the night. Mom had to drive and pick him up. But she never got mad at him for that.

On the day we left for the camp, I didn't want to go anymore. Ken was coming with me, and I thought that something bad was going to happen. But Mom said I had to go to the camp now because I said I wanted to go. She loaded our bags in the car and told us to get in. I asked Mom if she would come and get Ken if he wanted to come home, like when he called her from his friend's house at night sometimes. Mom didn't say she would or wouldn't.

It took us four hours to get to the camp. It felt like going to a different country. I saw buildings and towns that I had never seen before, and I was getting scared about being away for such a long time.

When we finally got there, Mom brought our bags and checked our names with a young woman in the office. There were many log houses in the middle of a forest. When she left, she held us both so tight that I couldn't breathe. Her cheeks were wet with tears.

"Mommy, what's wrong?" Ken pulled her shirt. She wiped off her tears and put her hand on her chest like she couldn't breathe.

"You're responsible for your brother now." Her voice was shaking. Then she turned around and quickly walked back to her car. Ken ran to her, but she closed the door and drove away. We watched her green car disappear, and I wished I had never said I wanted to come to camp.

Boys and girls stayed in different buildings. After dinner, we learned new camp songs and played games, but I kept thinking about Mom crying on the way home. She was alone now, and it was my fault. She would just sit by the window and wait for Dad to come home. When Lisa and I went back to our room, she showed me her new pajamas. We used a flashlight to stay up late and talk because we had to turn off the lights at nine o'clock. I had been so excited about camp, but now, all I could think about was Mom.

Someone knocked on our door, so we quickly hid our flashlight and got back in our beds. The door slowly opened, and our senior counselor Rachel called my name and asked me if I was Ken Johnson's older sister. Ken's name gave me a heavy feeling in my chest. She said I had to come to Ken's cabin now. She was with a young man, Matt, a junior counselor for the boys. He was taking care of the boys in Ken's cabin. I got out of my bed, put a sweatshirt and shoes on, and followed Rachel and Matt. On the way to Ken's cabin, Matt asked me if Ken was on medication or sick before he came to camp. I said no. I was the only person that knew Ken. Mom's voice came back to me: *You're responsible for Ken.* Matt said Ken was holding his stomach, crying, and asking for me. Matt had a man's voice, low, but not as deep as Dad's. I was half running to catch up with him.

As soon as I walked into the room, Ken grabbed my arm. I'd never held Ken like this before.

"What happened? Does your tummy hurt?" His face was all wet and red from crying. He nodded his head. Matt wrapped Ken's body with a blanket, and Rachel drove the van to the local doctor, a half hour away. I sat in the back seat, shaking, hearing Ken's sobs. The van cut through the black air and it felt like we were driving in the closet, except for the narrow headlights in front of us.

Dr. Reed met us in his nightgown. The hospital was connected to his house, which looked like a small log cabin. Rachel said that he was the only doctor around here, and if Ken was really really sick, they had to call a helicopter to get him to a bigger hospital in San Francisco. I started to tear up, but I bit my lower lip and blinked my eyes so I wouldn't cry. Dr. Reed touched Ken's stomach, then put his silver stethoscope on his chest. Once he did that, Ken stopped crying and got quiet.

"Does this hurt?" Dr. Reed carefully touched Ken's stomach and chest.

"No." He shook his head.

"How about here?"

"No, my tummy doesn't hurt anymore."

We all looked at Ken's face.

"Can you describe the pain you had in your tummy?" Dr. Reed crossed his arms.

"It was like a big bug eating my tummy from inside."

"When did this sharp pain stop?"

"When you put that silver thing on my chest," Ken pointed at Dr. Reed's stethoscope.

"I see." Dr. Reed touched his chin. "Well, I'm glad I could cure you so quickly. I must be a very good doctor." Dr. Reed smiled.

"So a helicopter isn't coming to take Ken away?" I asked Dr. Reed. He smiled and said not to worry about anything. He left me and Ken in the room and took Rachel and Matt into his office. They were gone for a long time.

"Your tummy really doesn't hurt anymore?" I asked Ken. He shook his head, put Dr. Reed's stethoscope around his neck, and pretended to be a doctor. I told him not to touch it, but he kept playing with it.

When Matt and Rachel came out of Dr. Reed's office, they said that we could go back to the camp. We drove through the dark again. Ken fell asleep. As soon as we got back, we took Ken to his cabin first. I helped him get into bed. Then Matt drove Rachel and me back to our cabin.

Matt turned around and gently talked to me: "Dr. Reed thought Ken's stomach pain was psychological, from being nervous spending a night away from home."

"You mean he was faking being sick?" I raised my voice even though I didn't mean to.

"No, not faking. Ken's stomach was really hurting. But he wasn't physically sick," Matt quickly explained.

"But why did his stomach hurt if he wasn't sick?"

"That's why Dr. Reed said 'psychologically.'"

"What's that?"

"It's hard to explain." Rachel touched my back. She said she would explain it to me tomorrow, but for now, we had to go to bed because it was after one o'clock already. I wasn't sleepy at all. I didn't want to go back to bed. I wanted to go home. I walked to my cabin and went to my room. Lisa was sleeping, so I tried not to make any noise. I stared at the dark ceiling for a long time, waiting for my head and eyes to get sleepy. I was Ken's sister, and I had to take care of him, but I didn't know how to be responsible for him.

The next morning, my arms were heavy, as if they had turned into stones while I was sleeping. My eyes burned when I looked outside. Lisa said that she had called my name five times really loud, but I didn't wake up until she shook me. We were almost late for breakfast because I moved so slowly. The cafeteria was busy, and I saw Ken sitting with some boys, laughing, like nothing had happened to him the night before. Rachel came over to me when I sat down with my banana, milk, and cereal. She looked pretty with her hair up in a ponytail. She didn't look tired at all. She told me that Ken was good this morning, but that he was going to go and see Mrs. Hyatt.

"Who's Mrs. Hyatt?"

"She's the director of the camp. She'll find out what Ken is thinking and feeling." Rachel pointed at her head and heart with her finger.

"Is she going to know if Ken was lying?"

"No, no. We know Ken wasn't lying. He really felt the pain because he thought he was sick." Rachel touched my back again. It all sounded very fishy to me. We couldn't get sick by thinking about getting sick. When I didn't want to go to school, I prayed to get a fever, but I never got one. Rachel said not to be angry with Ken, but if he faked it again, I'd tell Mom about it. Then she'd put him in the closet.

At eight o'clock there was a whistle, and all the girls from fourth through sixth grades went outside and got in line to go hiking. We sang camp songs while we hiked. Rachel led the girls, and there was another counselor at the end of the line. A few girls asked me about Ken's incident. Kelly, my next-door neighbor, said how romantic it was that the cutest counselor,

Matt, came to my room late at night. Kelly said his wavy dark hair and brown eyes were gorgeous.

"Did you know that junior counselors are eighteen or nineteen, freshmen or sophomores in college?" Kelly whispered, looking back at me and Lisa. Behind us, there were two more girls, Mandy and Alice. "And senior counselors are twenty or twenty-one," Kelly continued with her proud look. "In four years, I'll be sixteen. I could marry him." Kelly was twelve, the oldest in our group. She looked like a woman, and I could see that she was wearing a bra.

"Matt's dating one of the girl counselors," Lisa said. I knew Lisa was making up a story. She did that all the time. We all started matching Matt with the girl counselors, one by one.

"You know," Kelly licked her upper lip and put her face in front of me. "You said you left Matt and Rachel in the van last night?" Kelly's smile was growing. "Well, what do you think happened to them after you left?" Kelly looked back at me and Lisa, and then to Mandy and Alice. Mandy started laughing loud. Alice was giggling, too. Lisa's face got a little red.

"I think they went back to their rooms and went to sleep." I knew they wanted me to say sex, but they don't say it, like it was a secret word, and that was stupid.

"Helen, how old are you?" Kelly rolled her eyes. She knew I was nine. "Let me tell you, a man and a woman in a van late at night, they were . . ." Kelly didn't finish her sentence. Everyone was giggling. I saw Rachel leading the group, far ahead of us. I wanted to be as old as Rachel. She looked back to make sure that everyone was following her. Her ponytail moved left and right as her body moved forward. Someday, I would be like Rachel, taking care of everyone, being responsible, but for now, I was only nine.

That night, I woke up to Rachel's voice whispering my name from the door again. I jumped up even though she said everything would be all right. I got dressed and went out with my heart pounding. She took my hand and we ran to Ken's cabin. He was on the floor moaning, holding his stomach and sweating. Tears ran from his eyes, and Matt was holding him. When Ken saw my face, he cried even more.

"Helen, my tummy is going to break!"

"You mean it *really* hurts?" I sat by Ken on the floor. I couldn't stop shaking. Mrs. Hyatt came in and said we had to take Ken to Dr. Reed's again. Matt wrapped Ken with a blanket like the night before, picked him up, and ran to the van. All the way to Dr. Reed's, Ken moaned, and it sounded worse than the night before. Matt drove faster, too. I thought about riding in a helicopter with Ken and going all the way to the hospital in the city. Then we would be closer to home. Maybe Ken would be better at home.

Dr. Reed was wearing the pajamas again. He helped take off Ken's T-shirt, which was all wet from his sweat. Ken curled up on the table. Dr. Reed checked Ken's stomach with his hands and took out his stethoscope and checked Ken's chest. Ken slowly stopped moaning. The room became very quiet without Ken's sobbing. Ken didn't move, and his eyes were wide open, facing Dr. Reed, but I didn't know if he could see Dr. Reed's face.

"What's wrong, Ken? Are you O.K.?" I touched Ken's shoulder. Tears rolled down my cheeks. I thought he was going to die, and it was my fault that Ken came to the camp.

"My tummy doesn't hurt anymore." Ken looked at me.

"What?" I didn't know what was happening.

"It feels warm, though." Ken touched his stomach. Dr. Reed wiped off Ken's body with a towel and said that he wanted to talk to Mrs. Hyatt and Ken alone. I walked to the bench in the hallway with Rachel, since my legs were still shaking. Matt went to Dr. Reed's kitchen to get water for me. Rachel said that I was a good sister and a strong person. She said that because it was a nice thing to say, but I knew that I wasn't strong. I wasn't like

Rachel. When Mrs. Hyatt and Ken finally came out, I was half asleep on Rachel's shoulder. Mrs. Hyatt held Ken's hand and stood in front of me. Ken didn't look like he was sick anymore. We walked back to the van and drove back to camp.

The next day, during my drawing class, Mrs. Hyatt came in and asked me to join her in her office. Everyone watched me leave the classroom. Her office was crowded with piles of papers. Showing me to the chair in front of her desk, she asked me how I was. I said I was sleepy. She smiled and nodded.

"I wanted to tell you that the camp thinks it's in Ken's best interest to send him home. What do you think?" Mrs. Hyatt's smile was gone. I wasn't surprised. Everybody knew that Ken was too little to go away for such a long time. Mrs. Hyatt asked me if Mom and Dad both worked. I told her that Dad worked late, but Mom was home.

"That's what I thought." Mrs. Hyatt looked down and flipped some papers on her desk. "I've been calling both your parents all day, but I couldn't get in touch with them. I guess I'll try contacting Mrs. Hogan."

"Mrs. Hogan?"

"Her name is listed as an emergency contact. Who's Mrs. Hogan?"

"Our neighbor." I could almost smell her smoky breath just saying her name. I didn't understand. Mom was always home. She didn't really leave the house unless she was taking us to school. I didn't know where she went or why Mom wrote Mrs. Hogan's name on the form. Mrs. Hyatt smiled and said that she would take care of everything, and I was free to go back to class. When I got back, Lisa asked me what happened. I said nothing and tried to go back to drawing, but I couldn't think of anything to draw, so I drew circles on the paper until it was full of black circles.

Before dinner, Mrs. Hyatt came to my cabin. She was with Rachel and Matt. Mrs. Hyatt said she talked to Mrs. Hogan, and

Mrs. Hogan went to my house to talk to Mom. Then Mrs. Hogan called Mrs. Hyatt back from my house. I was trying to follow who talked to who, and I didn't understand why Mom wasn't talking to Mrs. Hyatt.

"It turns out that your mother won't come and get Ken. She won't come until the end of the third week. Mrs. Hogan couldn't explain why." Mrs. Hyatt's voice sounded a little angry. My cheeks burned red. I had to say something. Mom wouldn't come and get us because I had wanted to leave home. She was mad at Ken and me.

"I'm supposed to be responsible for him. It's my fault. I'm sorry." I didn't want Mrs. Hyatt to think Mom was a bad person.

"It's not your fault, and you are certainly not responsible for Ken!" Mrs. Hyatt stood up. "Ken really needs to go home though." Mrs. Hyatt turned to Matt and they started talking. I was there and heard their voices, but I wasn't hearing the words. My stomach was bouncing with something heavy inside and I thought I was getting sick like Ken. We left home, Ken got sick, and Mom wouldn't come and get him. What if she left us here forever? I sat still, my sweaty hands on my thighs. After a while, Mrs. Hyatt told me they had a new plan. I was to move into Ken's room. She thought Ken would be better if he was with his sister. I said o.k. Then everyone except for Rachel left. I started packing my clothes, and Rachel helped gather my stuff from the bathroom. Then we walked to Ken's room together, her hand on my shoulder again.

⌒

Every Friday, the camp had a special guest for "Friday Show for Kids." Everybody ate their lunch quickly on Fridays because we all wanted to sit close to the stage in the gym. On the first Friday, a magician came. We sat on the hard floor and waited for him to come out. He was skinny and tall, and wore a funny tuxedo and a long polka-dot tie. He opened his black suitcase and took out all kinds of magic stuff. My favorite was the soft blue scarf that he put in his hat and changed into a little rabbit. Ken talked about it nonstop before going to sleep in our room. I thought about Mom then. She would say that magic wasn't real. But I saw how the blue scarf really disappeared in the hat and became clear in the air. The magician was so funny. I didn't want the show to end.

All week, the camp counselors told us the special guest for the last Friday would be an origami artist from Japan. When I heard the word Japan, I jumped a little. No one knew what origami was, so Rachel showed us some birds and flowers made out of paper.

"Her name is Kyoko, and she is a professional origami artist," said Rachel.

"What's professional?" asked David. He was Ken's friend.

"Well, professional means that you're trained to do something very well, and you use that skill for your job. And you get paid to do it," said Rachel. I couldn't believe someone got paid for making something out of paper! No one was all that excited about this origami artist. I told Lisa not to tell anyone about my mom. She was the only person that knew that Mom was half Japanese. But she must have said something to Kelly and Mandy. When I was in line for lunch, they came and asked if Kyoko was my mom, then ran away laughing. I didn't wait for Lisa to go to the gym for the origami artist's show. She had made lots of new friends. I went there alone.

Ken was already at the gym. He was sitting with his new friends. Once I started living with Ken in the same room, he didn't have any more tummy pain. It was weird, but I didn't say anything to him. I didn't want him to remember being sick. Ken liked camp a lot and made two new friends. They played soldiers in our room and made gun noises at each other. Ken was the soldier that never died. Other boys got shot, so Ken was the hero that saved them. They even brought wooden sticks to our room for sword fights, until I kicked them out. I wanted to go back to live with Lisa again, but I also didn't want Ken to get sick again. At night, I thought a lot about going home. Every day was long and slow.

The lights came on and a woman in a colorful outfit walked to the middle of the stage. Everyone was surprised by her clothes, and we all stopped talking. A deep red cloth was wrapped around her body and tied with a thick gold and green belt. I had never seen anything like this. We all looked up at her from the floor.

"Hello, my name is Kyoko." She opened her eyes wide.

"Have you seen a dress like this? This is a kimono. Can you say ki-mo-no?" We all repeated what she said. Then she opened a big poster.

"Who wants to help me hold this big picture?" She looked around the crowd. Almost all our hands were up in the air. She went to the second graders' crowd and picked a little girl. She was only as tall as the picture, so she couldn't see the picture from behind it. It showed kids in Japan holding many different animals made out of paper. She said that all Japanese kids made origami in elementary school. Mrs. Hyatt passed square colored papers around. She usually didn't come to our classes, but it was a special day—the last day of camp. All the counselors were there, too. I got a piece of green paper. Down the row, Ken had red paper. Kyoko showed us how to make a cup. It was easy, so I tried the next one, a bird. She explained slowly how to fold the thin paper and kept telling us to fold gently. I saw Ken rip the side of his red paper and ask for a new one.

Kyoko walked around, and I saw her tan-colored hand teaching Ken's clumsy hands to make a bird. I made two flowers, a bird, and a cup. All the counselors walked around to help us. Kyoko didn't have time to walk over to my fifth grade crowd before she went back to the stage.

"I hope you had fun today. Do you have questions about Japan or origami?" Kyoko looked around the crowd.

The little girl with a yellow skirt stood up. "Do you have a boyfriend?"

Kyoko's face got red. We all laughed.

"Now, you heard what Kyoko said. The question has to be about Japan or origami, o.k.? Who else has a question?" Matt quickly said, but he was laughing, too.

"Do you know my grandma Ume?" Ken's voice jumped in my ear. Ken was standing up in the crowd.

"You have a grandmother in Japan?" Kyoko looked surprised.

"She died a long time ago. Her name is Ume. Did you know her?"

My cheeks were getting hot from the inside. I looked down at the floor and prayed no one remembered that I was his sister.

"There are so many people in Japan, so I do not think we met." Kyoko smiled.

"How about Shizuka? Do you know her?"

"Shizuka?"

"The ghost. Have you seen it?"

"No, I don't know that ghost. But *Shizuka* means *quiet.*" Ken didn't understand. He was being stupid. I told Lisa not to say anything about Mom, but I forgot to warn Ken. I wanted to take his mouth away from his face. I could hear everybody laughing. Lisa and some girls were looking at me and whispering. I looked down again at the floor, hard.

After the show, we went back to our room to get our bags, then went outside to wait for Mom to pick us up. Ken put his origami bird in his pocket. I told him to hurry up. He was slow, but I didn't want to help him. He dragged his bag, saying it was too heavy for him, but I kept walking ahead. There were many cars parked at the waiting area. I didn't see Mom's.

Many cars left and more arrived. Lots of kids were running to their parents. Ken and I stood together and waited for Mom. If she didn't come, where could we go? Every time I thought about it, my stomach hurt a little, so I quickly thought about something else. I didn't want to get sick like Ken did. Ken pulled the red bird from his pocket and held it.

"Did you like Kyoko?" Ken asked me.

"No."

"Why not?"

"Because you were stupid."

"I wasn't!"

"I wish you didn't say anything." I turned away from Ken and then saw Mom's green car. She opened her window with a little bit of a smile. I jumped up and waved my hand as hard as I could. When Mom got out of the car, Ken and I jumped into her arms. She was really here. She looked skinnier, but she was smiling. We threw our bags in the trunk and got into the car. As we left, I saw Rachel standing outside of the office, waving at me. I waved back. I was so scared that Mom might not come and get us that I forgot to say good-bye to Rachel. She waved for a long time until we turned off the main road.

"Guess what? Guess what, Mommy!" Ken jumped on the seat. "We met Kyoko. She taught us how to make origami birds." He showed Mom the red bird.

"Stop jumping!" I pulled his shirt. But I wanted to jump with him, too. I was so happy that Mom was here.

"But Kyoko didn't know Grandma Ume."

Mom's shoulder jerked.

"She didn't know Shizuka, either."

I saw Mom's face in the front mirror, getting pink as she blinked many times, breathing with her whole body. She put her hand over her mouth.

"What's wrong, Mommy?" Ken looked up. But she didn't say anything. Ken tugged on her sleeve, but she didn't look, and she sped up. We didn't say anything. We just watched her shoulders moving up and down.

I had no idea how long I slept, but I woke up when Mom took a sharp right turn. It was already dark. She passed our house and went straight to Mrs. Hogan's.

"You're going to stay with Mrs. Hogan until Dad comes home tonight." Mom stopped the engine.

"No! Why?" Ken shouted, but she ignored him and got out to open the back door.

"We don't want to go to Mrs. Hogan's house!" I grabbed the backseat and shouted as hard as I could.

"No!" Ken started crying when Mom grabbed his leg and started pulling. He kicked his feet at her arms, but she pulled him out of the car and set him on the ground. Outside, Ken's voice broke out like a fire. I grabbed the seat tighter when Mom pulled my ankle. I was stronger than Ken, and I knew what my body could do. I pulled and pushed my legs. But I saw Mrs. Hogan come out of her orange door.

"Go away! You can't make me!" I shouted with all my body. I just wanted to go home. I would stay quiet in my room. I wouldn't bother Mom. But Mom and Mrs. Hogan pulled me out of the car and put me on the ground. My fingers felt the burn of cloth on the car seat. I didn't know Mom's skinny arms were so strong. Mom whispered something in Mrs. Hogan's ear, and she quickly got back in the car and drove away. I couldn't see well with the tears in my eyes, but I got up and ran after the car. Ken shouted my name and ran after me. I heard Mrs. Hogan calling our names, but I didn't look back. Ken kept calling my name, so I took his hand and ran as fast as we could. We passed Joan's Bakery and Green Village Park and a small hill and big trees by the post office, and we ran and ran into the dark night air. The moon followed us, and the Earth was turning faster, pushing us to our white house on the corner.

The house was dark except for a little light in the living room. Mom's car sat at the top of the driveway, but Dad's car wasn't there. Ken tried the doorknob, but it was locked. We walked around the house to the living room window where the light was on.

"Mommy's in the house!" Ken shouted. Mom was standing in front of the mirror like a tree. Her back was as straight as a pencil. Her long black hair looked heavy on her thin shoulders. She was wearing her soft pink pajamas. Ken ran to the window. I followed him. I couldn't help it. We ran together to the big window in the living room.

"Mommy! Mommy!" Ken shouted and waved his little hands in the air.

"Mom!" I could reach the window, so I banged it hard.

Mom turned around. Her face turned white like an ice cube, and her eyes got bigger and bigger, looking at us. Her body started to shake. I could almost hear the sound of something bouncing inside her.

"No, please don't come close to me. Go away!" Mom cried out. If Shizuka really was in the closet, she would sound like Mom. She sat by the mirror and started to cry. She was shaking right and left fast and falling down on the floor. Mom covered her eyes with both hands. Ken stopped jumping.

"What's wrong, Mommy?"

"Let's go. Mom doesn't want to see us." I pulled Ken's hand.

"I want to see Mommy!" he cried, but I kept pulling his hand. I didn't want to look back. Something in me or Ken was hurting Mom. She was scared of us. We walked back to the front door and sat there for a long time until Dad's headlights pulled in the driveway and blinded me. We told him that Mom was inside crying. When we told him that Mom didn't want us inside, he looked really sad. He told us to wait there, opened the door with his silver key, and went inside. We ran to the back of the house to the living room window. I saw Dad holding Mom's body. She was saying something to him and slanted her head against his chest. He spoke into her ear, then she shook her head. He took her to a different room, so we went back to the front door. Later he came out with the bags that we brought back from the camp and told us to get in the back of his car. He said he was taking us to Uncle Steve's house.

"We're going away again?" Ken came close to me and held my hand.

"Just for a little while."

"I don't wanna go!" Ken yelled, but Dad got in the car.

I pulled Ken's hand and got in the backseat with him.

Ken started to cry. "What's wrong with Mommy?"

"I don't know," Dad said.

"Why don't you know?"

"No more questions, Ken!"

"Can I come home tomorrow?"

"Not tomorrow."

"When can I come home?" Ken pulled on Dad's suit from the backseat. Dad pulled his arm away, looked straight, and started driving. Dad fixed his glasses up on his nose. All the way to Uncle Steve's house, we listened to Ken's sobs. Even after he fell asleep, Ken's breathing sounded like sobbing. I didn't say anything. I just watched the pale moon follow me in the dark.

AUGUST 1975

"August 22, 1975. The famous child Ken turns six! Happy birthday!" Uncle Steve, my dad's younger brother, announced like a news reporter at lunch. Then Aunt Mary let me put six candles on the birthday cake. Aunt Mary wanted to invite some of Ken's friends, but Ken's school friends lived too far away from where we were living now. So it was just us: me, Uncle Steve, Aunt Mary, and Ken. Uncle Steve put his arms around me and Aunt Mary, and we sang "Happy Birthday." Ken giggled. Uncle Steve gave Ken a little box with a big bow. He tore off the wrapping paper and opened the box.

"Wow! Airplane!" He jumped up and smiled big. Then he ran around the room with his new toy. I sat by the window in the kitchen and finished my lunch. From there, I could see a small green pond down the hill. I used to think that San Francisco had the most hills in the world, but here in Tiburon it was worse!

We hadn't seen Mom or Dad for three weeks, but Dad had called us twice. Last week, he wanted to talk to me. He said he was going to send me and Ken to a new school in Tiburon in September. We were going to a private school, St. Mary's Catholic School, because we'd been through a lot. I knew Dad was talking about Mom.

"You mean we don't get to come home?" I asked.

"Are you unhappy there?"

"No."

"I know they take good care of you." His voice was tired, as usual.

"What about Mom?"

"She needs a little more time."

I wanted to ask Dad if she was still mad at me and Ken. But he said he was calling from his office and he had to go.

Uncle Steve was twenty-seven, five years younger than Dad, and his opposite. He always said hello to me with a big smile. He really liked taking us fishing, something we had never done before. The first time, we went to a river. Ken and I didn't catch anything, but Uncle Steve caught two pretty fish, though he told Aunt Mary that both Ken and I caught them. He was very handsome. Every day, he wore blue jeans, which made him look very blue, since more than half of his body was legs! Ken tried to climb those legs like they were trees. Uncle Steve was strong, too. When Ken and I sat on his feet, he walked like nothing was on his feet. He always had the radio on, and when a song he liked came on, he grabbed Aunt Mary and danced around the house. Sometimes, he even picked me and Ken up and danced with us, which we really liked. He showed us how to shake our legs to a fast song, but we couldn't move like him. Unlike Dad, Uncle Steve never wore a suit because he was a gardener and could go to work in his jeans. Mom had once told me that Uncle Steve was a good man, and she could tell by looking into his eyes. So I asked Uncle Steve if I could look at his eyes for a while. He looked surprised, but he sat still. His eyes were so pretty, with a sunflower center in the middle of a blue circle, but I couldn't tell which part was the kindness.

Aunt Mary kissed Uncle Steve every day when he left for work and when he came home from work. Mom and Dad never did that. Uncle Steve and Aunt Mary said they were newlyweds. They got married six months ago, but they didn't have a wedding because they don't like big parties. When I asked Uncle Steve how he asked Aunt Mary to marry him, he kneeled on his right knee down in front of me and held my hand.

"I had to beg her to marry me in this position," he winked at me. My heart jumped. Aunt Mary's curly red hair sparkled when the sun shone on it. She worked at the library on Tuesdays and Thursdays, and Ken and I went with her. She knew lots of fun books. I liked sitting behind the white counter reading books all day. I could finish a book a day sometimes. But Ken got bored quickly. He found someone to play with, and they always ended up playing war in the courtyard. Sometimes Aunt Mary said we could help putting books back on the shelf. Everyone at the library thought we were good helpers.

When we first came to Uncle Steve and Aunt Mary's house, they asked a lot of questions. They wanted to know everything. What time we used to go to bed, what we used to eat, what Mom used to say, what happened at camp, what Dad did at home. They always sat still and listened to us seriously like we were telling a great adventure story.

On Ken's birthday, Uncle Steve was taking us fishing again, so I changed into blue jeans and a yellow T-shirt just like Uncle Steve. Aunt Mary packed us goodies in plastic bags, even some chocolate bars. I didn't tell her that Mom thought sugar was poison. As soon as we got inside Uncle Steve's truck, Ken wanted to eat one. Uncle Steve smiled and said a birthday boy could have anything he wanted. When we were done eating the chocolate, Uncle Steve asked if we were finally happy. Ken said he wouldn't be happy until he ate another one, so he ate another one and said that now he was happy. I didn't know how to answer a question like that.

Riding in Uncle Steve's red truck was like sitting in the driver's seat of the school bus. I could see for a long ways. After we drove through some busy towns, Uncle Steve stopped by the bait shop near the ocean. He always bought a small package of worms there even though he didn't fish in the ocean. He said he liked river fishing because the river wasn't big and scary like the ocean. Ken and I waited inside the truck. We could see him opening the refrigerator in the back. I couldn't hear anything from here, but Uncle Steve was greeting and smiling at everyone in the store. Everyone liked Uncle Steve.

I liked fishing, but hooking a worm was my least favorite part. When the hook went through the worm's thin pink skin, its tail moved up and down, like when Ken had a tummyache at camp. If a hook went through my back, I would move like that, too. Uncle Steve showed us how to make a knot when we put on bait, but we couldn't do it. He always ended up doing it for us.

"Here we go." Uncle Steve handed us the rods and winked. My heart beat faster.

We threw our lines in the river and sat and waited for a long time. Fish picked which bait to bite, so if I was lucky, I was a good fisherman. Uncle Steve was always lucky. Two fish picked his bait. Then Ken got a small one. He was so excited that he wanted to get another one. I was getting bored since no fish came to get my bait.

Uncle Steve told us that the biggest trout he'd ever caught was as long as his arm. He put his arm straight. Dad had a long arm just like Uncle Steve's, but Dad and Uncle Steve were very different.

"How come Dad isn't like you?"

Uncle Steve smiled. "Well, what's your Dad like at home?"

"He's quiet. He wears suits every day. He works a lot. He comes home late. He doesn't sing and dance like you."

"You've never seen your Dad dance? James is such a good dancer."

"Dad?"

"Yeah, back in college, all the girls wanted to dance with him at mixers. He could make them look good. He knew the rhythm and lots of different moves. He was smooth. Doesn't he play Elvis at home?"

I shook my head. Maybe he was thinking of someone else, like his friend, but not Dad. There were many records on the shelf at home, but they were all dusty. I have never seen Dad play music in the house.

"When James danced with Anna, everyone watched. They moved like they were one, they looked so good."

"Mom danced, too?"

"Oh yes, on the dance floor, she was very confident. No one said anything mean about Anna then."

"People were mean to Mom?"

Uncle Steve's smile went away for a second. He shrugged his shoulders. "James's friends used to give him a hard time about dating Anna. Actually, I did, too."

"You were mean to her?"

"Not directly to her, but yeah, I have said some nasty things to James."

"Like what?"

"Like, 'Of all people, why do you want to date a Jap?'" Uncle Steve said in a low voice, and covered his face with his hands like he was embarrassed.

"What's a Jap?"

"It's a derogatory term for Japanese." Uncle Steve uncovered his face. Mom always thought everyone was watching her and talking about her, but I couldn't picture Uncle Steve saying anything mean to anyone.

"I'm a little bit Japanese, too," I said. I hoped that was O.K. Uncle Steve was nice to me now, but maybe only because he didn't know that I was a little bit Japanese. But I couldn't lie, because a liar was going to drown in the ocean.

"Helen, back then, I was seventeen and living with my family. We were against James marrying Anna, so I went along with them. But James didn't try to change my mind. He just said to me, 'Even if you're so certain about yourself, you could change. Such a possibility is always within you.' That was James, the philosophy major talking! I was so annoyed when he talked to me like that. Of course I thought to myself he was so wrong, he was the one with problems. But once he left for Vietnam, I got to know Anna. She was smart because she didn't try anything with me. She was just very kind to me even though I didn't talk to her at first. Eventually, you get embarrassed when you're acting stupid around people who are very nice to you. Anna actually reminded me a lot of James, too. He would just let you realize your stupidity on your own." Uncle Steve laughed a little.

"You think Mom and Dad are alike?"

Uncle Steve looked down on the river and sighed a little. He said Dad changed a lot since he came back from the war. He said he was lucky that he wasn't drafted, but Dad was really unlucky not just because he was drafted after his graduation from college, but also he went there when the war was getting bad.

That sounded like this fishing. Unlucky fish get caught, and we eat them. They must be sad and angry when they get hooked.

"Anna is depressed now, living with James. I would be, too. It's sad that she's more lonely now than when James was away. I think she should see someone, a good doctor." Uncle Steve looked at me straight.

"If you're lonely, you're sick?"

"Well, everyone has good days and bad days. But your mom has bad days all the time. You know when you see a sad movie, sometimes you're sad for a long time? Maybe that's how it is for your mom—she's sad from her sad memories."

"Why can't she forget sad things?" I didn't like this.

"It's not so easy." Uncle Steve put his hand on my head, but it didn't make sense. She shouldn't think about sad things if it made her sad.

Suddenly my fishing rod moved. I jumped up.

"Uncle Steve, a fish is eating my worm!" He jumped, too. He told me to be ready to reel the line in. I held it tight.

"Now!" Uncle Steve's voice shook my body. I reeled. A small fish jumped up in the air, almost flying, but with nowhere to go, like a dog on a leash. I didn't know what to do with it, so I held the line moving right and left.

"Bring her close to me, Helen!" Uncle Steve said, but it was hard to control something that was hanging at the end of a thin line. A brown and yellow fish with red dotted skin was shining in Uncle Steve's hand.

"Great job! A beautiful rainbow trout!" He took the hook out of the pretty fish's mouth. Blood dripped on his hand. He put her in his little fish basket.

"Is she o.k.?" The blood made me nervous.

"She's sleeping in the basket by now." Uncle Steve smiled. But on the way back to his truck, I could hear her moving.

"Maybe we should bring her back to the river," I told Uncle Steve.

"Why? We all got at least one this time. Fish for dinner tonight!" Ken jumped.

"I'm going to take her to the river," I grabbed Uncle Steve's basket.

"It's too late. This fish has been out of the water too long. It won't survive even in the river," said Uncle Steve. I held up the basket and felt her jumping around. I could almost hear her screaming, *let me out, let me out.*

KAMAKURA

I immediately feel sick to my stomach and out of breath, seeing a letter from Steve Johnson in the mailbox. I carefully take it out and open the envelope. My fingers tremble and almost drop it. *Dear Mr. Takagawa, My name is Steve Johnson, brother-in-law to your niece, Anna Johnson.* I put the letter back into the envelope as fast as I can with my trembling fingers. I don't want to read it further, not today, or at least not right now. My body moves the way it does every morning. I leave the rest of the mail on the kitchen table. I go to my office and get ready for work. But my hands are still trembling, and my mind is absolutely blank. I grab Shakespeare's *Henry V* and Walt Whitman's *Leaves of Grass,* but I can't remember which class I am teaching this afternoon. I need to leave this place as soon as possible. I place Steve Johnson's letter on my desk and walk out of my office. I put my shoes on, take the bag, and get out.

I walk so fast to the train station that I can barely breathe. I realize that I didn't say good-bye to Chiyo, that I'm teaching British literature today, and that my mind is scattered and terribly distracted, forgetting all my simple routines. My bag with its extra books feels heavy on my shoulder, but I command my feet to keep moving, to not consider turning around toward home. A train is coming into the platform, so I run to the station, down the stairs, and barely make it inside. As if I've been chased, I'm relieved once the door closes and the train starts moving.

It was foolish of me to leave the letter at home; I know it'll occupy my mind all day. It has been two weeks since I mailed my letter to Helen and Steve Johnson. Last week, a second before opening my mailbox, I froze, thinking that a letter from Helen would be there. When I didn't find one, I was disappointed and relieved. While I waited for their response, I thought about how Anna must have been terribly unhappy all these years; she might have been treated cruelly and perhaps suffered from hardships; in fact, she might have been abused and terrified all the time; she could be sick and dying now. Such assumptions progressed on their own and made me feel small. Now that Steve Johnson's letter is here, I'm too timid to learn about Anna. I have wondered why and how Anna's brother-in-law was helping Anna's family, and I would have found out if I had read the letter. Steve Johnson's letter was composed in such an adult manner, and there was nothing inexperienced about his approach, unlike Helen's. *I am a coward,* I tell myself, looking at the reflection of my flat and narrow eyes on the window in the train, and soon, the voice in my head is no longer mine, but Shinya's laughter—*I told you you'd catch Mother's weakness.*

Don't get close to Mother, or you will catch her weakness, Shinya used to say, ever since our mother attempted to leave us by going back to her family for a week when I was five. She left a note on the table explaining how she could no longer serve as a wife of the Takagawa family and asking for permission to return to her family. That morning, Shinya came to wake up me and Ume. Shinya calmly told us that our mother had left for good and we had to get dressed to go to breakfast. The maids came in and helped Ume get dressed. She was only three. At breakfast, Father was sitting and reading the paper as on any other day. I asked him if it was true that our mother had left. He said that was correct and began eating miso soup. He never explained why she left, where she went, or what was going to happen; therefore nobody said any more about her departure. I didn't really believe that I was never going to see Mother again, yet when she didn't return after three days, I began to feel nervous. Then, a week later, late at night, she came in from the back door to the kitchen and sat on the cold floor. I ran to her, but she told me to go get Father. I ran to Father, who had spent the evening in his library reading, and told him that Mother was home. He looked up slowly, gazed into my face, and quietly arose. I followed him to the kitchen. Mother was already surrounded by our servants, who were telling her to sit by the fire to warm up and drink some tea, but she stayed on the floor until Father came. As soon as Mother saw Father, she bowed with her entire body and began to apologize: *Please forgive me, such a foolish wife, for leaving. I was taken by an evil sprit and wasn't thinking clearly. My parents reminded me what a horrible mother I was to leave my children and abandon the duty of a wife of Takagawa. I beg your forgiveness to take me back to this household.* The entire time she spoke, she faced the floor as her body shook. Father just looked down at her and told her to pull herself together and that he expected breakfast at seven as usual tomorrow, then went back to his library. Mother, still facing the floor, began to cry. Perhaps it would have been better if Father went to her and slapped her face, but his life with or without Mother was manageable, as long as the breakfast was served at seven as he expected. If one's existence or absence does not matter in the slightest, one lives with the deepest sorrow, which was what I saw in my mother's eyes. Looking at my own face in the window, perhaps Shinya is right that I have caught weakness, but I won't blame Mother. I am in the midst of a battle with my own weakness.

Look, I told you, weakness is contagious and slips into you if you aren't careful. Shinya's dry voice spreads in my head, but I disagree. Shinya thought that being afraid was the sign of our weakness, and from the moment of his birth, he was taught to disallow any lenience. But he, too, must have felt afraid sometimes. He just rejected such a feeling completely within himself. Worse, yet, as if the pressure of becoming the future master of the Takagawa tradition and responsibilities of the silk farm business wasn't good enough, he signed himself up for the Youth Bravery Military Force to be sent to Manchuria. He often said that he was going to make the business bigger and more successful than what his grandfather or father had done, and to do so, the military was going to train and build him further. Father was quite proud of his dedication and commitment. In retrospsect, I'm afraid that Shinya was simply out of control and couldn't have imagined his death as the result of his commitment to strength. I, on the other hand, followed my mother's wish and pursued education. My mother's father was a professor who translated Russian literature into Japanese. He left his job when Mother was still little and formed a small publishing house for making Russian-Japanese dictionaries during the Meiji Era. I don't know how the two families became acquainted, but when the publishing business fell through, my paternal grandfather thought that welcoming a daughter of a college professor from a prestigious family in Tokyo to be his son's bride would sound "positively colorful and modern" to his community. Thus the marriage between Mother and Father long before they were teens was arranged, and in return, the huge debt Mother's family carried was taken care of. Mother often told me that involvement in a business could destroy one's mind since business was all about selling and buying, and even if selling and buying might be the most effective way to become wealthy, it led to the most worthless kind of life. I didn't take any of her speech seriously, since I knew her opinion was based on her resentment toward the Takagawa family. Mother made an arrangement for me to have access to the Hiroshima University Library, the largest library around, where I encountered texts from all over the world, and she told everyone how I, only a fourteen-year-old, was reading and studying books among older college students in the library, how dedicated I was, riding the bus three times a week after school to go to the library. My education became her weapon to rebel against the way of her life, but more importantly, the only way to express a part of herself.

While others thought I was honoring Mother's wishes, I just truly loved reading. I loved everything from Western mythology and Homer to modern Tolstoy and Dostoyevsky, but nothing stole my heart the way Shakespeare did, so I read everything the library had by and about Shakespeare. One of the professors at the university looked over my shoulder once and laughed because he didn't think I could understand Shakespeare, since I knew nothing about the history of England. But after he saw me sitting in the library all the time, captivated by Shakespeare's words and poetry, one day he gave me a copy of *Richard II* written in English. He said I must read the work in the original language if I truly wanted to understand it. I found out then that he was a professor of English literature and had even gone to study in Oxford for several years. This professor, whose name I do not recall, opened the text of *Richard II* and began reading in English. Back then, I didn't know anyone who had gone to a foreign country, or for that matter, someone who could speak English. I had no idea what he was saying, but the sound of the English words spread into soft sounds and covered my ears, as if I were listening to music. Although I didn't understand the meaning, the sounds themselves swept me away. I began spending hours using the English and Japanese dictionary, translating words one by one. I loved to translate, unlocking words into my world as the foreign words became more familiar.

The English words that were once musical to my ear felt sharp, reading Steve Johnson's letter, yet I still should have read it this morning. *You are a coward;* Shinya was right, and haven't I always been a coward? Every time I visited the school Anna attended, pretending to be just another generous volunteer who came to spend some time with orphans, I couldn't bring myself to introduce myself as her uncle, as I had no courage to face the

question to come—*If you are my uncle, why do I live in the orphanage?*
Nor did I have the courage to adopt her and watch her face the
cruelties of life in Japan. Many small children sat around me as
I taught them simple English. They especially loved counting in
English, which was like a song to them. My eyes kept singling
Anna out, and if I didn't control myself, I would have looked
at her the entire time. I made myself look around at all the children, but when my eyes met Anna's, I stayed there longer than
I was supposed to, for I was filled with joy. She was only five
years old, but I unfairly looked at her as if she were Ume, for
the sake of my longing for my sister. Over the years, each grain
of my sorrow has gathered into the center of my chest and
hardened like a rock. I have lived carefully not to break this
rock so that the sorrow wouldn't spread throughout my body
like blood. But in the end, I know it is better for whatever will
break my heart someday to break it now. This touch of the
truth will be painful, but I cannot stop Anna's presence from
walking directly toward me.

The cool air hits my face as I walk alone through Kamakura's
quiet night, full of nostalgic air. My mother used to say that
when we were feeling nostalgic, our ancestors' ghosts were right
behind us. I have always lived with a sense of nostalgia since
the death of Ume, yet never once did I feel as though she were
right behind me. She was gone and was never going to return.
Instead, I'm afraid that my father's dead face would be waiting
behind me. But when I turn around, all I see is the Tsurugaoka
Hachiman Shrine, standing with elegance up on the hill. I picture Samurai soldiers walking on this street hundreds of years
ago on a cold night like this, full of crisp air.

After a lecture and two meetings, I thought I would rush to
get home. But I have been wandering and walking around the
main street of Kamakura this evening. Ahead of me is the train
station, which I have already walked by three times. I'm acting

like a child, hiding to avoid a punishment. The train station is rather crowded with many people and businessmen in dark suits. I finally walk up to the platform and stand in the line behind an old man. His body seems fragile among young people in colorful clothes as they laugh about something. To young people, I suppose I must look just like this man, awfully small and frugal. Young people are handsome, much taller than when I was their age. I always thought we stopped growing during the war, as if something stopped our bones from growing. Young people today seem free to grow so wholeheartedly, and I envy their bright faces standing above our heads. When my train arrives, we all push into a small space. A group of young women are talking with laughter by the door; a couple in front of me are describing American films; a young boy and a mother next to me are discussing the entrance exam for a junior high school. There's a distance between me and everything else inside the train, as if I were a foreigner, and I'm afraid that we wouldn't understand each other, as if what matters to them is so different from what matters to me. I get off at the next station even though it's not my stop. I don't want to be carried in the same train among all these strangers.

Watching the train leave, I sit on the bench at the platform and look around. Somehow I was left behind while the world moved on. On the day I carried Ume's ashes in the train, unlike tonight, I felt connected to others, perhaps because we were all grieving. A sight of a man carrying an ash box on a train wasn't unusual right after the war, and people bowed to me with a sense of understanding. People died so often during and after the war that death and grief were as tangible as hunger. Over the years, the sight of people carrying an ash box on the street or in the train disappeared, but my mind remained in the train with the people who grieved.

A day after Ume's death, a man from the crematorium came to pick up her body, and I sat in the front seat of his car with him. Ume lived for twenty-one years, but her body took only two hours to become ash. How quickly a human body is reduced into gray powder. Ume's ashes were placed in a box wrapped in a white cloth, and I carefully held it and walked on the busy road to go home. That day, I noticed everything. The road was crowded that afternoon, and people were shouting from the markets, selling random items like soap, cups, ashtrays, children's toys, clothes, razors, radios, cigarettes, canned vegetables and meat with English labels. When I walked on this street every day from my apartment to the train station to go to the university, I never paid attention to any of the items that the people sold there, but the day after Ume's death, I felt as if the road had suddenly become longer. I smelled dust covering all the displays.

In my apartment, I placed Ume's ashes in a box on top of my bookshelf with a glass of water and incense sticks. That was the altar for Ume. I telegraphed my father about Ume's death, but I didn't hear anything from him. I was unable to sleep that night; I just sat on the futon and smoked cigarettes for hours. I felt exhausted, but my mind wouldn't allow me to sleep. I was sad, restless, and shocked that my sister had completely disappeared, but I didn't cry.

During the week after Ume's death, I wasn't myself; it seemed that I could only walk three times slower than usual and felt as if I could never reach my destination. I was working as an assistant to Professor Kudo at Tokyo University, who offered me a few days off from work and suggested that I go back to Hiroshima to see my father. Thanking him, I told him that was unnecessary; my father knew of Ume's death through my telegram, and as I suspected, he showed no response to her passing. I only took one day off for Ume's cremation and went back to work the following day. I hardly slept for over a week, but I needed to do something.

At work, I read and translated some passages from five British journal articles and stayed as late as possible in the office until the building closed at nine o'clock. On the way home, the night air felt painful on my skin, and I had a dull ache in my head. Every step I took to the train station made a loud noise in my head. All I wanted was to go to a warm room and rest on a soft futon, but the reality was that I was going back to my cold apartment where Ume's ashes rested on the top of my bookshelf. I lit a cigarette as I passed the busy crowds of foreign soldiers laughing with young women dressed in bright red and green. I could feel some of them staring at me in my old, dirty coat and shoes, a typical Japanese man who looked nothing like those clean and tall foreign soldiers. Standing next to a Westerner, my head only came to his chin. Their laughter seemed to follow me as if they were mocking me. I walked even faster, though I wasn't moving forward fast enough, as if the air had become a thick wall blocking my path.

By the time I returned to my apartment, it was late. One day, the landlady stopped me before I went up and gave me hot water. She came closer and whispered that a young woman had been waiting for me by my door since late afternoon. My head was feeling each beat of my heart from the cold night air; I couldn't think straight. I thanked the landlady and carried the hot water upstairs. There, by the door, a woman in a light blue dress was sitting on the floor, but as soon as she saw my face, she stood up quickly and looked at me straight. Her warm and light presence seemed out of place, which surprised me so much that I just stood and looked at her. I didn't know this woman. She bowed deeply, so I bowed back. As I walked closer to her, I noticed that her eyes were all watery. She said she had heard about Ume's death. I apologized to her for not knowing who she was. In fact, I didn't think Ume had any friends, but she shook her head and said she didn't expect that I would know her. I opened the door and invited her into my apartment.

The presence of a young woman standing among the dark walls of my old apartment felt strange, and I realized that Ume hadn't been well enough to stand up for the past few weeks. That room had absorbed much moaning and coughing, but the presence of this woman in her colorful dress created a different space. How easy it was for someone to disappear completely from this world, I thought. She saw the altar on my bookshelf. She pulled out two apples from a brown bag and placed them by Ume's ashes. Her eyes were full of tears.

"My name is Chiyo Furukawa, and I work at city hall, at the Home Guidance Center," she spoke slowly. Then I realized who she was. Ume mentioned that she had gone to the Home Guidance Center at the city hall, a new system created by the postwar government, and found out about the Christian Home for Children. While Ume was dying, she wanted to make arrangements for her daughter, though she never considered asking me to raise her. Ume told me that she met a kind woman at the guidance center, and she advised Ume to take her daughter to the Christian Home for Children. After all the arrangements had been made, Ume went back to see Chiyo to thank her. When Ume was hospitalized for a few days, Chiyo visited her several times. I worked until late in the evening, so I never had a chance to meet Chiyo or even to remember her name, but I often heard from Ume about the woman from the Home Guidance Center, very kind and graceful.

I asked Chiyo to sit down and thanked her for helping Ume with a difficult situation. She bowed deeply. She said she found my address by checking Ume's file, that she wasn't supposed to use the file to visit me, but she felt she had to. She looked at me with her black eyes full of tears and said she hoped that her guidance was appropriate. Chiyo was afraid that advising Ume to give up her child might have worsened her illness. I could see the guilt in her eyes. Immediately, I felt immense joy that Ume was deeply cared for by this woman. It may have been brief, but Chiyo went out of her way to care for Ume, which was something that Ume had never before received, not even from her own father. All of Japan seemed to turn against her and treat her coldly for having a child with a foreign soldier. No one would speak kind words, and instead, she was judged as a dirty betrayer, even by children. I was so filled with gratitude toward Chiyo that I began to cry. Ume died knowing warmth. My chest was filled with Chiyo's kindness, and for the first time since Ume died, I cried. In front of a woman that I had just met for the first time, I cried feverishly. I lost control of my breathing and felt dizzy. Chiyo cried with me. We didn't say anything and cried together for a long time.

When I stopped sobbing, Chiyo said she had to return home. It was quite late. I put my coat on and walked her to Mitaka station.

"Ume told me that she used to follow you everywhere you went. She told me about your family's silk farm," Chiyo said as we walked together in the cold night. I had never walked with a young woman before. I was so taken by the pleasantness and warmth in Chiyo's voice and wanted to continue listening to her soft voice that uttered Ume's name.

"I liked Ume, from the moment I met her. It's strange, but I liked her very much," Chiyo said before she bowed to me and walked to the platform. I watched her blue dress go up the stairs and disappear from my sight. Then I turned around and saw where we had just came from, the dark and long street.

Remembering Ume's death is always bittersweet, since I met Chiyo through Ume's death. I get up from the bench and start walking home. Something about tonight—walking through Kamakura or thinking about the letter from Steve Johnson—fills me with apprehension. I take big steps and move my legs quickly through the cold air, burning my face and lungs to get home where Chiyo awaits me.

SEPTEMBER 1975

On the night before the first day of school, Aunt Mary helped me pack my bag. She bought new schoolbags for me and Ken. I didn't want to go to a new school, but there was one thing that I *was* excited about. We had to wear a uniform—a navy blue skirt, a white shirt, a cream-colored vest, and a blazer for the winter. Ken had navy pants, a white shirt, and a brown jacket.

"Let's try them on for tomorrow!" Aunt Mary brought my uniform from the closet. Ken didn't really want to, but we made him do it, too. I put my skirt on first, then my shirt, and the vest. Aunt Mary brought two pairs of brown leather shoes. They looked so serious. Ken put on his uniform even though he complained. He looked like a little Dad in his dark suit.

When Uncle Steve's car came up the driveway, we ran downstairs. He was always home by dinner, but today, he called and said that he was going to be late. Ken and I stood in front of the door and waited for him to come in. He had never seen us in our uniforms. It's fun to surprise someone. The knob moved and the door slowly opened.

Ken yelled, "Surprise!"

"Surprise!" I yelled at the half-opened door.

"Hello?" It wasn't Uncle Steve. It was Dad. I stepped back a little. Ken stood behind me. We hadn't seen him for so long, since the night he dropped us off. I had no idea that he was coming today. He smiled, looked down, and just stood by the door. Behind him, Uncle Steve came in with a big smile.

"Wow, you guys look great!" Uncle Steve kissed my cheek, then picked up Ken. "Your Dad wanted to visit you." Uncle Steve smiled at me. Ken hid his face in Uncle Steve's chest.

"What's the matter? Why don't you give your dad a hug?" Uncle Steve tried to put Ken down, but he shook his head and didn't show his face. Uncle Steve turned to me because he wanted me to greet Dad. I walked to Dad.

"Hello, Helen." Dad kissed me. I could smell his hair and his gray suit. His skin felt moist. His eyes were bright blue like Uncle Steve's. I had never really looked into Dad's eyes before.

Aunt Mary walked to Dad, said hello, and kissed his cheek.

"Is Mommy here, too?" Ken looked around. Dad shook his head. He had the same tired look he had a month ago.

Uncle Steve walked into the dining room with Ken in his arms, so we followed him. Dad came last. I looked behind at Dad again. He smiled at me, then looked down. He didn't know where to look in this house. Uncle Steve asked Aunt Mary to make some coffee, then asked Ken to open the white box that he had brought home. Ken was acting shy, looking down. Uncle Steve's voice sounded extra cheerful tonight.

"Go on, open the box, Ken. It's for you." Ken still didn't move. So Uncle Steve turned to me again. I walked to the table and opened the box. It was a cake with big shiny strawberries on the top.

"It's a cheesecake. Your dad got it for you. For dessert." Uncle Steve's voice bounced in the room. I wanted to help Uncle Steve. But I didn't know what to say to Dad.

"Mom said cake is bad for us. She said sugar is poison," Ken mumbled. Dad opened his eyes wider, but he didn't say anything. He was standing with his hands in his pockets.

"This cake is special because your dad got it for you. It's actually good for you." Uncle Steve smiled and brought us plates from the kitchen.

We sat down and Aunt Mary cut the cake. Dad sat across the table from me. His shirt was wrinkled and his tie was loose.

He had red marks on both sides of his nose from his glasses. He slowly brought a creamy bite into his mouth. I'd never really seen Dad eat sweet food before. Uncle Steve and Aunt Mary kept saying that this was the best cheesecake ever. The table looked full with five people sitting around it. Dad didn't say much. Seeing Dad without Mom was strange; she was always there when he came home. Ken only ate half of his cake, then started to mash it into a flat shape with his fork. The white cream and the yellow cheesecake were mashed into a soft puddle, and he kept beating it. No one stopped Ken from playing with his food.

"Happy birthday, Ken." Dad's dark voice came from across the table.

"But it's not my birthday today," Ken said.

"I know. I'm sorry I couldn't be here on your birthday," Dad said.

Ken didn't look up. He nodded his head. Aunt Mary touched Ken's hair softly. When we were done, Uncle Steve cleared the table. Dad quietly wiped his mouth with a paper napkin. Aunt Mary was touching Ken's hair, and no one said anything. I felt like I had to say something, but I couldn't look at him. Aunt Mary got up and said we better go to bed since we had to get up early tomorrow. I stood up quickly and took Ken's hand. Dad watched us follow Aunt Mary upstairs. Nothing had changed. Dad still looked at us with that same tired face.

Aunt Mary didn't take us to our rooms, but to her and Uncle Steve's bedroom. She said that we could sleep there. We loved sleeping on their bed; it was so big that there was plenty of room for all of us. Uncle Steve said he felt like a king when he slept on it. I always pretended I was swimming in the covers. Sometimes when I had a scary dream, I came to their room. Then Aunt Mary always let me sleep right next to her. She rubbed my back until I fell back asleep. Sometimes, Ken came in, too. Aunt Mary tucked us in and kissed us good-night. She shut off the light and left the door half open. I could hear Dad's and Uncle Steve's muffled voices from below and the footsteps of Aunt Mary walking down the stairs.

"Why's Dad here?" Ken whispered to me.

"I don't know."

"Do you think he's taking us back home?"

"No, we're going to a new school tomorrow." I couldn't see Ken's face in the dark. The noise from downstairs was ringing in my head.

"I know the secret," Ken whispered again. "Mom's in the hospital. Mrs. Hogan said Mom's in the hospital." I got up quickly. Ken pulled my sleeve and said, *shhhhhhh*.

"Mrs. Hogan? When did you see her?" I glared at him.

"I didn't see her. I called home, and Mrs. Hogan answered the phone."

"When did you call home? You aren't supposed to. Dad said we couldn't call home, that only he could call us."

"Last week. I wanted to talk to Mommy."

"Why did Mrs. Hogan answer our phone?"

"I don't know. She said Mom wasn't home. She said Mom was in the hospital."

Ken whispered really soft when he said the word, *hospital*.

"She said we should go visit Mom."

"What's wrong with her?" I got closer to Ken.

"I don't know."

"Didn't you ask? Where is the hospital?" I grabbed his shoulders.

"I don't know. She didn't say. She was whispering on the phone. It was weird." Ken shook his head. Ken was so stupid! Mrs. Hogan should have talked to me. I would have asked more questions. I would have gone to the hospital to see Mom.

"Mrs. Hogan said Mom wants to see us. She said Mom just looks at the ocean from her window all day." Ken was too slow telling me what happened.

"I'm going downstairs to ask Dad where Mom is." I was getting out of the bed when Ken grabbed my sleeve to stop me.

"No, no! Mrs. Hogan said I'm not supposed to tell anyone about it."

"Why?" I pulled my sleeve away from him.

"I don't know."

He made me so mad. I went back to the bed, away from Ken, but he came close to me.

"We have to go visit Mommy," Ken said to my back.

"How? You don't know where Mom is." If Ken were older and smarter, if I could drive, we could find Mom, but we couldn't do anything.

"Mrs. Hogan said we shouldn't have left Mom." Ken shook my back.

I pushed him away. "We didn't leave Mom, remember? Mom didn't want to see us."

"But Mrs. Hogan said—"

"Shut up!" I got away from Ken, as far as I could go on the bed, and shut my eyes.

"Helen? Don't sleep!" Ken came back closer and shook my shoulder with his hands. I ignored him. He called my name five more times, but I kept ignoring him. Then he stopped and turned away from me. Soon I heard his quiet breathing and knew then that he fell asleep. Ken's breathing and the muffled voices of Dad and Uncle Steve entered my ears, not really making sense, but I had to hear them as long as I was awake.

For a while, I just gazed at the dark space and thought about Mom in a hospital gown. She took me to the hospital when I was sick once, and I had to wear a thin paper gown. I was little, maybe six like Ken, and sat on her lap. The doctor put his hand under my gown and listened to my heart. Mom held me tight with her arms around my stomach and kissed my head.

For a long long time, I counted. Eight hundred ninety-nine, and I was still awake. From downstairs, the muffled dark and deep sound of Dad's voice kept tickling my ears. His voice made me think of birds flying away somewhere far, so I kept counting birds in my head, until no more birds could fit. The sky was filled with so many birds that it scared me. Ken moved around. He moved too much when he slept. I didn't know what time it was, but it felt late. I opened my eyes just a little bit to see around. I could see a light out in the hallway. I slowly got up and walked through the hallway and came to the stairs.

From there, I could hear what Uncle Steve and Dad were saying. I came down two steps, sat, and looked into the living room. Dad was sitting on the couch, holding a glass half full of a brown drink. Uncle Steve stood in front of Dad, and he talked like he was angry. Their voices overlapped. They talked fast. I could hardly catch up. Their voices were getting louder. Then Aunt Mary walked in from the kitchen and said keep it down. They stopped talking, and the living room was silent. Uncle Steve walked to the window and stared outside. All the trees, flowers, and the pond in the yard were all black at night.

"James, please try harder." Uncle Steve turned to Dad.

"What do you want me to try?" Dad took a big sip from his brown drink.

"You're acting like you don't care about your family."

"I do care about them."

"I know you do, but Helen and Ken don't understand that."

Dad pulled out a cigarette from his pocket and lit it. He blew the smoke high up in the air.

"When I was lighting this cigarette, just now, what were you thinking?"

"What do you mean?"

"Just now, watching me light the cigarette."

"I don't know. I just watched you smoke. Why?" Uncle Steve shrugged his shoulders.

Dad looked down at his lighter and laughed a little. "This lighter won't blow up like Lieutenant Mayer's did right in

front of his face, but my head thinks it might. I have no idea
where he got that goddamn Zippo. It even said 'Made in USA.'
On patrol, Lieutenant Mayer always said, 'If it moves, runs,
hides, it's VC. Waste it. If it's dead, count it for your promo-
tion.' He never hesitated on anything. He even thought if you
got a Purple Heart from getting shot, that was stupid because
if you were smart, you wouldn't get shot. I couldn't believe
he'd say things like that. He thought we could move faster
than bullets? Anyway, a month later, he died from that stupid
Zippo blowing up in his hands. Can you believe that? Nobody
told the family how he died. They probably think he died in
combat. Who would want to be remembered as a fool, caught
by the Vietcong's goddamn trick?" Dad threw the lighter
against the wall.

"James, the war is over."

Dad got up and started putting on his coat.

"Why don't you stay here tonight? You should be here tomorrow morning for Helen and Ken. It's their first day of school."

"I'm sorry, but I better go." Dad took his briefcase and started
to walk to the door. At the door, his tired face turned around. I
could see his eyes all red and watery through his glasses.

"Steve, maybe my kids don't understand me, but it's better
that way. On the battlefield, I knew exactly what I was supposed to do. But now, I have no idea what to do. I can't be the
person I'm supposed to be." Then he walked out the door, like
he was never coming back again.

I got up and ran upstairs. I stayed at the top, hiding by the
wall, and listened to Dad leave. My bare feet could feel the outside air from the opened door. I slowly put my head out. The
headlights of Dad's car shone like angry eyes, slowly turning
around to drive away in the darkness. Uncle Steve stood in the
driveway for a while with his hands in his pockets. Before he
turned around to come back inside, I went back to the bedroom. I was blind in the dark room, so I touched the wall to

find the bed. There, I stepped on Ken's feet, but he didn't wake up. I put my cold feet against Ken's warm feet.

When I heard Uncle Steve's footsteps, I closed my eyes as tight as I could.

On the first day of school, Ken was so nervous that he started crying. He said that something hard like a rock was rolling inside his chest. He didn't want to go to a new school, but Uncle Steve said he had to. He promised to take us to get ice cream that night. So we went to school up on a hill surrounded by a white fence and many trees. Ken had to go to a different building from mine, so I was a little bit worried about him. Since we left home, he was always with me or Uncle Steve and Aunt Mary. But when I saw him during recess, he was laughing and running around with some kids. Ken was like that. He could change and forget about everything fast.

From the first day, Ken really liked school. At dinner, he always talked about his day. He didn't really talk about Mom or Dad anymore; I thought he may have forgotten about them. I liked the new school, too, but my teacher, Sister Margaret, was hard. She gave us a lot of homework. When we were studying poetry, she would start each class by reciting a poem. She didn't read from a book, but from memory. When she stood in the middle of the classroom and closed her eyes, we got quiet because we knew that she was going to read a poem.

> I have a small
> daughter called
> Cleis, who is
> Like a golden
> flower
> I wouldn't
> take all Croesus

Kingdom with love
thrown in, for her

After the reading, there was silence, and Sister Margaret waited
for a few seconds before she spoke to us.

"This poem is called 'Sleep, Darling' by Sappho. What do
you think it means to say someone is like a golden flower?"
Sister Margaret looked around. A golden flower? I have never
seen anything like that. It must be pretty if there was something
like a golden flower.

"Raise your hand if your parents call you honey, or sweetheart, or pumpkin?" Sister Margaret looked around, and many
hands were up. I raised my hand, too. Mom called me honey
sometimes. Dad called me Helen. Uncle Steve and Aunt Mary
called me many names.

"Good," Sister Margaret smiled. "The poet called her daughter a golden flower, and your parents call you a name that
means sweet. You can tell that your parents love you very much
when they call you that, right?" We all nodded to her questions
even though I didn't really know what she meant.

"This is what we call a *simile*." Sister Margaret wrote SIMILE
up on the board. "*Simile* means comparing an object or a person to something from your imagination by using *like* or *as*. We
probably use similes all the time without realizing it! We will
practice how to use them today."

Some boys in the back made the I-don't-want-to-do-it noise,
but she ignored this and wrote on the board: *Pick one person that
you love, and compare that person to five different things.*

It was a lot harder than I thought. I wrote Mom first, then
erased her name. Then I wrote Ken, but I would never say
Ken's like a golden flower. Ken is like a small puppy. Ken is like
a strawberry (his cheeks have freckles). Ken is like . . . Ken is
like . . . I didn't know more, so I thought about Dad. Dad is
like a stone. Dad is like a night. Dad is like his suit. Dad is like

. . . a big tree. Then I remembered the assignment. *One person that you love.* Do I love Dad? Do I love Ken? What did it mean? Uncle Steve said *I love you* all the time, so I said it back, too. I love Uncle Steve, so I wrote Uncle Steve. Uncle Steve is like a big tree. Uncle Steve is like his blue eyes. That didn't make sense. I just like his eyes. I wrote Mom. Mom is like a thin tree. Mom is like a white wall. Mom is like spring. Mom is like the ocean. Mom is like her pink pajamas. Mom is like a flower, but not a golden flower. What kind of flower is she?

Sister Margaret was walking around the class as we wrote our is-like assignment. Then she went back to the front and asked who wanted to read their five similes. Many hands went up. She picked Ryan in the back. He was a really loud boy.

"My dad is like a big car. My dad is like a strong soldier. My dad is like a super-strong storm. My dad is like a big tree. My dad is like a big steak!" Ryan read them fast and with a big smile.

"Why is your dad like a big steak?" Sister Margaret smiled.

"Because his stomach is big and soft." We all laughed, and Ryan looked like he was proud.

"And a strong soldier?"

"Because Dad was a hero in Vietnam. He was the strongest of all."

Sister Margaret thanked Ryan and asked for another volunteer. I had never raised my hand in this class. I gazed at my notebook.

"Helen? Would you mind reading yours?" Sister Margaret's voice was right on top of my head, and I could see everyone looking at me. My notebook was a mess. Ken, Dad, Uncle Steve, and Mom. Their names were everywhere and I didn't know what to do. I slowly stood up and found five lines at the bottom.

"My mom is like a thin tree. Mom is like a white wall." I breathed in warm air and kept reading, "Mom is like spring. Mom is like the ocean. Mom is like her pink pajamas." No one laughed or made noise. I just sat down and hoped that Sister Margaret wouldn't ask me any questions.

"Thank you." And she didn't ask any questions. Everyone's eyes went back to Sister Margaret up front, so I felt safe. She talked more about similes, until the bell for recess rang.

My cheeks were still warm from reading in class. I walked to the window and looked outside at all the big and thick trees. If I tied a big steak to the middle of the tree, then that was what Ryan's dad was like. Ryan's dad was the opposite of my mom. There were some small short trees by the fence. That wasn't Mom either. That was like me. A child tree. Five lines about me—I'm like a short tree, like a rainbow trout, I'm like . . . I'm like . . . red. My favorite outfit is my red velvet Christmas dress. But I could only come up with three things about me.

"Thank you for reading today." Sister Margaret walked toward me with her books.

"Yes." I looked up.

"I wanted to know what you meant by saying your mom is like her pink pajamas." Her eyes got bigger.

I didn't know how to explain.

"Does your mom have pink pajamas?" Sister Margaret's voice was loud enough that other people could hear us. I didn't want everyone looking at me.

"My mom's pink pajamas smell very good." I told her. I wanted to tell her that they smelled like spring air, spring flowers, they smelled soft. No one had that smell but Mom. I wanted to say the pink pajamas were mine, too. But I didn't know how to make them mine.

"I'm sure they smell wonderful. You must miss her very much." Sister Margaret squatted down to see my eyes.

"Who told you about Mom?" I looked at her. How did she know about Mom?

"Oh, your uncle told me that your mother is ill."

"Why? Why did he tell you?" I didn't understand why Uncle Steve had to tell her about Mom. I was being good and taking care of Ken.

"I just wanted you to know that you can come and talk to me about anything. I know you miss your mom. It's all right." Sister Margaret touched my shoulder. I looked away from her. She patted my shoulder again and walked away. She didn't understand. Mom got sick and dizzy when she saw me, and I was thinking about her pajamas.

"What's wrong with your Mom?" Ryan came from the back of the room. I didn't say anything. I didn't want to talk about Mom.

"Hey, is your mom Filipino? You look Filipino," Ryan said.

"I'm not Filipino."

"What are you?"

I didn't want to say Japanese. I didn't like that word.

"Are you sure you aren't Filipino? You look like our cleaning lady's daughter."

"I'm not Filipino!" I went back to my desk, took my paper, and tore it into many snowflakes. Then I walked to his desk and took what he wrote about his dad and tore it into snowflakes, too.

"What did you do that for!" Ryan pulled my hair. So I slapped his arm really hard. He punched my back. I coughed a little, but I pushed his back as hard as I could. He tumbled down and hit his forehead on the edge of someone's desk. Then dark red came down from his head. The blood looked so dark, almost purple. I always thought blood was red, but it wasn't. Ryan started to cry, and everyone was screaming. Sister Margaret came back to the classroom from the hallway. Her face turned white. She told everyone to stay where we were. She took Ryan and me to the school nurse. I was fine, I wanted to say, but she pulled my hand on one side and Ryan's hand on the other. We ran down the hallway together. Ryan's forehead was still bleeding. I watched his blood drip with his tears. I wanted to hide in the closet now. Now I wanted Shizuka to take me back to her world.

As bad as Ryan's forehead looked with his blood, once Sister Ann cleaned his forehead, his cut was really small. It was strange that so much blood ran from a small cut like that. My hands felt numb looking at Ryan's cut. He finally stopped crying when the nurse put ice on his forehead.

"You still need a few stitches, though." Sister Ann touched around the cut on Ryan's forehead. "I called your father and he is on his way to take you to the doctor."

Ryan's face got really pale when he heard that his father was coming. My stomach was moving right and left inside me, and I sat down on the floor.

"I called your uncle, too, Helen. He's on his way," Sister Margaret said sharply.

"Am I going to the hospital, too?"

"No, but you'll go home now. I need to talk to your uncle about today." Sister Margaret was mad at me. I looked down at the floor and followed the seams and pattern of the wooden floor. I didn't mean to hurt Ryan. I didn't know he was going to fall like that. I wanted to say I was sorry to Ryan, but I thought saying something was worse.

When someone knocked on the door, my stomach fell to my feet. I just prayed that Uncle Steve would be standing on the other side of the door. Maybe Uncle Steve wouldn't like me anymore. Maybe he wouldn't want me to live in his house anymore. No one liked a bad person. A tall and thick man opened the door and walked into the room. It was Ryan's dad. Ryan's similes were right. He was like a big steak. He was like a big tree. He walked to Ryan, looking at his forehead, and Sister Ann explained Ryan's wound. I stood up on the floor and tried to stay still.

"It's such a small cut. Are you sure that he needs stitches?" Ryan's dad checked Ryan's forehead closely.

"Yes, maybe two or three stitches, but yes, he needs to go to the doctor." Sister Ann nodded many times.

"Geez, I wish you didn't get into a fight, Ryan." Ryan's dad glanced at him. Ryan's neck went down like a broken branch. Soon, Ryan was going to point at me and tell his dad that I pushed him. I opened my mouth and was going to say I was sorry. But Ryan didn't say anything. Instead, he said he was sorry. Ryan didn't look at me at all. He just left with his dad.

Someone was running in the hallway. The sound got closer and suddenly changed into a loud knocking at the door. Before anyone said to come in, the door opened and Uncle Steve walked in with his light brown work shirt and jeans. His face was all red from running and breathing fast. He looked around the room and saw me in the corner. He ran to me with a worried look and asked me if I was O.K. I nodded. My chest hurt. I blinked my eyes many times to see him, but tears wouldn't stop coming out. I used both hands to wipe off my tears, but I couldn't catch up. I didn't know why my chest hurt so much. Uncle Steve held me with both of his arms. I was crying like Ken. But I couldn't stop. Inside Uncle Steve's arms, all I could hear was my own sobs.

❦

I watched the water from the bench by the bay and waited for Uncle Steve to come back from the ice cream stand. He came back, holding a big scoop of strawberry ice cream and green mint ice cream. The strawberry was mine. Uncle Steve hadn't said anything about me being bad and hurting Ryan. He just said everything was going to be all right. I felt bad that I was by the bay eating ice cream while everyone was in class and Ryan was getting stitches at the doctor. Uncle Steve licked his mint chocolate ice cream and showed me his green tongue to make me laugh. The green cream dripped on Uncle Steve's work shirt.

"When Sister Margaret called, I was getting ready to go to Mrs. Peterson's garden to arrange her trees." He wiped the spill off his shirt with his hand.

"I'm sorry." My mouth was so cold that talking was hard.

"Actually, you saved me from listening to her complain about how her thirty-year-old daughter hasn't gotten married." He smiled.

"Why does she complain to you?"

"Well, because Kate, Mrs. Peterson's daughter was my girl-friend when I was nine, like you."

"You had a girlfriend in fourth grade?"

"I know it's early, but I liked girls." Uncle Steve laughed. "You know, I was pushed by a girl when I was little, too." Uncle Steve licked his ice cream. "Kate came to school wearing a bracelet that looked like a snake. I was making fun of her, that she was a snake collector, that she had more snakes at home. She ran away from me, but I followed her and teased her all afternoon. Finally, she pushed me into the pond in my schoolyard."

"Really? Did you get wet?"

"I was all wet and muddy!"

"Were you mad at her?"

"No, because she told me that the bracelet was a gift from her grandfather. He just died that week, and she was close to him. I felt really bad and apologized to her. Then I became her boyfriend." He shrugged his shoulders with a smile.

That didn't make sense at all.

"Maybe Ryan likes you." Uncle Steve smiled at me. My face got warm, and I shook my head. He didn't like me, and I didn't like him.

"Should we go home?" Uncle Steve wiped off his hands on his pants and took my hand. My hands were sticky with ice cream, but he still held my hand as we walked to his truck. We drove home, going down the hill as I watched the ocean. I looked back up the hill, and all the leaves were moving along with the wind. Uncle Steve was looking straight ahead. The road was narrow and winding. I thought of Mom wearing the hospital gown, looking at the ocean.

~⌐

The phone rang and rang and rang, but no one was picking it up. It was so loud, I jumped up from the bed to answer it. The phone stopped ringing then. Everyone was asleep and the house was silent. The clock said twelve-fifteen. I fell asleep in Uncle Steve's truck on the way home from ice cream. After crying, I always get tired. I took a nap all afternoon. Aunt Mary tried to wake me up for dinner, but I was too sleepy to get up. She let me sleep, so I slept until after midnight, and the phone woke me up. Who was calling so late? I didn't know why Aunt Mary or Uncle Steve didn't answer it since the phone was right next to their bed. I went downstairs to the other phone. I slowly picked it up and put it next to my ear. There wasn't any dial tone. I could hear some fuzzy noise in the background. Someone must be on the other line.

"Hello?" I said.

Nobody answered. The fuzzy noise got louder and smaller like the ocean waves.

"Mom?" My stomach jumped inside. "Mom? Are you calling from the hospital?" I said it as loud as I could, whispering. It must be Mom. Mrs. Hogan said Mom could see the ocean from the hospital window. Mom isn't supposed to talk to us, so she must be hiding somewhere. When the fuzzy noise got louder, I thought Mom was walking outside by the ocean.

"Mom, wait there! We'll come, too!" I hung up the phone, ran upstairs on my tiptoes and went to Ken's room.

"Wake up, Ken! Wake up!" I shook him. He was sleeping hard. Ken rubbed his eyes and looked around.

"We have to go see Mom. She's waiting at the shore," I whispered.

"Really? Now?"

"She just called. She's looking for us."

Ken's eyes were wide open. I went back to my room and got dressed quickly and grabbed my coat. I knew it was Mom calling us. If she could see the ocean from her window, her hospital must be by the ocean. I knew how to get to the ocean from Uncle Steve's house. We could walk the shore until we saw the big hospital. Mom must be outside, waiting for us.

"Hurry up!" I shouted, still whispering. Ken didn't move fast enough, so I helped him get dressed. We tiptoed to the front door. Ken held on to my coat. I unlocked and turned the doorknob slowly. It made a little noise, so I stopped and looked around. Uncle Steve and Aunt Mary were still sleeping. I held Ken's hand, went outside, and closed the door as quietly as possible. Outside at night looked like a different planet. I ran, holding Ken's hand, down the hill. Our running was so loud that I thought everyone in Tiburon would wake up. The stoplight's red was extra bright at night. I stopped, looked right and left, pulled Ken's hand, and ran through the intersection, down the hill, all the way to the ocean.

We finally came to the stone stairs that went to the sandy shore. We couldn't run when we were on the sand.

"It's so dark! I can't see anything!" Ken screamed. There was no light, and everything was black. I couldn't even see my feet. It got so windy on the sand, and the sound of waves came from all over.

"We just have to walk parallel to the water! O.K.?" I shouted to Ken and pulled his hand. He was getting heavy. He didn't move forward.

"I'm scared. I can't see anything!"

"Move your feet!" I pulled him forward. I didn't know which way to the water, but we had to find it.

"What if the waves pull us in the ocean?" Ken yelled again.

"No, we won't go *into* the water! We'll walk *by* the water," I yelled back. But we couldn't find the water.

"Where are we?" Ken stopped.

I tried to follow the sound of the waves, but the sound came from different directions every time I took a step, as if the ocean pulled back a step, running away from us.

Ken came to a complete stop, so I tried to pull him, but he started crying.

"Where are we?" His voice was shaking. I looked around. We were in the pure black air. *The ocean was behind the wall of the closet,* Mom told us. Were we standing right behind the closet wall? Ken sat on the sand. The wind was swirling and making a scary noise. I sat down next to him.

"I'm scared." Ken came close to me.

"We should just sit and wait." I put my arms around him.

"What are we waiting for?"

"Mom will come and open the door."

"Open the door?"

"Yeah, we are behind the wall in the closet. Mom will come and find us soon." I knew we weren't supposed to look for Mom, but Mom would come and find us, wearing her hospital gown, and take us home. We couldn't be that far from her hospital.

We sat and waited for a long time, listening to the waves coming and going. Sometimes, the waves crashed, but other times, they were so gentle. The angry waves usually splashed white water, which I couldn't see tonight, but by listening to the sound of the angry waves, I could almost see the white water. I wanted Mom to open the door soon before Shizuka came and took us back to the ocean.

"Look!" Ken jumped up. I stood up, too. Small lights, like little stars floating up in the air, were coming toward us.

"Mom?" I called.

"Mommy?" Ken yelled. Mom must be coming to us with some lights, but she was far away. She couldn't hear us. We started to walk toward the light.

"Mommy!" Ken called out. We wanted to run, but our feet couldn't move fast enough on the sand. Suddenly, small lights became many lights in the air.

"Helen! Ken!" There was more than one voice.

We stopped and gazed at the lights coming toward us.

Many policemen surrounded us and put blankets around me and Ken. A young man carried me, and another man carried Ken, back to the road. There, I saw Uncle Steve and Aunt Mary standing next to the police cars with their shiny blue and red lights. They both came running toward us. They ran to us, screaming our names.

DREAM

From the corner of my house, I can hear the sound of the double bass. It's already eleven o'clock, unusually late for Chiyo to be practicing. I quietly open the door so as not to disturb her practice. She is in her pajamas, practicing Bottesini's concerto in the living room. Seeing Chiyo powerfully pulling and pushing the bow frees me from the restlessness I felt all day. I quietly pass the living room and go to my bedroom to change my clothes without disturbing her as she fiercely practices a phrase from the first movement repeatedly.

Chiyo sometimes gets this way, unaware of her surroundings while she practices her bass. Over twenty years ago, when she began learning this monstrous instrument, she would practice for hours, so completely focused that she often forgot the time. I would come home from work, and she would panic that she hadn't prepared dinner. Chiyo's love affair with the double bass started when we lived in England for my research at Oxford. Soon after we got married, I received a fellowship, and during those three years, Chiyo took day trips to attend London Symphony concerts. After she saw the performance of Mahler's Symphony no. 1, she came home running and announced that she was going to learn the double bass. I didn't even know what a double bass looked like back then. When I actually saw the instrument at the store, I couldn't believe my eyes. It was much bigger than she was, and for tiny Chiyo to even hold such a thing seemed impossible. When she held it and moved the bow with the other hand, I was certain that she wasn't fit to play such an instrument. I asked her if she would rather play something smaller like a violin, or, at most, a cello. But contrary to my thought, Chiyo was quite satisfied with the deep sound that came out of this instrument and said she would take it. When the store clerk told us how expensive it was—six months of my income—Chiyo didn't even flinch. She repeated, she would take it. Then she turned to me and said she was going to sell her mother's emerald pin—the only item she owned of her late mother. *My dead mother's emerald means very little to me; it doesn't remind me of my mother,* Chiyo said, but of course I couldn't let her sell her mother's pin. I went to the bank and somehow managed to get a small loan that took us two years to pay off. But this investment was worth it since her double bass gave Chiyo a place to pour her passion. While she worked at the Home Guidance Center in Japan, helping women with various family issues meant so much to her. She had to leave her job because of my research in England, and I felt guilty not only for Chiyo, but also for all the women who could have used Chiyo's kindness the way my sister did. Chiyo studied the double bass with a professional bassist at the Oxford School of Music, and after we returned to Japan, she continued to study with a bassist in the Tokyo Orchestra. She's quite accomplished now, and when she's playing, I try not to get in her way.

While I take off my suit and hang it in the closet, the music stops and I hear her coming to me.

"I'm sorry. I didn't hear you come in." She picks up my shirt from the floor and folds it.

"It sounded great, the Bottesini for the next concert."

"It's a frustrating piece." Chiyo sighs.

I laugh because that's what she says about every piece she plays.

I walk to the bathroom, and Chiyo follows me with my pajamas. The sound of her slippers comforts me. The hot water in the bathtub reaches me all the way to my bones. Chiyo must have picked citron from the garden this afternoon. The citron's skin, cut into small pieces, floats in the water, and its sour smell rises with the steam. I scoop hot water with both hands to splash my face with my fingers, all wrinkled from the hot water.

I wash my face with the washcloth and get out of the bathtub. The sour smell of citron follows me into my pajamas. Chiyo has already turned off the heater in our bedroom upstairs for the night and prepared our futons with a hot water bottle inside. I slip into the warm futon, lay my body inside, and close my eyes. My body knows that this is the safest place in the world.

The sound of Chiyo's slippers approaches and stops by our bedroom. She stands in front of the door for a moment but doesn't open it right away. Then I hear her come in, but I don't feel her body lie next to mine. I open my eyes and find her sitting by me, staring down at my face.

"What's the matter?" I place my hand on her cheek.

"What do you think is happening to Ume's daughter in America?"

"What do you mean?" I get up from my futon.

"The letter from Mr. Steve Johnson. You left it on your desk."

"You read it?" I didn't mean to raise my voice.

Chiyo calmly nods. "So what do you think is wrong with Ume's daughter?" Chiyo's question tightens my body as if my bones were squeezed into a tight knot.

"Is there something wrong with Anna?"

"Did you not read the letter?"

"I couldn't."

Chiyo gathers wrinkles on her forehead.

"I was overwhelmed. I stopped at the first sentence and I just . . ." Before I finish my sentence, Chiyo gets up and leaves the room and comes back with the dreadful envelope that I saw this morning.

"You must read the letter." She places it in my hand. I don't know what I'm afraid of. I have never regretted the decision to send Anna away to the Christian Home for Children or even to the United States. Making a decision is about abandoning other possible paths, but for Anna, a decision came to her since no other possible paths were available to her.

I open the letter. *Dear Mr. Takagawa, My name is Steve Johnson, brother-in-law to your niece, Anna Johnson.* Why a brother-in-law? I read this part over and over again.

"Are you reading the letter?" Chiyo pulls my sleeve.

"Just the first part, the first sentence."

"Why don't I read it for you, and you'll understand?" Chiyo slowly pulls the letter away from me and puts on her glasses.

November 25, 1975
Dear Mr. Takagawa,

My name is Steve Johnson, brother-in-law to your niece, Anna Johnson. I cannot thank you enough for writing to me. Helen told me about the letter that she sent to you. I'm afraid that her letter may have made you worry about Anna. I wanted to assure you that she is taken care of and we are hopeful that she will get better soon.

My brother, James, married Anna ten years ago, and they have two children. Helen is nine years old and Ken is six. Because of Anna's condition and James's busy work schedule, they are unable to take care of their children now. My wife Mary and I have been looking after Helen and Ken, and they are absolutely delightful. On more than one occasion, Helen and I discussed how it would be important for Anna to recover her roots by visiting Japan. However, she is not in a condition to travel currently, and my wife and I encouraged Helen to visit Japan for her mother. Although she is young, she is passionate about helping her mother, a strong sister to

Ken, and an inspirational niece to Mary and me. I am writing this letter to ask you if we could visit you in Japan and if you could help us learn more about Anna's childhood and her mother Ume. It would be a gift for Anna to have the memory and knowledge of her past in Japan, and I am quite certain that this knowledge will be important for Helen and Ken later. I have agreed to accompany Helen if meeting with us is possible for you. I can only imagine what a shock it must be to receive this letter, and I hope we did not upset you. Please write me back and share your thoughts on our visit.

Sincerely,

Steve Johnson.

Chiyo puts the letter and her glasses on the table and looks into my face.

"Ume is a grandmother now," Chiyo says. It's strange to be thinking of her this way, since she has always been twenty-one years old in my mind, but almost thirty years has passed since her death.

"You must write him back as soon as possible," Chiyo says, putting the letter back in the envelope.

"What should I say?"

"You must invite them to our home."

"Why?"

"It's your duty to invite them." Chiyo speaks without any hesitation.

"Duty?" I don't like that word and am surprised that she would use it. Chiyo must have read the letter and thought about it all day.

"You must invite them. What else can you say? Don't come? Absolutely not."

"I'll have to think about this whole thing tomorrow. For now, we're going to sleep." I get up to turn off the light and get under the covers. Chiyo is still sitting in the dark, and I know she wants to talk more about this. She is like this, not afraid of pain, but I need a minute. Here I am, inside the blanket, afraid. But why should I be afraid of meeting Helen? Everything that I remember of her mother is delightful. I held her for the first six months, cooing in my arms, and I can still remember the physical sensation of a warm and fragile being in my arms.

Chiyo lies on the futon and holds me from behind.

"You must write them back tomorrow and invite them." Her voice is as desperate as a bird in a cage. Without answering, I lie still and stare into the darkness. Chiyo's hand moves up and down on my back, but eventually, it stops moving, and I feel her quiet breathing, asleep, against my neck. Sleep is the only way to distance myself from being afraid.

〜

Chiyo's moaning wakes me up. Her eyes are tightly shut, but tears cover her cheeks, and her mouth moves slightly, uttering incomprehensible words. Her hands grip the sheets, her legs move as if running, and her entire body shakes, drenched in sweat. I hold her shoulders and call her name gently to calm her; I want to bring her back to our bedroom as gently as possible. She jumps a little, but wakes up in my arms. The tears sit still in her eyes like water in a well. Through the wall of water, she looks at me.

For the twenty-seven years of our marriage, she has had the same dream from time to time. She is walking with the people of Takiyama village in the middle of Manchuria. When the Soviet troops begin shooting from behind, in front, and from both sides, everyone jumps into the field, crawls on the ground, and hides behind the tall and thick leaves of Gaoliang—Chinese corn. The soldiers in their gray uniforms move toward the villagers, and soon, they are everywhere, turning the field gray. Then all kinds of sounds—the soldiers' deep voices, foreign words, footsteps, women and children's screams, shots, moaning—intertwine in the middle of the Gaoliang field. Chiyo gets down on the ground and prays that the earth will conceal her body from the eyes of the soldiers. Her teeth rattle against each other, so she grabs a handful of dirt and puts it in her mouth. Chewing dirt softens her shaking as it absorbs her saliva. She tells herself to concentrate on chewing, don't choke, don't move, don't make any sound, don't breathe; her feet slowly become soil, then her legs, thighs, hips, stomach, chest, neck, chin, nose, and eyes transform as they touch the ground. She feels suffocated and rolls her body over as she becomes the earth. The last thing she sees before disappearing into the soil is the blue sky spreading into millions of sharp glass pieces falling onto the ground. But instead of glass, she sees my face in the dark bedroom through her tears. Chiyo has never taken her dream seriously. *A dream isn't a memory; it's all dramatic and random*—she would dismiss it this way.

Chiyo's father was a military official who trained Japanese farmers to become armed immigrants before sending them to northeast China, to Manchuria. Chiyo's father himself was sent to Manchuria with the newly trained young soldiers to join the Japanese Guandong Army, the military force specifically organized for Manchuria. Soon after his settlement, he sent for his family. Seven-year-old Chiyo, her older brother Taro, and her mother also immigrated to Manchuria in the early 1930s. But after Japan's defeat in World War II, her entire family died. Her mother went missing during the evacuation and was recorded as "dead in Linkou, August 1945," and the death certificate was issued to Chiyo's family. Her father was executed in prison as a war criminal, responsible for many Chinese citizens' deaths. Her brother's troop unit was reportedly annihilated, just like my brother's unit. So Chiyo came back to Japan alone. *Once a heart beats fast out of enormous fear, we gain certain openness,* Chiyo told me once, *as our hands are capable of the unthinkable; I used to believe that I could not throw a living baby into a river as many women did in Manchuria, but I realize that I, too, would, if I had to.*

Chiyo wipes off her tears and gets up to find a towel and another nightshirt. When she comes back, she sits next to me. Her back is wet with sweat.

"I almost choked on the dirt tonight. That never happened before," Chiyo shivers. She unbuttons her shirt and places her hand on her chest. She breathes slowly, touching her neck, and takes off her shirt to dry her back. I take the towel and wipe off her back, which is covered in goose bumps; my fingers feel her backbone and follow it down to her hips. I lean my forehead on her back. Chiyo handles almost anything, though I know some memories sleep deep inside her, and she is careful not to wake them up. Over the years, I know she has wondered if her missing family members would be found alive in China and could come back to her. She has given up such hope long ago, but she never stopped thinking about them. As she went to sleep, she must have been thinking about Steve Johnson's letter—ghosts from the past.

The first night I held Chiyo, on our wedding night, she woke me this same way. I tried to rouse her, to save her from her nightmare, but she woke up screaming. Since then, I have learned to bring her back from the middle of the Gaoliang field by calling her name gently. Every time she woke up, she would tell me a story from the time she was living in Manchuria.

"I almost choked," Chiyo repeats. The scent of soap rises as I help her put on her shirt. We both get inside the futon, and I hold her close, though as I get closer, I imagine I can almost taste the dry Gaoliang field in my own mouth. I feel guilty for having Chiyo read the letter from Steve Johnson, which must haven taken her back to Manchuria.

"Tell me the story of Yalu River," I whisper to her.

"Yalu River?"

"The one about the ice."

"Right now?"

"Yes."

In a whispering voice, like telling a secret, Chiyo begins telling me the story she has told me many times.

"Before the war intensified, my father, mother, brother, and I had the most wonderful trip together. We took a train all the way to the Yalu River, the border between Korea and Manchuria, and stayed overnight at a small hotel. My father took us to see ice breaking into huge pieces and drifting down the river. I always thought the season of spring was gentle, but there, it was powerful. The hands of many people could never break the large river ice in China, but only spring could melt the ice from the outside edges, which broke them into pieces, and as they ran they bumped each other into a fast stream. I stayed awake all night at our hotel, listening to the sound of spring breaking the ice. I thought that the river was the throat of the earth, unable to breathe during the winter. The sound of ice breaking felt like the earth breathing. Can you imagine this sound?"

GHOST

Chiyo calls from downstairs and says that breakfast is ready. This is like any other day, getting dressed for work, Chiyo calling for breakfast, going downstairs, sitting down, and picking up the paper placed on the table. I always thought I was very different from my father, but our morning routine is exactly how my father arranged for his family. I put down the paper and watch Chiyo, moving quickly between three pots on the stove, making soup, watching the fish on the grill, and steaming some vegetables. I'm amazed by her organization and wonder how I haven't noticed that she did so many things at once every morning. I gaze at her from the table and smell the delicious aroma of grilled fish.

"I'm not so young any more to deserve your gaze." Chiyo notices and turns her face, already covered with white powder brushed with soft plum color on her cheeks. Her white apron makes her thin frame softer. I know she didn't rest well from the nightmare, but she doesn't show a bit of fatigue.

"I have never noticed that you made so many things at once." I watch her in amazement, and while I say this, she is already back at the cutting board slicing some pickles.

"You have to do everything at once, otherwise one thing gets cold while I'm making another, Professor." Chiyo calls me "Professor" when I lack common sense. She often says I don't know how to live simply and practically because I think and analyze everything too much, yet I give lectures on life through literature. Listening to her slicing pickles, I wonder what it's like to be simple and practical.

Chiyo places the bowl of rice and miso soup in front of me.

"You're very fortunate that Anna's family wrote you that let-ter," Chiyo says without slowing down. "If only I could get a letter from my long-lost family." She goes back to the stove, then returns with the vegetables and grilled fish. Her words instantly fill me with anger. She doesn't understand what is happening to me. How could she say that I'm fortunate?

"Would you call yourself fortunate if you heard from that pregnant woman you left behind?" I don't realize how sharp my voice sounds until all the words come out of my mouth. Chiyo stops and looks straight at me, recognizing my intention and desire to nail her down with her painful memory only because I am cornered by my own past.

"If she were alive and found me, I would be fortunate. But unfortunately, that will never happen because she's dead." She puts down the dish of pickles on the table and leaves the kitchen. I am weighed down by the sound of her quick foot-steps on the stairs and the warm breakfast that she prepared steaming in front of me. I don't know if I have ever spoken so sharply or cruelly to Chiyo before. What has gotten into me? I almost thought it was my father's voice coming out of my throat. Sitting alone, I feel sick to my stomach, thinking about his terrible face when he died alone—didn't he teach me how bitterness isolates us from everything and everyone that matter to us?

Chiyo left a pregnant woman behind in Manchuria during the horrific evacuation at the defeat of Japan in World War II. In Manchuria, Chiyo's father was sent to the military police division to oversee the local police and Japanese immigrant farmers near the villages. These villages were often attacked by a group of Chinese farmers who were forced to sell their land to the Japanese immigrants and leave their homes. Chiyo's fam-ily lived there along with the farmers in Takiyama village, but as the war intensified in the 1940s, Chiyo's father and brother, along with many men, were ordered to leave their farming duties in the north. Assigned to fight in the south, they left the village with mostly women, children, and elderly people.

Chiyo's entire village was ordered to evacuate to the south because the Soviet troops had begun invading Japanese-claimed lands and villages up north. Chiyo said all the women in the village got together, cut their hair, and put black charcoal pow-der on each other's faces to look like men. They tried to take a train, but the rails had been destroyed by the Japanese Guandong Army to prevent the Soviet army's entrance. They all walked for miles and miles as they hid from the occasional attacks by Chinese farmers or the Soviet army. They all stayed in one group and moved forward as a long line of fifteen hun-dred people.

Chiyo met a pregnant woman who had trouble walking, so she held her hand and pulled her along. Chiyo doesn't remem-ber her name, though she remembers that the woman said she was about Chiyo's age, twenty years old, and that she had a large red scar on her hand from a farming accident. She told Chiyo that she had accidentally cut herself during the rice sea-son, since she took care of all the farming while her husband was at the war in southern China. Chiyo and her mother stayed with this woman and took care of her during the evacuation. Since the plan to escape south by train failed, they walked into the forest, carrying heavy bags and pushing wagons they obtained from the Chinese farmers. The path wove around a mountain, which doubled the distance, and they walked on the mountain road, passed through swamps, and slept under trees. Each day, some people gave up walking. They all said they would catch up, but Chiyo knew what being left behind in the middle of the Manchurian mountains meant.

Some nights, Chinese men from nearby villages came and asked the women to be their wives and stay in their village. They also talked to the families with young children, wanting to buy them for five yen. They said that the journey was dangerous, and that the village needed young women and children for the future, promising to take good care of them. At first, no one would give in, but as more days passed and they became weak, some mothers and children went with the Chinese men. Even the pregnant woman was asked to stay in the village, but she refused to go.

After twelve days of walking on the mountains, they finally faced the river, which they had to cross by managing the river's swift current. First they abandoned all the wagons and some bags. The pregnant woman took a step into the river and froze, unable to take another step. She told everyone to leave her. Chiyo begged her to continue walking, but she said no, crossing the river was simply impossible. Chiyo's mother gave the pregnant woman her blanket, a bowl, dry crackers, a towel, while the woman just sat under a tree and waited for everyone to leave. But Chiyo couldn't leave her. She could give birth at any moment, out in the field. Then what would happen to her? Chiyo was pulled and pushed by her mother to cross the river, and from the other side of the river, the woman watched them move away as she waved.

I find Chiyo sitting on the cold floor of the bathroom holding her knees with her arms, looking like a child in fear. It's awful that I spoke so cruelly to her just because I am afraid of meeting Ume's daughter and her family.

"I'm sorry." I sit next her.

"I shouldn't have said anything. I'm sorry," Chiyo whispers.

"I was wrong to say such a hurtful thing." I don't know what else to say or do to save myself from Chiyo's sad gaze, which sickens me.

"In Manchuria, I was always scared of walking at night. But as the sun came up, I felt safer. In the dark, I imagined all kinds of horrible things, but in the light, at least we could see and grasp what was real."

Chiyo leans into my chest, and I'm grateful that she lets me hold her.

"If you ask me, the worst is over," Chiyo says in my chest.

A chill goes through my body. Perhaps Chiyo and I have been together out of a sense of necessity and awareness that we can see each other within ourselves, mirroring ourselves. How alone we have become, that we're each other's only family. But in the end, it is always Chiyo who, in a gentle way, disallows me to be buried by fear and pushes me to walk through fire.

OCTOBER 1975

We were in big trouble when the police found us by the ocean.
We had to ride in the police car to get home. On the way home,
I wasn't scared, but I knew Uncle Steve was scared because he
held my hand and didn't let go. The sand between our hands
hurt me. As soon as we came home, Ken and I went to the
bathroom, and we washed our feet, which smelled like salt. I
thought Uncle Steve and Aunt Mary would be mad at us. But
they didn't get mad. Their faces just turned really white. Aunt
Mary's lips were even purple, like she was cold. I wanted to say
I was sorry, but I was afraid to say anything.

Then we went to Uncle Steve's king-sized bed. Ken and I
got in the middle and Aunt Mary sat next to us and covered us
with a blanket. Uncle Steve sat on the chair in the corner and
watched us get tucked in, with his hand covering his mouth.
Uncle Steve asked if we were trying to run away from home.
We shook our heads.

"I answered the phone, but no one was there, just the sound
of ocean waves, so I thought it was Mom, calling from the hospital," I explained.

"The phone didn't ring tonight, Helen," Aunt Mary said.

"Yes, it did! It rang many times, but you didn't answer it."

Both Uncle Steve and Aunt Mary looked at the phone right
next to their bed, then at each other.

"How did you know that your mom was in the hospital?"
Uncle Steve's voice sounded dry and deep. I looked at Ken, who
pulled up the blanket to hide.

"It's all right. You can tell me." Uncle Steve came closer and sat by Aunt Mary. Ken wasn't going to come out from under the blanket, so I told Uncle Steve about Ken calling home and talking to Mrs. Hogan.

"I don't blame Mrs. Hogan. She must be desperate." Uncle Steve sighed.

"You know Mrs. Hogan?" I had never heard Uncle Steve say her name before.

"Of course. Right now, it's stressful for Anna to have any visitors. So only close family members are permitted to visit her in the hospital—just Mrs. Hogan and your dad."

"Why Mrs. Hogan?"

"She is Anna's mother," Uncle Steve said casually.

Ken threw back the blanket and quickly got up. "Mrs. Hogan isn't Mom's mom. Mom's mom died in Japan. Her name is Ume."

"I meant that Mrs. Hogan's your mom's adopted mother. When your mom came to the United States, Mrs. Hogan adopted your mom."

"You mean Mom lived with Mrs. Hogan?" I have never heard Mom calling Mrs. Hogan *Mom*.

"You didn't know about Mrs. Hogan?" Uncle Steve and Aunt Mary looked at each other.

"What's an adopted mother?" Ken pulled my sleeve.

Aunt Mary explained that when the real mother couldn't care for her child, someone else became the mother, and the new mother was called an adopted mother.

"So are you my adopted mother?" Ken said. Aunt Mary and Uncle Steve looked at each other again.

"No, sweetheart," Aunt Mary touched his face, "I'm your aunt."

Ken looked confused, but didn't say anything more. Mom and Mrs. Hogan didn't look like a mom and a child. Mrs. Hogan's sad face with narrow eyes came back to me.

The next day, Uncle Steve talked to Mrs. Hogan on the phone for a long time. Ken and I sat on the couch, listening. Uncle Steve didn't say very much. He mostly nodded and listened. When he hung up, he said that Mrs. Hogan would visit us here on the first weekend of October. Uncle Steve made us promise that we wouldn't tell anyone that Mrs. Hogan was coming to visit us, even our schoolteachers and Dad. We had another new secret.

∽

I went downstairs because I couldn't sleep even after I tried counting sheep. The big orange clock on the kitchen wall said three-fifteen. A few minutes later, Uncle Steve came downstairs too. He said he couldn't sleep, but I knew he came down to check on me. After our running away, we all slept together on Uncle Steve's big bed. He often woke up in the middle of the night and checked that we were still there. I shut my eyes tight and pretended that I was sleeping, but I knew he was checking on us. I wanted to tell him that he didn't have to be scared of me running away again. But I pretended that I didn't notice anything.

Uncle Steve poured me a glass of milk and put it on the table. I put a kettle on the stove. He covered his face with both hands and stayed like that for a few seconds. Then he crossed his arms on his chest and leaned his back against the wall. There were wrinkles by his eyes and his hair was all messy. Looking at his tired face, for the first time, I saw that Dad and Uncle Steve did look alike.

"I'm sorry," I said.

"Why?"

"I think Ken and I made Mom sick." I didn't know how to explain. I was sorry that I ran to the ocean, that I hurt Ryan at school, that Mom was sick. I was sorry that Uncle Steve was tired from taking care of me and Ken. Taking care of us made everyone tired. Dad knew it so he didn't want us around Mom anymore.

Uncle Steve looked at me hard with his blue eyes. "You couldn't have made your mother sick. Helen, do you know what a nervous breakdown is?"

I shook my head.

"The doctor said Anna had a nervous breakdown. She is extremely nervous all the time and wired up."

"Why?"

"I don't know."

Nervous breakdown—when she got nervous, did she break down? I thought about Mom standing in front of a mirror, and the mirror breaking into pieces, and Mom on the floor, also in pieces. I remember what Mom said to Mrs. Hogan. She said she got dizzy looking at me and Ken.

"Everyone gets nervous around me."

"I don't get nervous around you." Uncle Steve's blue eyes opened bigger.

"You looked scared at the ocean two weeks ago. You and Aunt Mary, running to us."

"When you were gone, I got nervous. I'm all right now because you're back." He smiled and winked. After that, Uncle Steve looked nothing like Dad again. Steam was shooting out of little holes in the kettle. Uncle Steve put his favorite apple cinnamon tea into a mug. The kitchen always smelled sweet when he made tea. The steam covered his face.

"Is Mrs. Hogan really coming tomorrow?" I wanted to know about Mom, but the thought of seeing Mrs. Hogan was a little creepy.

"She'll be here in the morning."

"What are we going to do with her?"

"She'll tell us about your mom. She gets to go home every other weekend from the hospital. She stays with Mrs. Hogan. She shouldn't be alone, and you know how busy your dad is."

I nodded. Mom was always nervous when she was waiting for Dad. Our house had big windows and a big mirror, empty and white. She wouldn't be able to wait for Dad alone in the house. She would have to have someone to listen to the story about Dad coming home on his motorcycle in his underwear.

"Since you are stronger than your mom and dad," Uncle Steve took a sip from his teacup, "you have to help them."

I wasn't stronger than Mom and Dad! They were so much taller and older! Besides, Mom was scared of me and didn't want me around her. Uncle Steve didn't know her. He'd never seen Mom when she was scared of me. He didn't know that she put us in the closet, or that she cut my hair in the middle of the night. I got up to grab a pen and paper and sat back down next to Uncle Steve. I wrote with a black pen: *Anna had a nervous breakdown. Anna had a nervous breakdown. Anna had a nervous breakdown.*

In the morning, when I woke up, Uncle Steve had already left to pick up Mrs. Hogan at the bus station. I ran to the bathroom and brushed my teeth, washed my face, and changed my clothes. We were having a secret meeting. Dad wasn't supposed to know that Mrs. Hogan was taking a bus all the way from San Francisco to come and see us. Mrs. Hogan would be sitting in the bus with many plastic bags of milk containers and cans. Ken and I sat by the window waiting. Rain was hitting the ground hard and making everything soft. The surface of the green pond in the yard was shaking all morning. My stomach hurt a little, making all kinds of noises. I sat down and put my hand on my stomach. I was so nervous my stomach and skin hurt, my fingers were cold, but my face was burning. Was this a nervous breakdown? Maybe I had what Ken had at camp last summer. Was he having a nervous breakdown? Maybe Ken and I get sick like Mom did.

"Are you all right?" Aunt Mary looked into my face. When her cold hands touched my forehead, cheeks, and neck, I wanted her to leave her hands there, but she quickly went upstairs and came back with a thermometer. She put it in my mouth, and I had to sit still for a few minutes. Aunt Mary said that I had a fever and I had to go back to bed.

"But Mrs. Hogan's coming," I said. But she was already pulling my hand and walking me to my bedroom. She promised that when Mrs. Hogan came, she'd wake me up, so I changed my clothes back into my pajamas again. I got into bed and closed my eyes. I felt Aunt Mary touch my forehead again as I fell asleep.

I had no idea how long I slept. When I opened my eyes, my room was all dark, and the sky out my window was blue and pink. I didn't know what day it was, but I thought it looked like early morning. I had to get ready to go to school! I went to the closet and got my school uniform. I pulled on my skirt, but couldn't find my shirt. I looked under the bed, in the closet and laundry basket, but I couldn't find it. My tummy hurt, but I had to move quickly because I didn't want to be late. I looked everywhere. I couldn't breathe well because my chest felt tight. I didn't know what was happening. What if I was having a nervous breakdown? I sat on the floor. Tears fell from my eyes, and I couldn't see anything. Then Aunt Mary knocked and opened the door. As soon as she saw me crying on the floor, she came and held me. She asked me if I had a scary dream, but I couldn't talk. There was a woman standing by the door, she looked familiar, but I couldn't figure out who it was. She just watched us, not saying anything.

"How're you feeling now? You were sleeping all day." Aunt Mary touched my forehead.

"What day is it?"

"It's still the same day. It's five o'clock in the evening." Aunt Mary patted my back. I tried to stop crying because the woman was watching me by the door, but I couldn't breathe right. I whispered in Aunt Mary's ear.

"Someone is by the door."

"Don't you remember Mrs. Hogan?"

I rubbed my eyes to see her. She looked like Mrs. Hogan, but it wasn't the Mrs. Hogan I remembered. Her hair was tightly put up in back, and she was wearing a long purple dress. But when she came close to me, I knew it was Mrs. Hogan because I could smell her smoky breath. She said hello. Her dry voice hadn't changed.

We all went downstairs together. Aunt Mary said that Uncle Steve and Ken went to the store to get some things for dinner. She pulled up a chair and told me to sit down. Mrs. Hogan sat across the table from me. I could see that she was wearing a little bit of red lipstick! She sat up straight and looked at me straight with her narrow eyes. Aunt Mary put a glass of cold milk and a slice of banana cake on the table for me and a cup of apple cinnamon tea for Mrs. Hogan. The house smelled sweet. Aunt Mary said that she had baked the banana cake with Mrs. Hogan that afternoon while I was sleeping. Mrs. Hogan was still looking at me, so I looked at my cake and cut it with my fork. I wasn't hungry, but I had to do something. I chewed.

"I think you've grown since I saw you last." Mrs. Hogan's hands moved a little like she was going to reach for my hands. I held my fork tight and moved the other hand onto my lap. I wanted to ask her about Mom, but I didn't know what to say.

Mrs. Hogan pulled out some pictures from her purse. The first one was a black-and-white picture of an old man and a girl, standing by a big tree. I thought I recognized the tree from somewhere.

"This man," she pointed to the tall man, "is my husband, and this is your mother. She was six."

I brought my face close to the picture.

"Your mother looks just like you," Aunt Mary said, but I didn't think she looked like me at all. The girl in the picture had long hair under a straw hat and was holding three white flowers. Her shoes looked so small. Her face didn't really look like Mom. They were standing by the tree at Mrs. Hogan's house. The house looked the same, but it was colorless. There were flowers in the garden by the front door. I'd never seen flowers at Mrs. Hogan's house. She flipped the picture over, and there was blue ink with writing on the back: *Anna's first day, July 1952.* The ink was smeared in the corner.

Mrs. Hogan said she took the picture when Mom came to her house to live with them. She gave Mom the flowers to welcome her, but she wouldn't smile at all. Mom looked tired, but Mrs. Hogan's husband had a big smile.

"My husband loved Anna. After all, we watched her from across the street. You see, we were the second family to adopt her. The first family and Anna had some troubles," she said.

"Mom had another family?" How many moms did she have?

"A young couple adopted Anna from a Christian orphanage when they lived in Japan. They adopted her when she was five. We used to live across the street from this family. I think Anna was very difficult for them. She didn't come out much, but every Sunday, we saw her at church. She had big brown eyes, always fiercely looking at the people during mass."

Mom's eyes in the pictures looked right back at me like she was angry. She didn't have that strong look now. When she looked at me, I always thought she was thinking about something else.

Mrs. Hogan put another picture on the table. There was a girl, sitting under a grand piano. She held her knees, not smiling, and a woman sat next to the girl.

"This is Anna when she was six, and that's me. Anna used to take piano lessons from my husband." The girl looked very serious. She wasn't smiling at all. Mrs. Hogan was very different. Her eyes were pretty, not narrow like now.

"What were you doing under the piano? Hide and seek?" Aunt Mary asked. Mrs. Hogan flipped the picture and the blue ink said *Under the piano, 1952.*

"Anna was always hiding. She didn't know very much English, so she hardly spoke to anyone at first. She always hid under things, like a table, bed, or our piano. But she loved the piano. When Anna came to our house, if she wasn't playing piano, she sat under it, and I often sat with her. There, she would talk to me a little." Mrs. Hogan said the first young couple was very upset with Mom. There was lots of yelling that she could hear from across the street. After a year of living with Mom, the couple mentioned to Mrs. Hogan that they were thinking about sending her back to Japan, to the orphanage. But Mrs. Hogan and her husband went to the couple and asked if they could adopt Mom instead.

"Why did you want Mom?" I asked. Why would anyone want a bad child who hid under the piano all the time?

"My husband was a bit older than I was, and he had two children from his previous marriage. So we didn't have any children together. But when we met Anna, we felt close to her. She looked like she was lonely, not belonging anywhere except for under furniture. When Anna went under the kitchen table to eat dinner, sometimes we would actually join her." Mrs. Hogan laughed. "Eventually, after two months or so, she told us that her Japanese mother's name was Ume, and that her own Japanese name was Shizuka."

"That's the ghost's name!" I jumped. "Mom said Shizuka lives behind the wall in the closet. Shizuka's a ghost!"

Aunt Mary and Mrs. Hogan looked at each other.

"In the closet?" Aunt Mary looked confused. I stopped talking because Mrs. Hogan gave me the look. Her stare meant that it was bad to talk about Mom putting us in the closet. I quickly changed the subject before Aunt Mary asked me more about the closet.

"How come Mom doesn't call you Mom?"

"We thought it was best not to pretend to be her parents. We were just her caregivers." Her dry voice bounced in my head.

Mrs. Hogan took out another picture from her purse and put it on the table. This one was in color. Mom and Dad stood together, and he had his arms around her. Mom was in a navy dress, and her black hair was up with a little flower by her ear. Dad looked like a soldier, wearing a brown uniform and a hat. I have never seen him in a uniform before. I picked up the picture and looked at it really close. Dad looked happy being a solider. I had never seen him smile like that either. On the back, it said *The wedding of Anna and James, 1966.*

"Mom doesn't look like a bride! She didn't wear a white dress?"

"Actually, they didn't tell me that they were getting married. One day, they just went to the courthouse. Then they got an apartment for themselves and stopped by my place to let me know about their marriage. I took this picture then."

"You must have been shocked," Aunt Mary said.

"Not at all. Anna was fierce like that. If she were to get lost, she wouldn't stay in one spot long. She would pick a direction and go for it. You see, there was a rumor that a married man didn't have to go to war. Anna was twenty, still in school, but she was determined to stop James from going to war. But meanwhile, our county board didn't get enough enlisted men that year, so they stopped accepting the marriage deferment. Anna was extremely upset when she found out that John's draft wouldn't be deferred."

Mrs. Hogan took out a black-and-white picture from a white envelope more carefully than she had taken out the others.

"This is the oldest picture of Anna." A young Asian woman was holding a baby in front of a large gray building. The corners of this picture were a little bit ripped, and there were some spots on it.

"Is this Grandma Ume?"

"No, this is Mrs. Tamura. She worked at the Christian Home for Children, the orphanage that took care of children like your mom—half Japanese and half American."

"If you were half Japanese and half American, you had to go to an orphanage?"

"No, not really. It's just that your grandmother Ume died when Anna was a baby, and her family couldn't take care of Anna. It was best to send her away."

Mom said Grandma Ume told her the story of the ghost, Shizuka, but Mrs. Hogan said Grandma Ume died when Mom was a baby. Maybe Mom made up stories. If she did, wouldn't a liar drown in the ocean?

Uncle Steve and Ken walked in the door with many plastic bags. Aunt Mary got up and went to the kitchen to start cooking. She said she was making her famous meatballs for dinner. When we first came here, Aunt Mary made a big turkey dinner, and Ken got scared. We had never seen a big bird cooked in the oven like that before. Mom didn't cook meat. She said Dad didn't like the smell of meat being cooked in the house. He didn't like the smell of any food in the house. Mom always made sure that the window was open after cooking. We always had the same things for dinner: rice, corn, tomatoes, green vegetables, and cheese. Ken ate corn flakes at home. We both liked school lunch.

Uncle Steve told me to show Mrs. Hogan my room before dinner, since she would be sleeping in my room that night. I didn't know that she was staying overnight. Mrs. Hogan followed me with her bags. My room's walls were covered with many drawings and paintings that I had made in school. Aunt Mary put them up on the wall. Mrs. Hogan walked around to see each paper.

"What kind of flower is this?" Mrs. Hogan pointed at the one above my bed.

"It's a hydrangea." I said it slowly because it was a hard word to say. I learned this word from Aunt Mary. Uncle Steve planted many hydrangeas in their garden in summer because Aunt Mary said it was the prettiest flower. Many tiny flowers gathered in the middle to make up one hydrangea. Mrs. Hogan nodded and kept looking at my pictures. Mrs. Hogan's pretty dress was like a hydrangea, many different purples making up one purple.

She saw me staring at her dress.

"I forgot that I had a dress like this in my closet." Mrs. Hogan looked down at her dress. "When you start forgetting, you stop caring about things, and soon, you don't even know what you have in the closet."

I nodded.

"When Ken saw me today, he asked me if I was your mother's fake mother," she smiled. I knew Ken meant to say adopted mother, but he couldn't remember the word, so he called her fake. Ken didn't know what was good and bad to say. I wanted to say I was sorry for Ken, but Mrs. Hogan was laughing, so she wasn't mad at him.

"A few months ago when I visited Anna at the hospital, she gave me an envelope and asked me to mail it to the Christian Home for Children. She said she wanted to ask them about her mother and family in Japan. Anna said that for all these years, she has wondered about them."

"Why?"

"I never stepped up to be her mother. I just thought it would be best not to take over her Japanese mother's place, but instead, I'm afraid that Anna was motherless all these years." Mrs. Hogan bit her lips, but smiled with her sad eyes. "One of the teachers from the Christian Home for Children remembered Anna and responded to her letter. After Anna read it, she let me read it, too. Then she asked me to give it to you." Mrs. Hogan gave me the white envelope with Mom's name and our home address.

"She wants you to keep it safe. That's all. You can have all of these pictures, too." Mrs. Hogan pulled out all the pictures and gave them to me. I liked the pictures. The letter looked important.

"Can I read the letter later?"

"Yes."

"Mrs. Hogan, when do I get to see Mom again?" I asked slowly.

"Soon," Mrs. Hogan said, touching my head. Dad said Mom would get better soon. He said soon because it was easy to say. Mrs. Hogan said I could see Mom soon, too, but I knew that meant not now, waiting, counting many more birds in my head.

⌒

I begged Uncle Steve and Aunt Mary to read the letter first. I was scared that it would say that Mom was actually a ghost. Mom said ghosts were real because they were once alive. Mom's real name, Shizuka, made me think that she was the ghost of the woman that drowned in the ocean. Uncle Steve or Aunt Mary would probably laugh if I said something like that. I sat across the table from Uncle Steve and Aunt Mary and watched them read the letter. They took a long time reading even though it was only two pages. Aunt Mary sometimes covered her mouth. I wanted them to read more quickly; I could see their eyes following the words.

When they were finally finished, they put the letter back in the envelope, sighed, and sat back like they were tired.

"It's your turn now." Uncle Steve passed the letter across the table. I opened it and thought I smelled Mom's pajamas.

August 3, 1975

Dear Shizuka chan,

I was delighted to hear from you, Shizuka. You may not remember me, but my name is Yoshiko Tamura, and I am one of the staff at the Christian Home for Children. We often lose touch with the children adopted by American families. Losing touch is usually a sign of their happiness. Some of them do not even remember that they were once with us. But we also hear from many graduates, and they often ask the same kind of questions you addressed in your letter. Many of them contact us in the hope of getting to know more about their birth mothers, since we were the last person to witness the togetherness of the children and their mothers. Though we have had over one thousand children pass through our home in the past twenty-eight years, I can remember each child, and I especially remember you because you were in the first generation of the Christian Home for Children, the first group arriving right after the war.

In your letter, you mentioned that you vaguely remember an English teacher who was kind to you, and you wanted to know if he still taught at the Home. I am quite sure that you are thinking of your uncle Hideo Takagawa, your mother's older brother. You see, your uncle often visited the Home to teach English to the children. He couldn't introduce himself as your uncle, so you probably never knew about his identity. Hideo, at first, came to the Home to leave money, and we were a little concerned, since back then, many citizens didn't have enough money or food for themselves. After Hideo got married, he and his wife, Chiyo, came to the Home to bring money. One day, we asked Chiyo how Hideo was able to manage such a donation every year, and Chiyo explained that Hideo took a second job to translate business transcripts for a British company in addition to his primary job of teaching English literature at Kamakura University. Chiyo said that Hideo worked all the time to do something for you and for his sister, and that they even seriously considered adopting you. But we all felt that sending you back to his community would be incredibly difficult for you, since people were cruel to mixed-blood children. Instead, we suggested that Hideo could visit and teach English to the children. He managed to come on Sundays, and we could see how much that meant to him. But shortly after, Hideo was appointed to be a part of a research group by his university, and he needed to go to England. He said he was going to be gone for one year, but it turned out to be almost three. When he came back to Japan three years later, he visited us again, but you were gone by then. He asked for your contact information, but unfortunately, we weren't allowed to provide it for him. He gave us his address and requested that we let you know. But again, we couldn't give you the information unless you contacted us with a request after you turned eighteen. So now, I enclose his address, in case you would like to contact him.

Hideo Takagawa
467-90 Kitagawa cho,
Kamakura-shi,
Kanagawa-Ken, 257, Japan

He is a professor at Kamakura University, teaching English literature. Although he no longer teaches English here at the Home, he is still generous and sends money every year. I think you are always on his mind. Hideo was memorable to all of us, since it was rare for a brother to care so much about his sister's daughter.

You asked if we knew anything about your mother and father. I remember your mother, Ume Takagawa, because she came with Hideo. It was very unusual that a family member, especially a man, accompanied a mother to this place. Ume was pale, thin, and constantly coughing. She was very ill. She explained that she was too ill to take care of her child, and she could not ask her family to take care of you. When you came, you were six months old, but you actually looked like a three-month-old. Hideo kept apologizing to me for asking us to take you. We asked Ume about the baby's father, and she believed that he had returned to the United States. Unfortunately, we do not even know his name.

Separation from the child is painful for most mothers, and your mother's case wasn't an exception. Ume just held you and rocked back and forth, crying and singing to you. We explained the legal process of accepting the baby, the possibility of sending a child for adoption, and the policies such as no contact from the biological family directly to the child unless the child contacts them. Hideo carefully listened and agreed to everything. When it was time for them to go, Ume cried and held you harder. Hideo helped his sister let you go from her arms. They both bowed to us many times, thanking me and asking me to take good care of you. As they walked away, they stopped and looked back. They bowed to us again and again. We waited by the door until we couldn't see them anymore in case Ume came running back and demanded her daughter. Some mothers came back to do this. But Ume never had a chance to return for you. A few months later, Hideo wrote us a letter explaining Ume's death, how quickly her illness became worse, and that she died soon after you were out of her care.

I remember how quickly you grew up to be a beautiful girl. You always loved the annual trip to the beach. Do you remember how you used to stand in front of a mirror and practice telling the story of Jesus before the Christmas show? That was your last Christmas at the Home, and we all loved your dramatic storytelling. But you were also very serious. One day, you asked me why your mother left you. You said you often thought about her as you looked at yourself in the mirror. You see, when I first started working at the Home, I used to believe that after time, the connection between the birth mother and the child would be forgotten, but many instances have proved me wrong. Throughout the years, many children asked us why their mothers left them. We told them that their mothers loved them enough to make the painful decision to give up their own children, so that they could be safe.

What delighted me the most from your letter was to read about your two children. Helen and Ken sound lovely, and when you mentioned that Helen is an avid reader, I thought of you. You were a great listener. Being a mother yourself, perhaps you can imagine your mother's hardship. We tried to teach the orphans never to blame their mothers who had to leave their children in the care of the Home. These young women were often the survivors of countless bombings that killed their family members and destroyed their houses, and they had no food, or places to go. In the midst of a destroyed land of ashes and complete aloneness, many of them slept on the street with bleeding feet and dirty clothes. Some of them came to our home with their feet bleeding. When American soldiers offered bread, soap, and clothes, how could they have refused?

From your letter, I gather that you and your husband have established a wonderful life in America, which is truly the best gift for us to hear. As I write this letter, I was looking through your file, and all the memories come back to me so vividly. All the children who have lived here are absolutely unforgettable. Every child who left for a new path faced some degree of difficulty, but we always believed that each one had an incredible ability to overcome such difficulties. You have shown us this valuable lesson. I continue to wish all the very best to you and your family.

Warmest wishes,

Yoshiko Tamura

When I put down the letter, Uncle Steve and Aunt Mary were looking at me, like they were waiting for me to say something.

"Why did Mom lie? We don't have a wonderful life in America." That was the first thing that I could think of to say.

"Well, maybe Anna thinks so."

"She's lying! She had a nervous breakdown. She doesn't have a wonderful life!"

"Some things have been difficult for her. But she sure talked about you admirably." Uncle Steve got up and walked to the globe by the window. I followed him. He pointed at a tiny island in the middle of the blue ocean, then turned it again and pointed at the big land marked *The United States of America*. "We're just about on the complete opposite side of the earth from Japan."

"How did Mom get from there to here?"

"By airplane. It must have taken a long time to get here back then." His finger made a line and crossed the ocean on the globe. I put my finger next to Japan. It was so small next to my thumb. I move my thumb like Uncle Steve's. I could cross the ocean in one second on the globe, but I pressed my thumb hard, so that it would move really really slowly on the ocean.

SHIZUKA

"Hideo ni chan—big brother Hideo," Ume used to call me, and before she said anything, I knew from her voice what she was going to ask me.

"Will you read me the tale of Shizuka?"

"Again?"

"Yes, again."

A few months before Ume gave birth to her daughter, she grew weak, and she rested on the futon all the time. I asked the landlady to bring meals for Ume during the day while I was at work, but Ume looked forward to my return every evening because I brought books from school to read to her. Old Japanese tales were her favorite. In fact, what she liked more than anything were short tales from history books. One evening, I stopped at a used bookstore that recently reopened after the war. The owner said he kept his books at his mother's place in northern Japan because he couldn't bear to throw any away, especially the rare history books that he had collected over the years. When I told him how my sister loved listening to old Japanese tales, he went to the back of the store and brought back a thin moldy booklet called *The History of Kamakura*. The booklet was made for young students to study local history in Kamakura, so the historical events were written like stories. That evening, Ume almost didn't let me sleep because she wanted to hear me read all the stories. She especially fell in love with the tale of Shizuka, a story about a samurai's wife, and the battle between two brothers. After that, she asked me to read

Shizuka's story every night, so I would open the old moldy book and slowly read it to her.

THE TALE OF YOSHITSUNE AND SHIZUKA

When Minamoto-no Yoritomo began ruling in Kamakura in 1185, Kamakura became the capital of Japan. Yoritomo's younger half brother, Yoshitsune, was an amazing archer and a great warrior, and he helped Yoritomo win the major conflict, the Genpei Wars, thus making his older brother the dictator of Japan. After the war, Yoshitsune joined the cloistered Emperor Go-Shirakawa without consulting about it with his older brother, and soon, the cruel rumor— Yoshitsune was going to kill his brother to become the leader himself—reached Yoritomo. He never forgave his younger brother and ordered him to be captured. Yoshitsune took his soldiers and his lover, Shizuka-gozen, to escape into Yoshino Mountain, but Shizuka eventually took a separate way back down the mountain. She was pregnant, and she knew that the continuation of travel on the cold mountain was dangerous for her and her baby. This separation at Yoshino Mountain ultimately became the image she repeatedly recalled later. After Shizuka was captured by Yoritomo's troops, Yoritomo and his wife Musako took her to the Hachiman Shrine to worship; there, Shizuka was ordered to dance as a gift in front of the shrine because she was known as a beautiful dancer. She performed her song and dance. Although lyrics celebrating the great rulers of the new shogunate were expected, she sang of her longing and regret for her husband, who was not trusted by his own brother:

Yoshino Mountain—
I walked forward onto the
white snow on the peak
I now long for the trace

he left in the divided snow.
Quietly, like
a thread that spins repeatedly
into a small ball,
I have no way to make
the past present, repeatedly

Yoritomo was furious, but his wife calmed him down by
pointing out Shizuka's courage to portray her honest
thoughts and longing for her husband. Shizuka later gave
birth to a boy, who was immediately killed at Yoritomo's
order and thrown into the ocean. After Yoshitsune was
caught and he took his own life, Shizuka cut her long black
hair and became a nun. Three months later, in 1189, she died.

Later, when I went back to the used bookstore to thank
the owner for recommending the book, he told me about the
re-enactment of Shizuka's dance that took place every April at
the Hachiman Shrine in Kamakura. When I told Ume about
this event, she begged me to take her there even though she
was weak. She wouldn't listen to my concerns for her health
and insisted that I take her. Though I was worried about her,
I was also thrilled to see her excitement, as if she were once
again my cheerful younger sister who used to beg me to take
her to the silk farm. We took the train from Tokyo to
Kamakura and went to the Hachiman Shrine for the dance on
a sunny Sunday afternoon. We walked around the wooden
stage where Shizuka danced over eight hundred years ago and
sat among the many people surrounding the large wooden
stage in the middle of the courtyard. There, we saw the
dancer, the re-creation of Shizuka in a white and orange
kimono, moving slowly as she sang her sorrow. Ume was captivated by the graceful yet firm movement of Shizuka, and her
eyes followed every move of the dance.

When Ume's daughter was born, she said she wanted to name her daughter after Shizuka, not for her strength, but for her ability to name her sorrow. Ume said such openness and honesty—something simple like being able to cry—was admirable. Such a simple task is difficult, as it was difficult for our mother who used her life to serve my father. For her daughter, Ume had this simple wish: *May this child gain the ability to cry.*

⌒

November 20, 1975

Dear Mr. Johnson,

Is Anna able to cry? My sister wished her daughter could cry honestly so that her sadness would be known and visible to everyone. I think Ume knew that such a simple wish was the most difficult.

I wish to meet you and Helen. I would like you to come and visit me and my wife, Chiyo, as soon as possible, perhaps during Helen's Christmas break. Please forgive me for making such a direct request without considering your schedule. But I am not confident to wait for our meeting for a long time without changing my mind. I hope you understand this and don't mind making an arrangement to visit us soon.

Sincerely,

Hideo Takagawa

I reread the letter once, fold it, place it in the envelope, and seal it. It is far from appropriate and hardly going to make sense. But the blank paper is filled, and this is the best I can do.

Ume should have given her daughter a different name, wishing for her happiness instead of her ability to cry. But she would never have wished something unreachable. The thought of happiness wouldn't have crossed her mind back then. Instead, I know Ume wanted her daughter to cry as loud as she could so that the world would know that she was alive.

CONCERTO

From the middle of the concert hall, I imagine what goes through Chiyo's mind, standing under the bright lights, holding her double bass and facing all these people. As if my heart were a Taiko drum, my blood beats it loud in the center of my chest and runs throughout my body, making my hands sweat and shake. I think about how I woke up earlier with Chiyo's head on my chest. She was listening to my heart. *For a moment, I thought you were dead, sleeping so deeply without making a sound. You looked so peaceful. So I checked your heart, and do you know what I discovered? Your heartbeat is a perfect tempo for Bottesini's concerto! When I get nervous, I always play fast, so I'll remember your heartbeat for today's performance.* Then Chiyo smiled like a summer sunflower, and I could barely keep my eyes open to her brightness. On the stage, Chiyo stands with the same brightness, while enthusiastic applause welcomes her and a violin soloist, Tomoko. Sitting here and thinking about the pressure of performing, I lose my nerve. It's rare for Chiyo to perform with an orchestra, but she was asked by the Kamakura Youth Orchestra to appear for one of their annual concerts, performing *Gran Duo Concertante* by Giovanni Bottesini. The Kamakura Youth Orchestra is known for its serious teen musicians, and they often give wonderful concerts. They have many amazing violinists for solos, but they don't have a bass soloist. *Not many people want to study an instrument like this; only an odd person studies double bass,* Chiyo often laughed about the fact that she played such a large instrument. Tomoko is only fifteen years old.

Looking at them standing together on the stage for a moment, I think they could be mother and daughter.

When the music begins, Chiyo and Tomoko are focused as if they don't notice hundreds of eyes on them. I used to think that Chiyo devoted herself to music for an escape, a momentary release from herself, and I wondered what it was like to focus on something so closely that she seemed to even forget who she was. I envied her and even foolishly considered learning an instrument as well. I thought I could walk away from the world for a moment, like taking a break from myself, from constantly knowing what I really was about. Literature seemed to require me to walk *into* myself, while listening to music took me to another part of me, as though I were expanding.

I have had this unpleasant thought about myself—a vision of a small fly, the same kind that crawled among the corpses that I saw daily while I was in Indonesia during the war. Back then, I walked around the countless dead bodies of men, women, and children every day and never had much feeling toward them—no shock or even sympathy. They reminded me of silkworms that die as cocoons in boiling water before the silk thread is removed. I thought of death simply as leaving one's body, so corpses seemed like empty shells or houses to me. I walked by the bodies and even ate meals near them. I was in my early twenties and expected that I was going to die soon, which mistakenly made me believe that I was already dead. I cared very little about anything. When I returned to Japan and faced the death and dying of my own family, I was shocked that I had stayed alive and felt fearful about having a life, as if I hadn't owned it until then. For the first time, remembering all the corpses and flies frightened me. Why didn't I at least find out who the dead people were? Many of them were women and children, killed by Japanese soldiers, but I saw them all as empty beings, certain that I was going to die like them. I was afraid that deep within myself, I was an indifferent

and unkind being, like those flies who flew from one corpse
to another.

Chiyo looks so alive when she plays her double bass. Over
the years, I have come to realize that music demands Chiyo to
give everything she has, and such complete involvement is the
opposite of an escape from oneself. *I wanted to actually become the
double bass, but the closest I can get is to the middle of the music—there, no
one can touch me, not even me,* she said when she first heard the third
movement of Mahler's Symphony no. 1 in London. The third
movement began with a melody played by the double bass:
steady, slow, and repetitive, like walking forward, its voice was
immense, quiet, and deep. Paralyzing Chiyo with emotion, the
music was a mixture of sorrow and nostalgia. This piece took
Chiyo to the dry land of Manchuria. *If the dead could talk, they
would have a voice like the double bass.* That instrument was meant to
stay in the back of the orchestra, to provide deep sound, so other
instruments could sing the melody. But once in a while, the double bass takes over and sings a melody, releasing a sense of thick-
ness in the air as if the voice of something large, sleeping for
years, suddenly awakes. Then Chiyo's dream, the image of walking in the war-ravaged field, comes back to her.

Up on the stage, Chiyo is untouchable. She takes a deep
breath, as if the music controls her breathing. She says that
breathing is the most important factor in playing a double bass,
and she practices breathing every day. Her arms move as she
inhales the air going up the scale, and exhales as she moves
down. *The sound created by a body without any air inside has a sense of
desperation, whereas the sound formed during inhaling promises a sense of
growth, to the climax or the main theme. Can you hear the difference?*

The double bass sounds like the voices of the dead to Chiyo,
but to me, its dark vibrations overlap with Chiyo's whispering
voice. In music, melody itself is the story. Certain melodies
remain in my mind, repeat themselves, and become a part of
my body. Chiyo's voice is a part of me now.

I don't remember how long I walked before I heard bullets, and my neighbor Mr. Sasaki fell in front of me. Blood streamed down his neck. "Russians!" someone screamed. I couldn't see any Russians, but the shots came from all directions. I remember running then. My mother pulled my hand. Everyone ran into the Gaoliang fields. We ran through the tall leaves of Gaoliang, and they hit my face. All I could hear was my own breathing and the leaves against my face. We ran for a long time, maybe two hours, one hour, or even ten minutes. She finally stopped and pushed me onto the ground in the middle of the field where piles of human waste lay. I was covered in it, but I didn't smell anything. I inhaled and exhaled slowly, to avoid making any noise, but no matter how hard I tried, my breathing sounded loud in my head. I thought the Russian soldiers would hear my breathing and find me. I wanted to call Mother's name to make sure that she was still near me, but I couldn't open my mouth. My entire body was wet and heavy with waste, and I couldn't feel my legs. I waited and waited; when I finally emerged from the pile of human waste, it was dark, and I was alone. I screamed for my mother, looking for anyone. I was so scared that everyone might have died without me, that I would be left alone to kill myself. I put my hand into my pocket to feel for a packet of potassium cyanide. My village leader gave it to all the women and said that if the Russians were to hurt or embarrass us, especially women, we were to take it, because in the name of the emperor, we, the citizens of Imperial Japan, must act with pride. But I didn't know if I had the strength to take it alone. I got up and ran for what seemed like hours until I fell over and couldn't move. The pure black air covered my body; I thought if I were to die that night, I would become a part of the black.

But I opened my eyes again. I was covered in old rags and blankets, and my mother was washing clothes as she talked to me in Chinese. "Ma, ni wei shen mo jian zhong wen?"—Mother, why are you speaking in Chinese? I wanted to say more, but I was terribly sleepy and fell back asleep. When I woke again, I felt pain at my feet and realized that I wasn't dead. An old Chinese woman came into the house with water, and told me that I had to get ready to leave. She said she had cared for me for a day after she found me in her field, but I was Japanese and she was afraid to be called

Hanjian—Japanese sympathizer. She could be taken to prison for helping me. She said that Japan lost the war. I didn't believe her and thought she was trying to trick me. I left her house with sharp pain running through my body from my swollen feet. I didn't know where I was and what I was going to do, but I commanded my legs to walk on the gravel road.

I wandered around alone for a night in the mountain forest until I met a group of Japanese farmers from Qitaihe, and I walked with them toward Mudanjiang. Then we encountered a group of men from the Guandong Army, also heading south. When they confirmed the defeat of Japan, we suddenly understood our dangerous position as invaders in a foreign country. The soldiers were headed toward Fangzheng in the west and agreed to lead us, but they also said that they would be covering sixty kilometers each day. Since it was impossible for small children to cover such a distance, they ordered mothers to abandon their children or to take their lives to save them from the misery of a long brutal journey. The soldiers said that the upcoming journey would be intolerable for anyone under eight. Hearing this order, all the faces of the mothers with young children became pale, though no one could argue with them. We spent the night in the dark forest, and by the next morning, some mothers and small children were missing. No one asked or talked about them.

We walked for what seemed like forever, days and nights, passing by the dead bodies of Japanese women and children who had committed suicide. Such sights were becoming common, and every time I passed, I looked at the corpses closely in case I recognized them. So many horrible scenes—a pregnant woman giving birth alone on the side of the street as she screamed, "Don't look!"; children sitting in a circle in the middle of a forest, abandoned by or separated from their parents; a group of women who threw their children into the river; a man and a woman, walking as if possessed, not even seeming to notice that they were carrying their dead babies on their backs. I was beginning to understand the value of potassium cyanide.

A long time ago, I asked Chiyo what she was thinking or seeing during her performances, and she said nothing in particular—all black with my eyes closed, an intense, pure feeling without any logical thoughts. Her body breathed, and she became her feelings.

When Chiyo held her double bass inside her arm, her music was like liquid, rushing through even the smallest holes inside me and making me absorb all that she carried. *When you come to my concert, close your eyes and tell me what happens,* Chiyo said this morning while her face was still on my chest. I'll tell her that my heart expanded, her river of music filled my lungs, and I longed for more air. When the music stops, Tomoko and the Kamakura Youth Orchestra receives standing ovations. The audience doesn't stop applauding for a long time as if we all want to somehow reach out to and embrace Chiyo and Tomoko; their music was so raw and immediate to us.

Instead of going home after the concert, Chiyo says she wants to walk for a while. After concentrating her mind so vigorously, she doesn't know what to do with herself. Her face looks exhausted, as if she has been running for hours, though I know how alive she felt while playing. At one time, being alive seemed like a punishment to Chiyo, but while she played her double bass, she allowed herself to enjoy living fully for the sake of music.

"Let's go to the Hachiman Shrine." Chiyo begins walking toward the entrance and crosses the bridge. She stops by the red portable store where a man is selling apples dipped in candy syrup. Chiyo takes the apple candy on the stick and waves at me.

"Do you have a wallet with you? I didn't bring mine." Chiyo smiles and walks away from the store, holding her candy. She's acting like a young girl, carrying the sweet and sour apple candy, anticipating it melting in her mouth. While I pay for the candy, Chiyo is already running up the stairs, her white coat moving as she takes a step. I follow her as though I'm chasing a small white rabbit. I have to stop in the middle to catch my breath, but Chiyo runs all the way to the top.

I sit on the bench as my entire body feels the blood running through it from the stairs, and Chiyo sits next to me and unwraps the candy. There are many visitors here at the Hachiman Shrine on Sunday.

"Try the candy. It's good." Chiyo puts it in front of my face, and the sweet sugar smell covers my nose. I take a bite, and the sweet candy and the sour apple melt in my mouth.

"We're too old to be eating this sort of candy. Only small children walk around with sweet candy on a stick," I say.

"Nonsense." Chiyo laughs.

"Chiyo," I swallow the sweet taste all the way inside my throat, "I wrote to Steve and Helen Johnson. I told them that they should come and visit us soon, very soon, before I change my mind."

Chiyo's smile changes into a serious gaze.

"You did?"

"Yes."

Chiyo sits up straight and stops eating her apple candy. "Do you think they'll come?"

"I think so."

Chiyo smiles with a lonely gaze. "There are so many people who could come back and haunt us as long as we're alive. If you were my father, he would be having angry guests the rest of his life. I'm just glad that your guest is a lovely little girl."

She's right about her father. Chiyo always said that if Chinese people knew her father the way Chiyo knew him, they would have let him live, since living with the knowledge of his cruelty would have been the real punishment. Until Chiyo returned to Japan and searched for her father's record of execution, she had no idea that her father was ordering the arrest of fifty to a hundred suspicious Chinese guerrillas in Manchuria every week and torturing them. The torture was listed as beating, burning, and water hosing. *Water hosing—you place the hose deep inside their throat and run the water, which goes inside the stomach; it grows like a pregnant woman's belly, and if you go too far, the stomach breaks; one of the most painful ways to die,* Chiyo described to me once.

Finding out about her father broke Chiyo's heart. As a child, she thought of her father as a strong man with authority over the Chinese people, which he used only to protect them. *There were some incidents that didn't make sense to me when I was a child. When everything became clear after I read the record of his execution, my father, especially the memories of him as a kind man, was also taken from me.* Chiyo remembers the incident when a Chinese woman came running to their house in Fengtian screaming that her husband had been taken by the military police. She said that her husband worked for the printing company, and the owner and workers of the company were all arrested for planning a secret bombing to rebel against Japanese forces. Chiyo knew this woman, who sold Mautou—yellow buns made of corn—on the street, and also played with her three daughters after school. The woman didn't look like herself; she was disoriented as she grabbed Chiyo's father's arms and begged him not to use the water hose. *My father took her out, and my mother ordered me and my brother to go back to our rooms. Later he told me that the woman was crazy. I believed him because who, in their right mind, would run to a Japanese officer's house in the middle of night and scream not to use the water hose? How could I have imagined that my father would order such a torture during the day and come home in the evening to have dinner with us?*

Sitting alone on the bench with an apple candy, I almost feel as though Chiyo is going to cry out for her mother and father like a little girl. But no one will ever come for her from the past. Chiyo's escape in Manchuria ended when she was captured by Russian troops in Fangzheng and was placed in a refugee residence for Japanese in Harbin. She survived the winter until the order to return to the mainland finally came to Japanese immigrants in spring. She came back to Japan alone, leaving her mother missing in a Manchurian field, her father and brother away at the war. None of them came back. I move closer to her and touch the back of her neck. Her eyes are filled with tears.

NOVEMBER 1975

Uncle Steve had been on the phone with Dad for almost an hour. He listened for a long time. I could hear Dad's deep voice shake the phone going into Uncle Steve's ear, sounding angry. When Uncle Steve said "No" or "I can't," Dad's deep voice got louder. Then Uncle Steve pulled the phone away from his ear, pointed at it, and winked at me. I whispered and asked him if Dad was angry. Uncle Steve just smiled and shrugged his shoulders. Then Dad's voice was suddenly gone. Uncle Steve called his name three times. He sighed and hung up the phone.

"Your dad just hung up on me." Uncle Steve sat next to me on the couch.

"Is he mad at you?"

"Very."

"What did you do?"

"Mrs. Hogan and I found out that the couple that adopted Anna first lived not too far from Mrs. Hogan's house. I wanted your dad to come with us, but he said no. He told me to stop acting like a detective."

"The mean people?"

"Actually, they were courageous to adopt Anna, I think. Will you come with me to visit them next weekend?"

"Why are we going to visit them?" Mrs. Hogan said Mom didn't get along with her first parents. I didn't want to meet people who tried to send Mom back to the orphanage.

"I thought they could tell us more about your mom."

"But Mrs. Hogan already told us about her." I looked down. "Do I have to go?"

Uncle Steve got up and went to the kitchen table, then came back with a paper and pencil. Then he drew a big straight tree.

"Do you know how a tree grows?" Uncle Steve asked.

I shook my head.

"When you cut a tree," he drew a line through the middle of the trunk, "what do you see on the surface?" He drew a circle and gave me a pencil. It was like science class.

I took the pencil and drew a small circle in the center and added many more circles around it until there wasn't any more space.

"This smallest circle in the center," he pointed at the middle, "is the size of this tree when it was planted. A tree gains a layer each year, so you can find out how old the tree is by counting the layers." Uncle Steve counted the circles that I drew and said that my tree was seven years old.

"Suppose your mom is a tree; how many layers does she have?" Mom was so skinny that she didn't look like she had that many layers.

"Mom's skinny. She's more like a branch."

"Or more like an empty tree." Uncle Steve colored the middle circle with a pencil. Now there was a black hole in the middle of the tree. "A tree needs strong ground to let the roots grow. If she didn't have a place to grow strong in the beginning, then the core," he pointed at the black hole again, "is empty. An empty tree isn't very strong. When the wind blows, it can break."

I thought about Mom standing in front of a mirror. If I cut her in half, she must have a hole in the middle of her body.

"I think we should meet the first family. Anna deserves to be understood," Uncle Steve said.

"Can they fix Mom's empty tree?"

"I don't know. But do you know what I do when I see a weak tree?"

I shook my head.

"I add a couple thick sticks next to the tree and tie them to it. This gives strength and support, so it doesn't fall. You can be one of the thick sticks to help support your mother." Uncle Steve drew two thick sticks on the paper. "You and Ken are the only sticks your mom has." Next to the sticks, he wrote Helen and Ken.

"What about Dad?"

Uncle Steve drew a house next to the tree. Inside the house, he drew a person. "This is where your dad is, in the house. He can see that the tree is a little weak, but he's too afraid to go outside to find out what's really going on."

"Why's he afraid of an empty tree?"

"It's hard to admit that someone you love is empty."

Uncle Steve got up and taped our tree drawing on the refrigerator. Now I was responsible for Mom because she was an empty tree, and I had to be her stick. Dad was too scared and Ken was too little.

⁓

When Uncle Steve knocked on the door, my chest got tight. I thought a big man with a mean face was going to answer the door, but it was an old man. Uncle Steve called him Hector. Hector said hello and looked at me from head to toe. I just said hello and stepped behind Uncle Steve. He had a little gray hair on his head, but long hair was coming out of his ears. His skin had many brown spots. He was skinny, but his tummy stuck out like a pregnant woman. He walked slowly, taking us to the living room. Mrs. Hogan was there and said hello from the brown couch in the middle of the room. She was wearing the same pretty purple dress, and her hair was tightly put together on the back of her head. She looked exactly the way she did when she visited us. Hector went to the green chair by the window, and his brown pants pulled up when he sat down on the chair. I could see his bright red socks. They looked funny.

"Help yourself to coffee in the kitchen. I would pour you a cup, but I would spill it all over with these hands." Hector lifted his arms and pointed at the kitchen. His hands were shaking. His nails were all white and thick.

"Are you cold?" I asked Hector.

Hector laughed a little and said, "No, I just shake. I've been shaking for the last five years, and I don't know how to stop." Hector lifted both of his arms, and they shook fast. "Everyone calls me Shaky Hector."

I followed Uncle Steve to the kitchen. The kitchen was small with all bright green walls. There were three cups on the counter already, by the coffee.

"Is Shaky Hector sick?" I whispered to Uncle Steve.

He nodded his head and poured coffee into a cup. I was so stupid to have asked if he was cold.

When we went back to the living room, I looked at the floor and tried not to look at Shaky Hector's hands. I sat between Mrs. Hogan and Uncle Steve. The room was dark because the curtains were closed and the carpet was dark brown.

"I'm sorry that you had to come so early on Sunday, but it's the only time Carol isn't home. She's at church," Shaky Hector said. On the way here, Uncle Steve told me that when he first called them, they said they didn't want to see him. Later, Hector called him back and said that we could visit him at eight on Sunday morning because that was when his wife would be at church. So we had to leave home at seven in the morning to get there by eight o'clock. It was like going to school.

Shaky Hector pulled a pack of cigarettes from his pocket and put one in his mouth, looking at Uncle Steve, who got up and lit it for him. Shaky Hector inhaled slowly and then the smoke was everywhere on his face, shaky like his hands.

"It's still hard for Carol to remember Anna. Things didn't work out between us, but we cared for her." Shaky Hector's voice, smoke, and Mom's name, coming from his mouth. That was so strange.

"Good thing Carol didn't meet you. You look like your mother when she was little." Shaky Hector stared at my face. His eyes looked gray in this dark room, like the eyes of the dead rainbow trout I caught. I looked down at his funny red socks. Aunt Mary said that I looked like Mom, too, but I didn't think we looked alike at all.

"I wanted to know how you found Anna in Japan," Mrs. Hogan said to Shaky Hector, but he just kept smoking, and his cigarette got shorter in his hand. When it was gone, he looked at Mrs. Hogan, Uncle Steve, and then me. His eyes stopped at my face again, so I quickly looked at his socks again. Shaky Hector took out another cigarette and looked at Uncle Steve, who lit it again. Mrs. Hogan looked too scared to say anything. I didn't know how long we had to sit here and watch Shaky Hector smoke. The bright orange light flamed from the tip of the cigarette, was gone, came up again, and was gone. A lot of smoke came out of his mouth, and he put out the cigarette on the table next to him.

"Carol would kill me if she found out that I met you all. She was furious when you called us," Shaky Hector said to Uncle Steve. "But I guess I don't think it's a big deal. I don't mind talking about Anna." He scratched his face with his shaky hands, then he laughed a little.

"When I was drafted to Japan after the war, I was too stupid and young to understand why I had to go there *after* the war had ended. Eventually, I figured out that I was a part of the occupation force."

"Occupation force?" I whispered to Uncle Steve.

"That's the group that doesn't fight. They just help occupy the country," Shaky Hector said, looking right at me.

"Occupy?"

"It's like soldiers were sent to rebuild the country, I guess," Uncle Steve said. I thought all soldiers carry guns, wear green clothes, and walk through jungles to fight like Dad did. Shaky

Hector opened his eyes wide and stared at me from head to toe again, so I stopped asking questions and sat back deep in the couch.

"I grew up in a small town outside of Santa Monica. After high school, I worked fixing cars. That was my life. All I knew about Japan was what the newspaper said during the war. To me, Japan was an exotic country somewhere far away. I had never been to a foreign country before. I was twenty-five when I was drafted, and for two years, I stayed in Japan." I tried to think of Shaky Hector as a young person, but he was so old and shaky now that I couldn't really picture it.

"I was supposed to be there just for a year, but my stay was extended, so I called for Carol to come too. We lived near the Yokosuka base, and Carol volunteered at the local church. That's how she became acquainted with a teacher from the Christian Home for Children. Carol wanted a baby so badly. So we went to the Home and requested an adoption."

"Why didn't she have her own baby?" I asked, but it must have been a bad question because Uncle Steve elbowed me.

Shaky Hector didn't answer my question. He pulled out another cigarette from his pocket. He sure smoked a lot. It was strange that Mrs. Hogan wasn't smoking at all.

"When Carol first told me about adoption, I thought it was a crazy idea. I mean, adopting an orphan from Japan? That was unheard-of back then. But Carol insisted, and we met some children at the Christian Home for Children." Hector leaned over and his gray dead-fish eyes were right in front of me again. "When we met Anna, she was only two, very shy, but a lovely girl. We immediately wanted her. It's strange how a place becomes familiar once you live there. If we had been in the States, we'd have never considered adopting a child from Japan, but we knew the streets and train stations and people. Then before you know it, we were trying to adopt a Japanese child."

I wanted to look down to his red socks again, but he was talking to me, so I couldn't. I felt like he was talking just to me.

"We really wanted to raise your mother. It was illegal for Americans to adopt a Japanese child back in 1948, but even so, we begged the principal at the Home. She had to pull all kinds of strings to make it possible. It took a long time, a few years, for everything to be official. We came back to the States without Anna, but we never gave up. You don't know how happy we were when the principal called and told us that Anna could finally come and live with us. We were so happy. Do you understand? It's important that you understand this." Shaky Hector started to speak faster and louder. He wasn't angry, but he was talking just to me still. I sat closer to Uncle Steve.

"You understand Hector, right sweetheart?" Uncle Steve touched my head gently, so I nodded.

"Maybe things would have worked out if Anna could have come sooner, if she had come when she was still little. By the time she actually came to us, she was already five years old." His hands were shaking harder on his lap. "When she arrived here, she was already a complete human being. I know it sounds strange, but she was already five, a person with her own mind. She didn't understand English. That first day, we told her that her new name was Anna, and that we were her parents. But the next day, Anna packed her bag and was ready to go back. I explained to her again that she was going to stay for good. But she didn't understand a word I was saying, so I took her bag and unpacked it in her room. She just sat on the bed and watched me unpack. Every day for the first month, when she woke up and saw our faces, she'd start crying. We didn't know what to do. We just felt her pain." Shaky Hector looked like he was getting upset.

I wondered if Mom cried when she had to leave her friends and teachers at the orphanage in Japan. I was sad when I went to camp for only three weeks. On the last day, I was so scared that Mom wouldn't pick us up. Mom was only five, half my age, leaving Japan alone. She must have been really scared.

"How did you communicate if she couldn't understand English?" Uncle Steve asked.

"By teaching her English. And things got better as Anna slowly learned, but it got worse again when we sent her to school. She was teased because she didn't speak English well. Other kids called her stupid things like Jap or yellow monkey." Mom didn't look anything like a monkey! Mom doesn't have a yellow face. Her face is pale like an ice cube.

"Anna didn't want to go to school, but we made her get up and go every morning. We wanted to make sure that we actually saved a girl from the orphanage. If she didn't have a better life here, what the hell was the point of coming here?" Shaky Hector's smoky breath came to my nose, and I wanted to move my face away from him, but that would have been rude.

"Do you like going to school, Helen?" Shaky Hector smiled with his yellow teeth.

"Yes."

"Good girl. Does your uncle take good care of you?"

"Yes." I looked at Uncle Steve.

"Good. You see, I didn't do good like your uncle, Helen. I suddenly became the father of a five-year-old one day. I didn't know what the hell was going on." His dead-fish eyes turned to Uncle Steve, who didn't say anything, just blinked his eyes.

I didn't like Shaky Hector. He was just like my dad. Dad didn't want me and Ken around, so he took us to Uncle Steve's house. He promised that he would come and get us, but he hasn't. Shaky Hector didn't want Mom, so he gave her to Mrs. Hogan.

"Why did you yell at Mom all the time?" I stood up and said it loud to Shaky Hector.

"Yell?" Shaky Hector's eyes got bigger.

"Everybody could hear you yelling at Mom. That was mean!"

"Who is everybody?"

"Mrs. Hogan said everybody could hear you yelling at Mom."
Uncle Steve pulled my sleeve and Mrs. Hogan's face got red. But
I wasn't scared of Shaky Hector or Dad. I was the stick to Mom's
tree, so I was going to yell back at Shaky Hector if he got mad
at me. But he didn't get mad or yell at me. Instead, he just smiled.

"I yelled at her when she hid all kinds of places in the
house before going to school. When we found her and forced
her to come out, she would scream and throw things at the
windows. She broke three windows in a week once. In the
morning, she would hide under the table and say that she
wouldn't go to school. Carol had to go under the table and
pull her out."

I tried to think of Mom breaking windows, but instead I
remembered Mom screaming at me and Ken not to come close
to her after camp.

"In our old house, we had a big closet in the guest bedroom.
There were some shelves in there, and Anna climbed all the
way up in the corner. She fit so perfectly in the corner that we
couldn't reach her. We talked calmly, reasoned with her, yelled
at her, tried to bribe her with candy, but she wouldn't come out.
The house was old and we had no locks on the doors. No matter what we did, she'd still get in the room, then into the closet.
She would stay in the closet for the entire day sometimes. Carol
used to sit by the closet and beg Anna to come out, but she
wouldn't. It was getting bad. Carol wasn't sleeping well, was getting sick and depressed. I had to protect Carol, so I finally told
Anna one day that if she didn't come out, we'd send her back
to Japan. But it was like she didn't hear me. She was singing
and talking to herself in Japanese." Shaky Hector put his hand
on his forehead and closed his eyes for a moment. I had no idea
that Mom sat in the closet, too.

"Later, we sent Anna to the head doctor." He pointed at his
head. "He's the one who said that we should send Anna back

to Japan because according to him, her behavior was 'a manifestation of her attachment to her home.' We wanted what was best for her, so we were going to contact the Home. But when Mrs. Hogan talked to us, we thought Anna should have one more try in America. I guess I didn't want to fail her completely." Shaky Hector waved his shaky arms up in the air. His breathing was getting short like he had been running.

"But you all came to the church every Sunday, as a family. I remember that," Mrs. Hogan said in a small voice.

"Anna willingly did that—who knows why. I prayed and prayed for Anna to become normal, but she didn't get better. You must think we were horrible to Anna," Shaky Hector said to Mrs. Hogan and Uncle Steve. Then he looked at me again.

"I know you're still little, but I want you to remember this. When Carol and I met your mother, there really was a connection between us. But when she actually came here, she was a complete stranger. She didn't want to absorb anything from us." Shaky Hector shook his head, got up slowly, and walked into the back room. When he was gone, I whispered to Uncle Steve that I wanted to go home. Uncle Steve leaned as far back as he could to see what Shaky Hector was doing. I could hear him moving and dropping something on the floor. Then he came out with a brown shoebox. He walked to Uncle Steve and gave it to him.

"The first year I was in Japan, I wrote many letters to Carol, almost one a week." He pointed at the box. Uncle Steve opened the top, and there were many envelopes addressed to Carol Gandini. Hector walked slowly back to his green chair, sat down, and looked at Uncle Steve. "You should read those letters before you go to Japan."

"You're going to Japan?" I turned to Uncle Steve, who looked surprised, his eyes wide open.

"I haven't told them about it yet," said Mrs. Hogan. Now we all looked at her. Mrs. Hogan smiled and said I should go to Japan and meet Mom's uncle.

"Mom's uncle?" I remembered reading about him in the letter from the teacher at the orphanage. He brought Mom to the orphanage with Grandma Ume. Why did she want me to meet Mom's uncle? Shaky Hector tried to send Mom back to Japan. Maybe Mrs. Hogan was trying to send me back to Japan, too.

"Are you sending me back to the orphanage in Japan?" I asked Mrs. Hogan. Her narrow eyes got bigger, then smaller when she burst into laughter.

"Goodness, Helen! I'm not going to send you anywhere. You aren't going alone anyway. I thought perhaps you," Mrs. Hogan looked at Uncle Steve, "would go with Helen."

"Me?" Uncle Steve opened his mouth wide to say something, but Mrs. Hogan spoke first.

"We never forget where we come from—I'm sure you agree. I was hoping that you could help Helen and travel to Japan with her."

"But going all the way to Japan? I don't know if I could . . ." Uncle Steve looked scared.

"You won't really understand unless you go there," Shaky Hector said.

Uncle Steve looked at the floor like he was thinking about something.

"If we go and visit Mom's uncle, Mom will get better?" I asked.

"I doubt it." Shaky Hector pulled out another cigarette. Uncle Steve was still looking down and didn't see, so he didn't get up to light it.

Shaky Hector put the unlit cigarette in his mouth. "It's just that Anna deserves to know where she came from."

Uncle Steve said Mom deserved to be understood. Now Shaky Hector said Mom deserved to know where she came from. Every time she deserved something, I had to do something scary. To visit Mom's uncle, we would have to go over the ocean. I'd be scared. Uncle Steve wanted me to be Mom's stick holding her up, but I didn't know how.

On the way home, Uncle Steve didn't say very much. We just listened to the radio. He stared at the road with his serious face. In the truck, I was thinking that I was in an airplane and thought about flying for ten hours to the opposite side of the earth. Uncle Steve sighed many times on the way home.

When we got home, Uncle Steve sat at the kitchen table, going through Shaky Hector's letters in the shoebox all afternoon. He had to clear the table for dinner, but after dinner, he was back at it. Aunt Mary, Ken, and I were watching *Wild Kingdom*, but Uncle Steve missed it for the first time. Since Ken and I came here, every Sunday, after taking a bath and doing our homework, we'd watched this show in our pajamas. It was Uncle Steve's favorite show, too. We loved watching all the wild animals running in Africa. Mrs. Hogan said that we had to go to a place to really know it, but watching *Wild Kingdom* made me feel like I was in Africa. I felt bad that Uncle Steve was missing it because they were showing a lion family. Ken was pretending to be the guide. He explained how strong the lions were, how they could eat a person in ten seconds. Aunt Mary put her hands on her cheeks and pretended to be scared.

During a commercial, I got up and went to the kitchen. There were envelopes and papers everywhere. Uncle Steve looked up and said hi to me. I sat across the table and asked what he was reading. He just pointed at the letters.

"What did Hector say in the letters?"

"He described a lot about Japan when he was there. Do you want to hear some?" Uncle Steve pulled a letter from the shoebox. I wanted to go back to *Wild Kingdom*, but I said O.K.

"On November 12, 1946, he talks about the streets and the people in Japan. *All the men and women are skinny and wearing torn and filthy clothes. I can tell that many people are struggling here. But there're so many stalls on the street. They sell almost anything you can find, like soap, kimonos, socks, and even old newspapers. I can feel that they are desperate to get up again, and they have incredible energy and enthusiasm, which surprises me."*

On TV, soldiers were always running and firing their guns. But instead, Shaky Hector was shopping at street stalls.

"Hector said he really liked using the trains in Japan. *On December 12, the last cart of each train is specially reserved for u.s. soldiers, and we can use the train anytime for free. Even the subways in Tokyo are free to use, but the subways are always packed. There are rumors that just by standing on the platform, we could get typhus. In the crowds, we can get lice and the lice could deliver it to us."*

Shaky Hector could only walk slowly now, but when he was young, he rode a train in Japan.

"Listen to this. *December 20, 1946. Dear Carol, I am visiting the town of Mito in Saitama now. I was sent to the Air Force base yesterday because one of the jets needed to be repaired. As soon as I got in Mito, I worked six hours straight, and then I was free. I thought I would go look for your silk in town, but I was told that the town of Mito outside the base is off-limits to u.s. soldiers. Two days ago, one of the GIs got drunk, started shooting randomly, and mistakenly shot an eighteen-year-old girl and her father. The girl died immediately, and her father died three days later. A representative from our base is going to the wake tonight to apologize to their family. The family will cremate the girl tomorrow. We were ordered not to go into the city for a while. Even though I wasn't involved in this incident, I was shocked and terrified. I thought about the family. It reminded me of why I was sent here. I was drafted after the war and I didn't have to fight. The war seemed like a forgotten past. I was just intrigued by the hard-working people and the beautiful silk. Then there is an incident like this."* Uncle Steve covered his mouth a little.

"I didn't understand why Hector wanted me to take these letters. Now I can see why he wanted to adopt your mom." Uncle Steve nodded many times, but it didn't make sense to me at all. I didn't know how Shaky Hector's letters could help Mom's empty tree. Uncle Steve put all the letters back into the box. There were so many letters. A long time ago, Hector's hands could still do anything—like write letters.

"Is Shaky Hector really sick?" I asked Uncle Steve.

"He has the same disease Mr. Hogan had."

"Mr. Hogan? You knew him?"

"No, I never met him. He died when your mom was in high school."

"Did he shake all the time like Hector?"

"Yes, it was worse. He couldn't walk, stand, or sit, and soon he was in bed all day. Then he got Alzheimer's and forgot everything."

"Alzheimer's?"

Uncle Steve stopped his hand from putting the letters in the box. "It's a disease that affects your memory. He first forgot Anna, then Mrs. Hogan. He didn't even know who he was in the end. He lived like that for a year."

"You mean he forgot his own name?" Ken forgot things all the time, but even he could never forget his name. I thought about Mrs. Hogan's sad narrow eyes. I felt bad that I thought of her as a weak and slow old person. Mom forgot about me a lot, too, when she put me in the closet. But she didn't have Alzheimer's, she had a nervous breakdown.

"Can you imagine forgetting everything?" Uncle Steve's serious face looked straight at me. "Maybe if Anna knew a little more about where she is from, she wouldn't feel so alone."

"Mom feels alone?"

"I imagine so."

But I thought she wanted to be alone. She didn't want me or Ken near her.

Uncle Steve finished putting all the letters into the shoebox and put it aside on the table. Then we went back to the living room. We all squeezed onto the couch to watch the rest of *Wild Kingdom*. Ken got up again to show Uncle Steve that he was a guide to the lions in Africa. Uncle Steve covered his head and pretended to be scared. He looked much more scared when Mrs. Hogan talked about him going to Japan.

~

I kept having the same strange dream after I went to see Shaky Hector. In my dream, Mom was wearing a navy suit standing in front of a mirror in the backyard of our house. She started sinking into the ground. I thought about going to pull her out, but I couldn't move my feet, so I just watched her sink from behind a tree. The dream wasn't really scary, but it always woke me up in the middle of the night, and staying awake in the dark was scary. The house was alive at night, making all kinds of noises. I told Uncle Steve about this dream. He said that I should go and see the dream doctor.

"A dream doctor? You're making that up!"

"Oh no, there's a doctor for everything." He smiled.

"Is there a doctor for gardening?"

"Sure."

"How about for cooking? If you are a bad cook, is there a doctor for that?"

"Absolutely."

"What about eating chocolate? Is there a doctor for eating too much chocolate?"

"That," he made a serious face, "is the only kind of problem that there is no doctor for."

"Why?"

"Why would you want someone to stop you from eating too much chocolate?" He laughed. I guess I wouldn't want a chocolate doctor. Instead of taking me to the dream doctor, Uncle Steve pretended to be the dream doctor. He said the bad dream might go away if I stopped sleeping with Mom's baby picture under my pillow. But I didn't want the picture to get lost while I was sleeping. So I kept sleeping with it.

One night, I woke up again after having the same dream, so I got up, turned on the lamp by my bed, and took out the picture.

I got out of bed and I took out the letter from the teacher at the orphanage from my desk drawer. I touched the address of Mom's uncle, Hideo Takagawa, on the envelope. I wanted Uncle Steve to write a letter to Mom's uncle, but I didn't want him to be scared anymore. His face turned pale when Mrs. Hogan asked him to go to Japan with me. He hadn't said anything about going to Japan since. Maybe he didn't want to go so far away. So I took out a piece of paper from my notebook and started writing a letter to Mom's uncle. I had no idea what to say, but I had to write because I was the stick next to Mom's tree. Sometimes, I had to do things by myself.

Even though the letter was short, it took me a long time to write it. I folded it in half and into an envelope. Then I tiptoed downstairs and opened the top drawer in the kitchen. Aunt Mary always kept her stamps there. I didn't know how many stamps I had to put on for this letter for going all the way to Japan. I guessed and put ten stamps. I didn't want it to go halfway and come back in the middle of the sky. The stamps covered half of the envelope. I went back to my room and put the letter in my schoolbag because there was a big mailbox in front of my school, and a mailman in a light blue uniform always came and opened the box with a key in the afternoon. Tomorrow, I would walk there and drop off this letter. I would ask the mailman to take my letter to Japan. I would ask him not to lose the letter. I could do this all by myself. And if Mom's uncle wrote me back and said that I could come to Japan, maybe Uncle Steve would go to Japan with me. It would be scary to fly for hours, but we would be going back the opposite way that Mom came from many years ago when she was only five, half of my age.

HOMECOMING

The first thing I saw—a Japanese woman wearing a bright green dress and red lipstick, kissing an American soldier—shocked me not only because she was kissing an American, but because it was in the middle of the day on a public bench. The woman's eyes were shut tightly, her arms were around the soldier's neck, his arms around her waist. My troops, wearing dirty brown uniforms covered in white DDT powder, walked off the boat at the Yokohama port, returning from Indonesia. We all stood there and blankly gazed at the kiss between the Japanese woman and the American soldier in his clean, sharp Navy uniform. I had come back to a changed Japan. I had been gone for nearly three years and never imagined that I would encounter the sight of a public kiss. My unit had been captured as prisoners of war right after the defeat of Japan in 1945, but was fortunate enough to be released back to Japan in February 1946. On the way home, we were told that all the major cities in Japan were bombed, and that General Headquarters had taken control of everything. We stood in the middle of Yokohama port and gazed at the mixture of tall foreign soldiers and Japanese crowds. Foreign soldiers drove away in jeeps, waving at children, with smiles. Japan never had so many foreigners at once. I, along with the men from my unit, felt embarrassed in our dirty clothes, and stood there like fools. Eventually, we went our separate ways to our own homes.

While I was learning English as a student, there were two difficult words for me to comprehend. *Homecoming*—it seemed so peculiar that the home was coming to us instead of us coming home. Shouldn't it be *Cominghome*? And *bittersweet*—what food could offer such a paradoxical flavor? When I saw the kiss of a Japanese woman and an American soldier in public, both words, *homecoming* and *bittersweet,* entered my mind. It was my home that was coming to me in a changed shape and form, and homecoming tasted both sweet and bitter.

The first thing Chiyo saw in Japan when she returned from Manchuria was a young woman's buttocks covered in white DDT powder right in front of her face, so close that her nose almost touched it. Before arriving at Maizuru port, all the men, women, and children were ordered to take off their clothes and go into a small room in the boat where they all knelt down as white DDT powder covered them. They looked like dirty homeless people. Chiyo felt ashamed and embarrassed as a failed immigrant, returning home as a survivor, but a moment after she landed on the ground where her mother and father were born, the most important thing was that she was alive and home, the closest place she could come to be with her family in spirit even though she had nothing left in Japan.

In three days, Helen and Steve Johnson will arrive. What is the first thing Helen is going to see? Ume's name has been so private, like a code only Chiyo and I understand, but the thought of meeting Helen feels like homecoming and even fills me with a bit of nostalgia. Something so familiar, the memory of Ume, is returning to me through Helen. Although Japan is closely rooted to her through her mother and grandmother, this place will seem strange to her. I hope her visit will be filled with much sweetness, but I know there is always a bit of bitterness in homecoming. How is she going to relate to this strange place?

Because I had changed and my home had changed while I was at war, I didn't know how to relate to, or function in, my own country when I returned to Japan. I felt at a distance, which was why I urgently looked for my family, who were missing amidst the chaos after the war. After arriving in Yokohama port, I went to Tokyo to look for my aunt's house, where my mother, Ume, and I used to live. After my father was drafted and left the silk farm in Hiroshima, Mother quickly left for her sister's house in Tokyo, not able to tolerate the cold treatment by my father's sister, Aunt Fuyu. She used my entrance to Tokyo University as an excuse to move away with me and Ume. When I was drafted, I suggested that she leave Tokyo, which was becoming more and more dangerous. But she never considered returning to the silk farm.

The entire neighborhood in Tokyo looked different from how I remembered; some small shelters had been rebuilt, but the land was mostly empty. The neighbors didn't know what had happened to my family. Sympathetically, they told me that the bombing worsened after I left, and that our area was severely bombed on the March 10th Tokyo bombing. They said not even a single house in the neighborhood survived. Since they hadn't seen any of my family for almost a year, they assumed that either they had died, or if they had survived, perhaps they had moved to the countryside. I walked around the city and visited schools and hospitals, asking if they had any records that indicated that my mother or Ume had come, but I didn't find any trace of them.

In the evening, I walked back to Tokyo station to buy a ticket to Hiroshima; I thought they might have returned there after losing their house. As I approached the station, markets began to appear, and the street became crowded with people selling, yelling, and buying and exchanging materials for food. I inspected each face that passed me in case it was my mother's or sister's. At the station, there were hundreds of men, women, and children, homeless and sleeping on the floor, so I walked around, calling Ume's and Mother's names. I arrived at the station too late for the train that went to Osaka, then to Hiroshima, and the next train wouldn't be leaving until the next morning. I spent the night at the station with the injured soldiers and homeless people. Occasionally, orphans got up and ran as a group to foreign soldiers walked by, because they often gave candy and chocolate to the children. I couldn't have imagined myself sleeping at the train station before I left for the war, but now everything had changed.

The next day, the train ride from Tokyo to Hiroshima was over fifteen hours, and I didn't arrive until eight o'clock that night. On the train, I felt nervous thinking about Hiroshima. Even though I had heard about the damages from the atomic bomb and the black rain, the image of the rivers calmly running through the city to the sea stayed deeply in my mind. An old man who came to Tokyo to sell oil products told me that other cities like Fukuyama and Kure had all been bombed severely by B-29s. I absentmindedly listened to him and thought about our house on the hill, how it must have been an easy target. Nothing really registered in my mind until the train arrived in Hiroshima, where all the large concrete buildings—movie theaters, department stores, banks—were gone. The downtown area where the small stores, cafés, and restaurants used to be was simply empty. The old man said that nothing would grow there for the next seventy years. Hiroshima was my home, and to this day, I don't know how to describe what I saw—words like *complete destruction* don't quite describe what I saw. Everything was black, bare, and vanished. I hurried to the street train to get to Kusazu, my hometown. The train ran through the city, and nothing was familiar to me, except when it ran by the deep black ocean—the only recognizable sight to me that night.

When I saw my house—burnt fields and broken houses abandoned up on the hill—I thought I just wasn't seeing very well in the dark from the bottom of the hill. But I kept walking, squinting my eyes and eventually running up the hill to small piles of wood, metal, and broken glass. I sat down and blankly stared at the sight, trying to remember what the place used to look like.

"Hideo chan? Is that you?" A woman in a white apron came up the hill. I quickly stood up and walked toward her. It was Mrs. Kataoka, who worked for Takagawa Silk Company and lived down the hill with her husband and children. Mrs. Kataoka held my hands and bowed deeply as she said that she had been praying for the safety of the Takagawa children. Mrs. Kataoka had known me since I was born and always called me Hideo chan, the way she also referred to small children, even after I began high school. Looking at our destroyed house, she described how the airplanes flew over Kusazu on the way to Kure City, where the large Naval Base was. American airplanes didn't target small towns, but one night in the middle of June, Mrs. Kataoka saw fires and heard bombs. She thought Kusazu was safe because it was out of the city, but she took her family to the air raid shelter in her yard just in case the planes changed their direction. She heard them fly by and the bombs being dropped closer as the ground shook hard. But it was only for two or three minutes, then the area became quiet immediately after the planes flew farther way. She stayed with her children underground all night, and in the morning, when she slowly came out, she saw her house along with her neighbors' houses standing. But up on the hill, my father's place—his house, storage buildings, silkworm rooms, and factories that took three generations to build—were all destroyed and smoking.

Mrs. Kataoka told me to come down to her house, and as we walked down the hill, she explained that my father had returned from the war. He was living with my Aunt Fuyu, in Koi.

"I will send my son to your father tonight so that he will know that you have safely returned." She walked quickly as if she couldn't wait to get to the house to send her son to my father. I asked Mrs. Kataoka about my mother, Ume, and Shinya. She said Shinya hadn't returned yet, and as for my mother and Ume, she wasn't certain what happened to them. She sympathetically explained that when my father returned from the front and saw the destruction of the silk farm, he was like a madman, uncontrollably angry, throwing logs against the hill, crying and screaming. His employees gathered on the hill and tried to comfort him. When he found out that my mother left for Tokyo as soon as he had been drafted, he became terribly angry and said protecting the house and farm was her duty, the least she could have done as the wife of the Takagawa Silk Company's master. My father went to Tokyo and looked for my mother and Ume. Mrs. Kataoka didn't know what he would do if he found my mother, and was afraid for her. When he returned, he said that my mother had died, and that Ume was the same as dead. Since his rage and resentment had worsened, Mrs. Kataoka was too afraid to ask what he meant. The thought of my mother's death made me feel heavy, though I was more frustrated with the ambiguous statement about Ume.

"Your father seems like a different person since he saw his burnt home. For a week, he visited the farm and just sat on the ground. Watching your father, I almost wished that the big bomb was the one to destroy the farm. The east side of Kusazu was blown away by the atom bomb, but not the farm. I think your father felt insulted that a small airplane destroyed what his family took years to build. I told him that his employees would help him reconstruct the farm again, for the silk farm was your father's life, but he kept saying that it was over. Eventually, he stopped coming." Mrs. Kataoka was certainly aware of our family dynamics.

As soon as we came to her house, Mrs. Kataoka opened the door and called for her fifteen-year-old son Yukio, telling him to bike to Koi and tell my father that his son had returned. Yukio came running from the hallway.

"Welcome back, Hideo san." He bowed to me deeply. When he lifted his head up, I saw that the right side of Yukio's face was discolored with red and purple skin, swollen, and pushing down on his eyes; he had no eyebrows, and his hair was thin like an old man's. His neck was inflamed and discolored. I stared at his deformed face for too long. Yukio used to come to the train station, waiting for the arrival of the three o'clock train that I took after high school. He would tie my schoolbag behind his bicycle and walk home with me; I would tell him many tales of Western mythology that I had learned from my tutor. But now, youth was gone, and I was horrified by his face. When I finally realized that I was staring, I quickly took off my hat and bowed back to him. I felt ashamed for my terribly offensive gaze.

"Don't worry. I don't mind when people stare at my face for the first time." Yukio smiled as if to comfort me, but his smile also horrified me. I tried to say something, but no words came out of my mouth. Yukio bowed again and left with the familiar sound of his bicycle, moving away from the house.

Mrs. Kataoka looked at me sadly. I took off my boots and sat on the floor.

As she prepared tea, Mrs. Kataoka said that all the students from Yukio's high school had been ordered to work at a factory making army uniforms near Hiroshima port, and he was only 2.5 kilometers away from the location where the bomb was dropped.

"Yukio is obsessed with flies now." Mrs. Kataoka poured hot tea for us.

"Flies?"

"There were millions of flies in Hiroshima. Thousands of dead and burnt bodies were left for days throughout the city. Flies tried to lay eggs on the open wounds of even the survivors. If the flies left eggs, the wound would become infested with maggots. I stayed up many nights with a rolled newspaper, killing the flies that came after my son's burnt face. When he got well enough to sit up, he sat with a rolled newspaper and killed flies all day. Now, in February, there are no flies, but Yukio still thinks he hears flies buzzing above his head and wakes up in the middle of the night."

I felt nauseated thinking about the burnt remains of my neighbors and the flies. I had seen the death that Mrs. Kataoka described—corpses and flies swarming around their bodies as a sour odor infected the air in Indonesia—but I never felt so ill as I did imagining the dead bodies piling up on the ground of my hometown. Such a reaction was ignorant, but while I fought on the battlefield, I never fully comprehended it as someone's hometown and never felt strongly about the corpses, since everything was just the result of battle and a part of war. Until I had the image of the dead bodies piled up in Hiroshima, I hadn't really grasped the odor of death.

"How did Yukio survive, being so close to the bomb?" I asked desperately.

"Most of his classmates' entire bodies were burned. They walked along the port, and some of them ran into the ocean for relief. Yukio tried to stop them. The salt water would hurt their wounds. But some of them must have been unbearably hot, thirsty, and delusional, so they jumped into the ocean and died. Later on, many of his classmates' parents came to ask Yukio if he knew how his friends had died. He couldn't tell them about the ocean; he just told them that they died immediately from the blast. But poor Yukio, he says the black dead bodies floating in the ocean are on his mind all the time. He said he thought about the story you told him, something about world and hell and journey . . . ?"

"*Odyssey*, the underworld?" I immediately remembered the lines:

If thou art
numinous and hast ears for divine speech
O tell me, what of Odysseus, man of woe?

Is he alive still somewhere, seeth he daylight still?
Or gone in death to the sunless underworld?

The *Odyssey* was Yukio's favorite of all Western mythology.

"Yes, yes," Mrs. Kataoka said. "I didn't know that someone wrote a book with the image of a burning city long before Hiroshima happened. How frightening!" She shook her head. I wanted to tell her that the story was a Greek epic from long ago, not American, and also that the burning city was not what Yukio remembered from the *Odyssey*, but the ocean, the underworld, where the dead stayed. But to the mother of a child whose face was melted, the sight of Hiroshima should have been unimaginable.

"He's lucky to have survived, but he says that he wishes he'd died with his classmates. I don't blame him. You saw his face." Mrs. Kataoka sighed. The loss of my home was suddenly a small thing compared to flies trying to land on Yukio's half-melted face or burnt young students floating in the ocean.

A few minutes later, I heard the sound of a bicycle. Instead of Yukio, it was my father who came running into the house. As soon as he saw me, his face fell in disappointment. Even though it was only a matter of a second that his face changed from full excitement to letdown, his disappointment was immediately obvious, not just to me but also to Mrs. Kataoka, that he hoped for a different son's return.

"Hideo, I see that you have returned." My father gathered himself and nodded to my deep bow.

"I'm glad that you had the strength and opportunity to serve our country and emperor." He spoke rather formally. I hadn't seen him for five years and was shocked by his aged and exhausted face, yet his aggressive gaze and thin lips had not changed at all. Mrs. Kataoka told my father to please come in, but he said he was going back to Aunt Fuyu's house and told me to get ready because I was going with him.

As we walked on the dark road, Father asked me where I had gone to fight for the Imperial Japanese Army and the emperor. He still spoke overly patriotically without any warmth in his voice. I told him about my service in Indonesia, but after that, he didn't ask anything anymore, and we silently walked together in the dark, to the Jizouzen station. Seeing my father didn't comfort me; rather, I struggled with the silence and loneliness between us. All my life, I never expected Father to be kind. I used to believe that his tenderness and compassion were absorbed by the millions of silkworms he cared for. In raising silkworms, workers washed, fed, and took care of them by hand, and even with such hard work, it took a few thousand silkworms to produce only a small amount of silk. I saw my father lift many silkworms carefully from one bamboo tray to another, which was my only memory of his gentleness. In June, after the fourth molting of larvae, they had to be fed five times a day and twice at night. Father and his employees took turns feeding them, and we hardly saw Father right before the spinning of the silk. After providing such care for thousands of silkworms to bring success to the family, I could understand that he wouldn't have much energy or patience left for us. After the silk farm was taken away from him, I imagined his heart had sunken down to the bottom of the deep river.

While we waited for the train to come, my father suddenly glared at me sharply.

"I'm disappointed that you went to Tokyo to go to the university. You had an obligation to protect our property. Your failure has caused all of us a great loss. What's a business if the family doesn't commit our lives to protect it? Americans, when they smelled the weakness, dropped their bombs. The house was destroyed because of your weakness." His face from the side looked stiff, directly gazing at the empty space in front of him, and his hands shook. I knew his remarks were meant to hurt me, but instead of feeling hurt, I was surprised to witness his unwillingness to admit that everything had changed, causing him to be terrified.

"Hideo, stand up and recite the great wisdom of Kanji Kato. You still remember the words, don't you? I won't forgive you if you don't." Father stood up and ordered me with his chin. How could I forget the words he required his children and employees to recite every morning for years? Father cherished books by Kanji Kato, the principal of Japan National High School in Yube, who promoted the importance of farming as the ultimate way of life for all Japanese citizens. He admired how Kato defined farming as the spirit of the Japanese, for working with nature, requiring our complete devotion. This also became a metaphor for serving our country with complete selflessness. Kato worked with the government and military officials to develop the plan to send thousands of farmers to Manchuria. His words described my father's ultimate dream of expanding his business to the world while promoting the Japanese way of life.

"What are you waiting for? Don't you remember the words? I knew I couldn't trust you." Father's glare made me think that he hated me. I stood up and recited, as diplomatically as I could, just the way Father taught us to do.

"*Small beings can only think about themselves instead of how they relate to a larger world. If we could perceive ourselves as large beings, then we could think about our family, which would let us consider our village, our country, and eventually our world as a part of ourselves. Devotion to something large begins through individual effort and sacrifice, which is ultimately what it means to be Japanese.*"

"So you do remember. If only you lived by his words, we could have saved our farm." He sat back down and shook his head. He resembled the homeless soldiers that I saw at Tokyo station—while he fought for the country and his community, his community was destroyed, and what was left was his old self, too inflexible to start over. Bitterness overfilled him by coming home.

"Father, please tell me about Mother and Ume?" I hesitantly spoke.

"They're dead."

"Both of them?"

"Don't ask me about them again. They betrayed me." His enraged glare stopped my voice. When the train came, we got in, not saying a word all the way to Aunt Fuyu's house.

Aunt Fuyu seemed surprised to see me; Father must have told her that he was going to see Shinya. As he walked in the house, he loudly commanded her to bring sake to him.

"We don't have any sake," Aunt Fuyu said timidly, sensing his anger.

"Then go buy some at the market."

"But they're closed."

"Then go knock on the neighbor's door and find some."

Aunt Fuyu sat there with a troubled face. Then he pushed her against the wall.

"I told you to go find sake, now!" His face was red. I jumped and stood between them. Father grabbed my shoulder and started hitting my face as he called me a worthless son—a betrayer. Aunt Fuyu quickly got up and came between us.

"I'll go and find sake. Please stop hitting him. Hideo just returned from the war." Then she went to the kitchen, put some food into a small bag, and left the house. She would go around the neighborhood and try to exchange food for sake. Father sat on the floor and turned away from me. His back looked small, and his fists shook on his lap because he had wanted to see Shinya.

My father never imagined the defeat of Japan, the u.s. occupation, or the emperor being overthrown. Along with all these changes, not only was his dream of expanding Takagawa Silk Company to the world shattered, but worse yet, the hard work done by our ancestors was also destroyed. My father's family had devoted itself to producing silk, which began with my great-grandfather in the 1850s. He began by raising over a hundred thousand silkworms three times a year, in May, July, and September. My great-grandfather sold these cocoons to a silk factory where they produced silk threads. Over the years, he learned the operation of a silk factory and developed his own, producing very fine quality raw silk threads, which he sold to the most prestigious kimono makers in Kyoto. My grandfather, on the other hand, was more of a businessman who popularized Takagawa silk by dealing with both Western clothiers and kimono brokers, and he also created thinner yet stronger silk threads for dresses and blouses. By the time my father took over the business, he was responsible for over 1.5 million silkworms a year; thirty-five employees and their families, working and living in the houses on his property; and ten acres of mulberry fields, as well as fifty silkworm rooms, a large boiling room, and two work rooms for weaving and dyeing silk threads. While most silk businesses considered raising silkworms and producing silk threads to be separate operations, my father often proudly talked about how the Takagawa Silk Company did both and strived to create their own line of special silk.

I often wondered what would have happened if the farm had survived. If my father had been able to continue his work, he perhaps could have achieved his goal of expanding his business to the world. If Shinya had come home, he would have reconstructed the farm with Father. But without his silk farm or Shinya, he couldn't revive strength enough to start over again. That night, Father blamed me for not being Shinya, but instead of hating him, I felt sorry for him.

"Father, please tell me about Mother and Ume," I said firmly, breaking the silence. Father gave me the hateful look again and shook his head.

"Ume told me your mother died after the Tokyo bombing." I felt remorseful for leaving my mother alone. *Forgive me, my poor mother; your sons and daughters were away when you needed us the most.*

"What about Ume now? Is she safe?"

He turned to me with his red eyes, filled with tears. I had never seen my father's tears before. His gaze paralyzed me.

"You must forget that you ever had a sister."

"What do you mean?"

"You don't have a sister." Father looked away from me. Seeing my father's deep pain, I didn't have enough courage to continue asking him about Ume. As soon as Aunt Fuyu returned with half a bottle of sake, he ordered me to pour sake for him. As if my hands were no longer a part of my body, I couldn't move them. I felt as though I were turning into solid ice. Father took the sake bottle away from me and poured it for himself. After taking a sip, he wiped off his mouth and threw his cup on the floor, yelling that he'd never tasted such horrible sake. He got up, shouted that he was going to sleep, and stormed out of the room. He shut the sliding door, and a few minutes later, the light went out.

As Aunt Fuyu began to clean the floor, she apologized to me for my father's terrible behavior.

"Please don't misunderstand him. He's glad to see you. But he doesn't know what to do without the silk farm."

I didn't trust Aunt Fuyu. Over the years, I was told that Takagawa Silk Company's success was earned by hard work, support, wisdom, and devotion shared by the wives of the masters, especially my great-grandmother and grandmother. My mother was a disappointment. Aunt Fuyu was always telling stories about my mother's uselessness—when she first came to the family, she was put to work in the field, picking mulberry leaves, which wasn't heavy work, but she was slow and couldn't tolerate the long hours of physical labor. Aunt Fuyu sarcastically compared Mother to silkworms—they were easy to handle, though very delicate; they only ate mulberry leaves, unless they were wet or withered, then they wouldn't touch them. When Aunt Fuyu ridiculed my mother's worthlessness in front of her children and employees, Mother disappeared into her room and didn't come out all day. Aunt Fuyu said that Mother turned herself into a cocoon.

That night, I wanted to blame Aunt Fuyu for driving my mother away from the farm, and for her death, which was just as unreasonable as my father blaming me for not protecting the farm from the bombing.

"Tell me about Ume, or else I will never forgive you for my mother's suffering and death. Why do you think she moved to Tokyo while everyone was moving away from there?" I was giving her the same sort of hateful glare as my father did to me. I was even surprised that I was capable of such a statement, but I couldn't control my anger toward my father, which I unfairly threw at Aunt Fuyu. She used to never accept such treatment, but she sadly looked into my face and didn't resist.

"After the Tokyo bombing, after your mother died, Ume came back to Hiroshima. But our house had also been destroyed. We had lost everything and couldn't offer her any help, so we had to send her back to the factory."

"Factory? Was Ume working at a munitions factory, too?"

"You didn't know? Her school assigned everyone to work at a factory in the outskirts of Tokyo. She was lucky that she had a place to live, in the dorm there."

I knew that most of the junior and senior high school students were taken to work at various factories toward the end of the war. It was arrogant of me to assume that Ume, the daughter of Takagawa Silk Company, would be treated differently, as if the government would have a special plan for her. Still, I was enraged at Aunt Fuyu for not taking care of Ume.

"How could you send Ume back to the factory?" I glared at Aunt Fuyu in the most disgusted manner.

"I know, and I'm sorry. It's just that so much had happened, and I had to take care of my family." Aunt Fuyu started to shed tears. That was that first time I realized that her children weren't there. She had a son who was in Yukio's class, and a daughter Ume's age. I was afraid that I had been blaming Aunt Fuyu without knowing something important, and just as I feared, she told me that both children worked at the factories in Hiroshima city, and they were missing after the atomic bomb was dropped. She found them at the local hospital, but they died three days later. I was beginning to understand my father's terrible behavior, which came back to strangle him. And now I acted like him, freely blaming others out of my own desperation.

"Where is Ume now? Is she still at the factory?" I asked Aunt Fuyu as I swallowed my urge to cry out.

"In Omori, a suburb of Tokyo, there is a place called Komachi-en. She works there." Aunt Fuyu looked away from me.

"Komachi-en?"

"Yes. If you go and see her, please tell her that I'm terribly sorry that I couldn't take her in." She covered her mouth, got up, and ran to the kitchen.

I didn't have to ask Aunt Fuyu what sort of place Komachi-en was. I felt numb and sat silent for awhile. My only clear thought was that I needed to go back to Tokyo immediately. I got up and gathered my bags and put on my boots. It was already midnight, and although it took me fifteen hours to get there from Tokyo that day, I couldn't wait another minute to get back and find my sister. I knew trains weren't running at that hour, but I would rather sleep at Hiroshima station, which seemed closer to Tokyo. Aunt Fuyu came running after me, sobbing and apologizing, which irritated me more. I had to get out of that place as soon as I could. She grabbed my arm and begged me to stay, but I shook myself free and rushed into the street.

"Wait, please take this." Aunt Fuyu ran after me and forced some wrapped money in a white cloth into the pocket on my chest. I tried to take it out, but she covered my pocket with both hands.

"This is for Ume. I want her to have it. Promise that you'll take it to her!" Then she fell on the street and cried as if she were on fire. As she sobbed, curled up, she resembled my mother, who lived with a broken spirit and enormous fear. I should have shared some kind words to console her, but instead, the best I could do was not return the money. I left her crying in the middle of street. I was certain that Father heard us, but he was hiding behind the sliding door, as if it would protect him from everything that he wasn't prepared to face.

There were no more street trains, so I walked to Hiroshima station, following the railroad in the dark, next to the black ocean. Each step I took sounded like the moaning of those who went into the ocean after the bomb. Yukio's face kept appearing right in front of me. I stopped and threw up. I was disgusted with myself and everything that had happened to the people around me. How did it all happen? What had I been doing for the last several years? How did Ume come to be so alone? I was her last hope, though I had no means to help her. I sat at the station for a few hours, and in the morning, I dragged my body onto the first train to Tokyo. It was another fifteen-hour train ride, during which I tormented myself with unanswered questions to the point of dizziness. I had had no sleep for two days, and had only had one sweet potato to eat, but I felt no hunger. I was filled with the rage that was lit by seeing my father, which continued to boil until I arrived in Tokyo.

I walked directly to the police station from the train. When I quietly asked the police officer the direction to Komachi-en, he looked at me with a strange gaze and told me that the place was not for Japanese men. A rush of embarrassment burned through my body, but I gathered myself and told him that I was visiting someone there. Even though the officer gave me directions and warned that no visitors were allowed at night, I desperately needed to go and see Ume that night.

At Komachi-en, when I saw a long line of foreign soldiers from the front door all the way to the outside entrance fence, I almost thought that I was back in Indonesia. As soon as I tried to walk in, a few soldiers yelled at me, but I ignored them and walked faster to the front door. There was a middle-aged woman speaking English and selling tickets to the soldiers.

"No Japanese men allowed." The woman waved at me.

"I came here to see my sister, Ume Takagawa, please."

She looked up my face. "No visitors allowed right now. Please come back tomorrow, mid-afternoon."

"This is my military identification." I pulled out a card from my pocket, but she didn't take my card.

"Come back tomorrow, please."

"Is my sister here?"

"Yes," she nodded.

I stepped back, slowly turned around, and walked away. The soldiers were laughing and yelling at me in English. I left feeling nauseated that she was working there. But at the same time, I said to myself, my sister is alive, Ume is alive.

That night, I walked around burnt-out Tokyo, not knowing what to do or where to go. After a few hours, I ran into Professor Kudo at the train station. He was my mentor at the university, and I worked for him as an assistant before I was drafted. He was one of those people who could sense another's burden, so he didn't ask me anything, just offered to let me stay at his house until I found my own place. This meant sharing their food, which was a serious sacrifice for them during that time. I was so exhausted that night that without properly thanking him, I followed him home. When I arrived at his house, I passed out at the entrance door and did not wake up until the next morning.

As soon as I woke up, I went back to Komachi-en, wearing Professor Kudo's clothes instead of my dirty soldier's uniform. Komachi-en appeared quite different during the day without the lines of foreign soldiers waiting to get in. The building was a traditional Japanese structure, which appeared strangely too clean and proper to be a comfort house. Instead of the middle-aged woman, a young woman was sitting at the front desk that morning. I took off my hat and calmly introduced myself as Ume Takagawa's brother and requested to meet with her. The young woman looked at me from head to toe and told me to wait there. A few minutes later, she came back.

"Ume doesn't wish to see you. I'm sorry," she said bashfully.

I was stunned. It was naïve of me to think that she would be thrilled and come running out to see me. We hadn't seen each other for three years. I took a moment to breathe in and talked to the woman politely without losing my calmness.

"Will you tell her that her brother, Hideo, has returned from the war." I didn't want to be mistaken with Shinya again; Ume would have been too frightened to face Shinya. The young woman looked concerned.

"We don't want any trouble again. Please leave."

"Something happened before?" As I spoke, I pictured my father's angry red face.

"Ume's father came here once and beat her and said terrible things at the entrance."

A chill ran through my body, thinking about my father's thick hands slapping Ume's face.

"Was she hurt?"

"The MP came and took him away. It's not just him. Some relatives come here very angry. They come back from the war and find out that their wives, sisters, or daughters work here. We don't want any more beatings." The woman gave me a fearful look.

"I'm not angry. I promise that I won't touch Ume. Please go and tell her that Hideo is here." The woman didn't seem convinced, but unwillingly walked back down the hallway again.

Father used to slap my mother when she didn't do as he expected. He despised even the slightest alteration of his routine, properness, and perfection. Ume's situation pushed him beyond the edge of his patience.

The woman was gone longer this time, but eventually, she came out with Ume. There were a few other women behind Ume, and they all looked terrified for her. She and I just stared at each other, looking so unfamiliar and familiar at the same time. Her simple appearance—pale face against a white shirt and dark blue *Mompe* pants—surprised me as if I had expected to see someone completely different, like the woman in a bright green dress with red lipstick, kissing an American soldier.

"Ume, I returned," I said as gently as I could. Her eyes were filled with tears, and she quietly nodded her head. She didn't come close to me, nor did I move even slightly, not even my fingers.

"Poor Hideo ni-chan, I'm sorry." Ume bowed deeply to me. I was speechless. Ume told the other women that she was safe and that she was going for a walk with me. They were worried and insisted that they come with her, but Ume reassured them of her safety. I could only imagine how violently and embarrassingly my father must have treated Ume. He rejected all unacceptable matters from his life, even if that meant abandoning his children. Ume had understood this so she probably simply let him beat her.

We walked through the busy street and went to a quieter road by the riverbank. My chest was filled with so many emotions, and I could barely talk or even look at Ume's skinny shoulders next to mine.

"You must have gone to see Father. He was terribly angry when he found me at Komachi-en. Understandably so, to find a daughter at such a place." Ume smiled sadly.

"Did he beat you badly?"

She shook her head. "When he saw me, he grabbed my hair and pulled me outside. Then one of the women tried to stop him and yelled not to kick a pregnant woman. That stopped him from kicking me, but it was worse because he found out that I was pregnant."

"Pregnant?" I looked at her as if I didn't know the meaning of the word.

"Father didn't tell you?" She looked at me in shock at first, which became a lonely gaze. "I suppose he said I died with Mother during the Tokyo bombing."

I wanted to say something comforting and kind, but didn't know how to respond.

I told her that I was getting a small job at the university again, and that as soon as I found an apartment, I would come for her. But she just shook her head.

"I'm having a baby. It would be awful for you. When people see my baby, they will call us names. You'll be asked to leave the apartment."

But those things were irrelevant to me, perhaps because I didn't understand or know the reality of how cruel people would be to us, and because no matter what, I couldn't leave my sister. I promised Ume that I'd come for her within a few days.

As soon as we parted, I walked around town visiting a few houses and apartments, and finally found an available place for us in an old run-down building. I met the landlady who told me that the building was mostly occupied by students on the first floor and families on the second floor, and none of the rooms had a kitchen or a bathroom. The residents shared one kitchen and two toilets on the first floor. Everyone went to the bathhouse a few blocks away for bathing. She gave me the only room that was available—a small floor of six tatami, one large window that shook when the wind hit it, and a sink. When I told her that I was moving in with my sister who was pregnant, she looked hesitant and wanted to know about my sister's husband. I said her husband died in the war, and I gained her sympathy. To pay for the rent, I used the money

Aunt Fuyu gave Ume, which wasn't enough, but she said I could pay the rest when I got paid next month. I wanted to move in right away, but she said I couldn't move in for two days. Waiting for two days to pass seemed like two years and drained me, thinking what Ume must go through during that time. I busied myself by constantly asking Professor Kudo to let me do some work for him. The night was the worst; I dreaded the time between getting into the futon until I actually fell asleep. The empty space in my mind, as if there were a mirror inside me, invited random images—Yukio's burned face, my father beating Ume, and the long line of foreign soldiers at Komachi-en. I got up and shook my head as if all the images were attached to my hair.

On the second day, I thanked Professor and Mrs. Kudo for their tremendous generosity, and left for Komachi-en. Ume was surprised that I was ready for her so quickly. Ume quickly packed her things into just one bag, and she carried it with both arms as though she were holding a baby. As Ume walked away from Komachi-en's entrance door, she stopped and looked back several times to bow to the other women who were left behind, who waved at her. All the way from Mitaka station to our apartment, the street was full of people selling and buying at the markets. Ume held my sleeve walking through the crowd, and I was filled with gratefulness for my sister's survival up until then, and immense fear for our survival from then on.

When Aunt Fuyu mentioned Komachi-en and Ume in the same sentence, she didn't have to explain what sort of place it was. I knew that comfort houses always had names that resembled the names of gardens. In fact, one of the comfort houses in Indonesia was called Sakura-en, the garden of cherry blossom. That facility was for exclusive use by Japanese officers. Being the lowest rank of private, my duties were preparing meals, cleaning and washing officers' clothes, and occasionally, I was ordered to deliver rice balls to the comfort houses for the volunteers who worked as comfort women. Back then, I truly believed that they actually volunteered and got paid to do what they did, and I had no sympathy for the young Korean, Chinese, and Filipino women, nor did I pay any attention to why Korean or Chinese women were working in Indonesia. I just delivered the rice balls and walked by a few women sitting in the resting room, all quiet. What torments me even now is how I glanced at them with a sense of disgust, thinking how disgraceful they were to do a job like this, for money. Once, an officer ordered me not to serve lunch to a group of women. An officer was trying to punish those who weren't serving as fast as other women in a different location. The thought of them starving actually satisfied me that day since I had no respect for them. When I brought their dinner, they all came running to me and grabbed their food. I thought they were repulsive creatures, like stray dogs.

If the Japanese had officers' clubs in Indonesia, it shouldn't have been any surprise to me that a similar system was created for foreign soldiers when Japan was defeated. As I walked by the line of foreign soldiers, those women in Indonesia with dark skin, sitting in the resting room as they held a rice ball, became Ume in my mind. I never imagined that my sister would be associated with such a place.

I blamed myself for Ume's suffering, as if my indifference and terrible behavior during the war caused her to sacrifice herself. The most aching part of homecoming has always been facing myself, what I had done, and what I failed to understand with my eyes wide open. Often, I got lost in deep hatred and doubt about myself. Those who committed crimes, like Ume and me, hope to be forgotten altogether; our past becomes our secret. Home always awaits us with a ruler of certain measurement, and all the immeasurable crimes that we conducted in the name of war have no place at home, so we bury them deep within us. Helen and Steve Johnson's visit will be bittersweet.

What I want to tell Helen is that all these years, I have remembered how her grandmother loved chasing the ocean waves as a little girl. She said that if we chased the waves, they would always chase us back. She would play this game all afternoon. I realize now that I have always wanted to meet Helen, because I have always wanted Ume to be remembered more than anything, even long after I die.

DECEMBER 1975

When it was time to make Christmas ornaments, Sister
Margaret said we had to work with partners. Partners always
were a boy and a girl. I never liked working with partners.
For Thanksgiving, we had to make a turkey. My partner was
Christopher, and he wanted to make our turkey blue, so he
picked out blue construction paper. But turkeys aren't blue.
He drew a blue turkey, and said that was what his mom's
turkey looked like after she cooked it. Christopher's mom
must be a bad cook. Uncle Steve said there was a doctor for
everything except for eating too much chocolate.
Christopher's mom should go to a cooking doctor. Sister
Margaret brought Indian corn and told everyone to use it to
make a turkey. Even after that, Christopher still wanted to
add blue feathers, so I told him that the turkey's eyes could
be blue, but the feathers had to be brown, white, and red.
Out of fifteen turkeys, our turkey was the only one that had
blue eyes.

"Susan and Christopher," Sister Margaret called the first pair
for Christmas ornaments. I looked back at Susan's face. She
raised her hand and whispered something to a girl sitting next
her. I was so happy that Christopher wasn't my partner this
time. I wish we could make our own ornaments.

"Helen and Ryan." Sister Margaret called my name. I looked
at Ryan, who looked back at me. He raised his hand.

"Helen?" Sister Margaret called my name again, so I raised
my hand, too. Since Ryan and I fought, I hadn't talked to him.

He didn't tease me anymore or get loud around me. He said hello to me once, but I got nervous, so I just looked down and didn't say anything back.

Sister Margaret said that each group would make three ornaments, and we'd decorate the big Christmas tree in the cafeteria. I had never decorated a Christmas tree before I came to Uncle Steve and Aunt Mary's house. Mom and Dad never had a tree at home. We didn't really do anything for Christmas except for Mom leaving a present next to our pillows on the morning of Christmas day. She gave me soft teddy bears, a red velvet dress, books, and paintbrushes. I kept them all in my room. I waited for Christmas morning all year long.

Sister Margaret said that an angel was going to be on the top of the tree. She shook a baseball cap that had our names inside. Whoever she picked could make the angel that went on top of the tree. The room became quiet.

"Helen and Ryan," she said, smiling.

"You're so lucky," Kate whispered to me from behind, but I didn't feel lucky at all. I'd never made an angel before, and I didn't know how. I didn't know how to talk to Ryan either, but Sister Margaret clapped her hands and we had to get up and find our partner. I just sat still. My chest was getting tight.

Ryan came over to my desk and stood by me.

"Can we work at your desk?" He didn't sound angry.

"I guess." I looked at his forehead, but I didn't see a scar. Ryan pulled up a desk and put it next to mine.

"You can make the angel if you want," he said.

"I don't know how to make it."

"Me either. I only know how to make a truck and baseball stuff."

"Baseball for a Christmas tree?" On the tree at Uncle Steve's house, Aunt Mary and I decorated it with many colorful shiny balls, but no baseball bats or trucks.

"Sure, ornaments can be anything. My Christmas tree has a dog, bird, butterfly, baseball cap, bat, a truck, cars . . . I can't remember everything." Ryan talked fast. His tree sounded heavy.

Ryan got up to go get some paper, glitter, cloth, and glue. Then, in his notebook, he drew a little girl with long hair, wings, and a circle on her head. He made a cone with white construction paper and said it could be the angel's body, which should be covered in silver glitter. I cut some yellow yarn for her hair. Ryan made wings from white and cream-colored construction paper, and I made a ball with tissue paper and covered it with white cloth to make the angel's head. Sister Margaret said that she could find a thin wire to make a circle that went on top of the angel's head. Ryan had lots of ideas. His fingers moved quickly to cut out wings and put glue on the edge of the construction paper to attach them to the angel's body. I put the silver glitter on the body cone.

"You're really good at this," I was so surprised that Ryan had so many ideas.

"My mom makes dolls. She makes me help her."

"You make dolls?"

"I just help my mom. Don't tell anyone." Ryan's cheeks became pink. I laughed a little, but he didn't get mad at me. He laughed, too.

"Did your mom come back?" Ryan asked.

I shook my head. Mom didn't leave; I did. But she wasn't at home, either. No one was living there except for Dad, but he was gone all the time, too. I didn't know how to explain everything. Ryan stopped cutting the wings and picked up the yellow yarn.

"Do you like spaghetti?"

"Spaghetti?"

"This yellow yarn looks like spaghetti. This angel is going to have spaghetti hair."

Having spaghetti hair was so silly, but I liked it. We made long hair and glued one string of yarn at a time onto her head.

Then we stepped back to see our angel. She looked funny with her big head and hair.

"What color should we make the angel's eyes?" Ryan asked me.

"I like blue eyes." I was thinking about Uncle Steve's. I'd tell him later that I gave blue eyes to the Christmas tree angel because I liked his so much. I made two blue circles in the middle of the angel's white face.

Everyone came and saw our angel when we took it to Sister Margaret. She said it was lovely, and we started laughing because the angel looked so clumsy with her big head. Sister Margaret asked what her name was.

"Do you know a cool name?" Ryan quickly turned to me.

"Shizuka," I said, almost whispering.

"Shizuka? What's that?" Ryan said it slowly, too. When someone else said her name, it sounded different.

"It's a ghost."

"O.K." Ryan shrugged his shoulders and said to Sister Margaret that the angel's name was Shizuka. She looked surprised and tried to say the name, but it didn't sound right.

Ryan made a truck ornament from construction paper, and I made a velvet dress by cutting red felt and gluing it to some dress-shaped construction paper. When everyone finished making their ornaments, Sister Margaret took the angel Shizuka, and we all followed her to the cafeteria with our ornaments. There was a big green tree in the middle of the room. Sister Margaret got up on the chair to put the angel Shizuka on the top. Then we all went up and put our ornaments on the tree. Ryan put his truck next to Christopher's yellow star. I hung my red dress, too. Kate hung paper flowers. The tree was full of ornaments. Sister Margaret told us to step back from the tree, so we stepped back and made a circle around the tree. When Sister Margaret turned on the switch, all the little Christmas lights became bright and twinkling. The angel Shizuka's hair looked like gold. She looked nothing like Mom, but her name was Shizuka, and Uncle Steve's blue eyes were smiling at me from the top of the tree.

Uncle Steve picked me up after school. He looked like he was going somewhere nice, wearing a white shirt and brown pants.

"I'm taking you on a date," he said as soon as I got into the car.

"A date?"

"Has anyone taken you on a date before?"

My cheeks got warm. I thought only older boys and girls went on dates.

"I don't go on dates."

"Why?"

"I'm only nine."

"Then this is your first date." Uncle Steve started driving down the road in the opposite direction from our house. He was smiling like something good had happened.

"Just us two are going to dinner?"

"Just us." Uncle Steve smiled.

The restaurant was by the bay and we could see all the lights in San Francisco. The place was pretty, and big and shiny like a castle. When we walked in, a man in a black suit opened the glass door and said good evening once to Uncle Steve and once to me, looking right at me. There was a huge Christmas tree covered with silver and blue balls. Up on the ceiling, shiny white lamps were everywhere. Uncle Steve walked toward another man in a suit standing by another door inside. The man had a soft voice, called Uncle Steve *sir* and said that he would take us to a table by the window. Uncle Steve talked to the man like he knew him, so I thought he'd been to this restaurant a lot, but when we were following the man to our table, Uncle Steve whispered that he had never been to a nice restaurant like this before. Our table had a white tablecloth and pink flowers and candles in the middle. I was the only little girl at the restaurant. There weren't even young people like Uncle Steve, just older people with white hair, wearing big shiny clothes, having dinner. I was still wearing my school uniform. The man in a suit pulled out the chair, and I didn't know what to do. Uncle Steve told me to have a seat. As I sat, he pushed the chair in. He must have never had a little girl in his restaurant. I could pull my own chair, but I didn't say anything to him because he was being nice.

There were too many silver forks and spoons on the table. I opened the menu, but didn't understand any of it. Uncle Steve said he'd order for me because he was my date tonight. I didn't know that a date had to order for the girl. I went to the last page of the menu. At Mike's Diner near Uncle Steve's house, the last page was usually the dessert page, but this restaurant's menu didn't have any dessert. Uncle Steve said that the dessert menu only came after the meal. This restaurant was like school! I had to eat the whole meal before seeing the dessert menu.

The waiter in a white shirt and a black ribbon around his neck came and took our order. I thought Uncle Steve was speaking words from another country. The man didn't write down anything; he just nodded. Then he bowed and walked away quickly. All the waiters looked and walked alike. They all had the same outfit on, like at school, and their hair was wet with oil.

"Did I surprise you tonight?" Uncle Steve asked.

I nodded.

"Do you know why we came here tonight, just the two of us?"

"No."

"Did you know that today is your dad's birthday?"

"Really?" I knew that everyone had a birthday, but it was still strange to think that Dad had one.

"A long time ago, he wrote me a letter, asking if I could take you out to a special place on his birthday every year so that you wouldn't forget about him."

"Why would I forget Dad?" Forgetting about Dad would be like Mr. Hogan, except that he was sick and he forgot everybody, even his own name. But I wasn't sick.

"He wrote it when he was in Vietnam. He was worried that he would die out there. I think he didn't want you to forget that he was your father."

"But Dad didn't die. He came home."

"Yeah, he did. Helen, you might think your dad doesn't think about you, but that's not true. I want you to remember that your dad wrote me a letter asking to take care of you. Can you remember that, Helen?"

"Why are you saying all this?" I got scared like Uncle Steve was going to say good-bye to me. I hated that feeling of worry. Uncle Steve's serious face got a little softer.

"I'm telling you all these things because it's your dad's birth-day, and I was thinking about him. I miss my brother."

Uncle Steve talked to Dad at least once a week. But they were always fighting on the phone. I had no idea that he liked Dad and that he missed him.

The dinner was a little confusing because the man in a white shirt had to bring each food separately. First, he brought our soup, then salad, which had pretty flowers. Uncle Steve said we could eat the flowers! Then a small chicken was served to Uncle Steve, and shrimp and green beans for me. I didn't know why he wouldn't just bring everything on a big plate. It took a long time to get to the dessert. The dessert menu was a small book. So many kinds of cakes were listed: strawberry, chocolate, lemon, ice cream, carrot, and more names that I had never heard of. Uncle Steve said I could get anything I wanted, so I ordered chocolate, and it came on a big plate with flowers, just like our salads. The cake looked like a tiny brown brick house with a small garden on a shiny white ground. Uncle Steve laughed because I didn't want to break the pretty house with my fork. The cake was soft and melted in my mouth before I could chew. Inside my mouth was all sweet. After eating the whole thing, my stomach was really heavy. Mom said that sugar was poison, but she never said it would feel like this.

"Did you enjoy your first date?" Uncle Steve leaned forward.

"This doesn't feel like a date."

"Why?"

"Because you're my uncle."

Uncle Steve smiled. "When you are on a real date, I want you to make sure that he loves you as much as I love you, O.K.?" His deep voice was a little bit like Dad's, but Dad would never say something like that.

"Helen, I know you wrote a letter to Mr. Takagawa." His voice got deeper when he said *Mr. Takagawa*, and I almost jumped hearing his name. "Why didn't you tell me about the letter, Helen? I'd have helped you."

"I'm sorry," I said right away. My letter wasn't a secret, but Uncle Steve looked so scared when Mrs. Hogan talked about going to Japan. No one wanted to fly up in the sky. I just didn't want him to get tired or scared around me anymore. I asked Aunt Mary every day if a letter came for me, but she always said no. Mr. Takagawa didn't write me back, so I thought the mailman lost my letter.

"After Mr. Takagawa read your letter, he wrote to me. So I wrote him back, asking if we could come and visit him," Uncle Steve said.

"You did?"

"Yes, and he said we could visit him."

"Really?"

Uncle Steve pulled out a thick envelope from his chest pocket and opened some papers with many numbers and words that I didn't understand, except for our names.

"Here are our tickets. We are going to visit Mr. Takagawa during your Christmas break."

"You mean next week?"

"Yes!" Uncle Steve had a big smile.

I looked down at my dirty plate. There were only flowers and chocolate sauce left, but no house.

"Helen?" Uncle Steve called me, but I didn't look up. Stupid Helen! In my letter to Mr. Takagawa, I asked him to write to Uncle Steve so that we could come and visit him in Japan. I wanted to help Mom. I thought I wanted to go to Japan, but now that everything was planned, I didn't want to do it anymore. Uncle Steve started talking about winter in Japan, and he gave me another present in a small box. I opened the box and there was a red winter hat.

"That's for you to wear in Kamakura. Mr. Takagawa said this winter is especially cold there. He said it might even snow!"

"Uncle Steve, do we have to go to Japan?" I didn't want to cry, but tears were welling up in my eyes. My hands felt numb.

Uncle Steve looked surprised. "I thought you wanted to meet your great-uncle?"

"I changed my mind. I don't want to go anymore."

Uncle Steve's bright blue eyes looked sad. "But now, we have to go. You'll be O.K. You're a brave girl, Helen."

I didn't answer him. I kept pushing the flowers into the chocolate sauce with my fork until they were all brown. I could feel that my nose was getting wet from my tears, and I didn't feel like a brave girl at all. *Helen Ume Johnson, you're going to fly, you're going to Japan, you're never coming home.* I hated the voice in my head so I crushed all the flowers into pieces in the chocolate puddle.

⁓

Mom, the sky is one big blue roll of air, and I'm in the middle of it. I can see far far away. We don't pass anything, just blue air everywhere. Is this what you saw when you first came to America? I thought flying would be so scary, but it's like magic. I look down at my feet and hands, and I don't feel any different. Inside the airplane is just like being inside a house. A young woman in a blue suit brought lunch with a glass of orange juice for me and Uncle Steve. We can eat meals like we do in the house. There are bathrooms and we can even watch movies! This place has everything.

Uncle Steve says that we're moving fast, five times faster than when he drives his truck, but I don't feel like we're moving at all. But Mom, I know I'm really flying when I look all the way down to the bottom, which is all green. Uncle Steve says that the ocean looks green from up here in the sky. He let me sit by the window because I love watching outside. I have birds' eyes now. Did you think the ocean is green, too, when you saw it from the sky?

Uncle Steve said by the time we get to Japan, it will be a new year. He says we lose a day, going to Japan, but we'll get that day back when we come back to America. Do you know where the day goes? Does it stay in the sky until we come through here again? There are many people in the airplane, and they all come back on a different day. There must be so many days wrapped in the sky, but Uncle Steve says everyone gets a day back. What about letters? When we send a letter to Japan, does it lose a day, too? Uncle Steve says I always have so many questions, but he likes my questions.

Mom, do you know how the airplane finds its way to Japan? There are no signs or buildings in the sky. Uncle Steve says that the pilot knows his direction, and he won't get us lost in the sky. I'm not as scared as I thought I'd be. We're just floating up, up, up like the balloon that you bought for Ken a long time ago. It got away from his hand and went really high up. When we couldn't see it anymore, you said the sky swallowed it and it wouldn't come down until the sky let it go. I think the sky will let us go when we are above Japan. Until then, we are floating up above the green ocean.

ARRIVAL

A tall man with dark hair holds the hand of a young girl with a bright red winter hat. He looks around; his eyes stop moving when he sees my sign, *Mr. Steve Johnson and Miss Helen Johnson.* His face brightens, and he walks toward us. Nervous sensations run through my body, and make my hands shake a little. The airport is filled with tall foreigners and businessmen in dark suits, but my eyes are glued to the young man and the girl walking toward me. Among the many people waiting for the passengers to deplane, Chiyo and I stand by the arrival door. They stop in front of us, and the young man reaches his right hand out and politely introduces himself as Steve Johnson. He enthusiastically shakes our hands. I introduce myself and Chiyo, just as I practiced in my head while waiting for their arrival. When I call him Mr. Johnson, he asks me to just call him Steve.

"And this is Helen." Steve steps aside to reveal Helen, who has been shyly standing behind him. She looks straight up at me. Even though she appears perfectly Caucasian, the first thing I recognize is her resemblance to her mother when she was a child—large brown eyes, smooth fair skin like pink silk cloth and dark hair down to her chin. Helen slowly goes back behind Steve, who smiles and touches her head. I have imagined this moment many times, but what is happening in front of me feels like a dream. As if my head is filled with water, everything that I hear and see isn't quite tangible, except that Helen's eyes and gaze concretely take me back to Ume. My body is filled with so much pressure that I can barely feel my fingers.

Chiyo pulls my sleeve because I'm gazing at Helen so intensely, and invites everyone to walk to the exit, taking my hand to walk with her.

Helen holds Steve's hand, staying right beside him.

"Was this your first time flying?" Chiyo asks Helen.

"Yes," she shyly nods.

"Did you like it?"

"Yes."

"She's quite a brave girl." Steve smiles at her, but Helen stays behind him even more. Steve interacts with Helen affectionately as he talks to her and smiles at us. They look like father and daughter. His gentle manner toward Helen somehow places me at ease and even lightens the anticipation that had developed within me. I had imagined that tremendous awkwardness and agonizing feelings would run through me when I finally met Helen and Steve, and I prepared myself to face the discomfort. But Steve's manner is so unexpected that I don't quite know how to respond.

"It's cold outside." Helen puts on her jacket. It's a sunny day, but the air is crisp, burning my cheeks while we wait in line for a taxi. Helen looks right, left, up and down.

"So we're really in Japan?" she asks Steve.

"Yes, we are."

"I don't feel any different."

"You're standing on the opposite side of the world from your home in California."

"So Aunt Mary is standing upside down?"

"Or sitting upside down!" Steve smiles.

Helen looks down at her feet. Watching Helen stare at the ground, I can almost see what she sees: Anna standing on the other side of the earth, connected by her feet.

∼

Chiyo makes fried chicken for dinner, something that we never do at our home, but not knowing what Steve and Helen like, we thought fried chicken was a safe choice. We simply assumed that fried chicken was the ultimate American food that everyone eats, but it turned out that Helen isn't keen on fried chicken. Steve is very polite, explaining that Helen and her brother Ken didn't grow up eating much meat or sweets.

"Really? I always thought American children love candy." Chiyo smiles at Helen.

"Mom said sugar was poison."

"Poison?"

"And it's not real happiness."

Chiyo and I look at each other, astonished.

"I'm afraid that it wasn't a good idea to buy dessert." Chiyo regretfully looks at Helen. Earlier, we went to the bakery, and Chiyo brought her face close to the counter, carefully looking at many different kinds of cake, choosing each one with Helen in mind.

"Oh, Helen does eat dessert. In fact, dessert is her favorite meal, isn't it?" Steve turns to Helen, and she cheerfully nods.

Chiyo lightly gets up and returns with a white box with many small slices of cake inside, and Helen's eyes brighten. Chiyo invites Helen to pick out any one of them, and without hesitation, Helen points at the strawberry shortcake.

I try not to stare at her face, but Helen's dark hair keeps grabbing my attention out of the corner of my eyes. And from deep inside my ears, Helen's voice feels familiar, even though it's unlikely that I would recognize my sister's voice as a little girl. I know that we can believe anything that we want to believe. I tell myself not to stare at Helen. If I didn't consciously control myself, my hand might unconsciously reach out to feel Helen's hair. Ume's black hair felt thin in my hands when I washed it while she was dying. She closed her eyes when I rinsed and said that she felt as if she was the empress. I hesitated washing her hair while she was so sick, since my apartment was so cold; her illness could get worse lying around with wet hair. But Ume insisted and thanked me many times. Looking at Helen, the sensation of Ume's thin hair suddenly returns to my old hands, alarming me. I take a piece of fried chicken and tell myself to focus on breaking it into pieces with my chopsticks.

After dinner, Chiyo shows Helen how to use the bath. She is surprised that we don't have a shower. Chiyo explains slowly that we wash our bodies outside the bathtub, and once we are clean, we get into the tub and also share the water with the entire family. Helen nods and looks around nervously. She walks into the bathroom with her pink pajamas and red bathrobe and closes the door. While Helen takes a bath, Steve makes a phone call to his wife in the hallway, and Chiyo is back in the kitchen, busy washing dishes. I go upstairs and rush into to the other bathroom, open the window, and stick my head out as if I had been suffocating. As the cold wind and the sound of the ocean fill the room, I stand in front of the mirror and look at my old face closely in the dark. Thirty years ago, I couldn't have imagined that I would live long enough to welcome Ume's granddaughter to our home.

Poor Anna. *Sugar isn't real happiness*—I empathize with Anna, how a simple task like eating can become terribly complicated. And I suppose sugar feels detrimental, since the sweetness is always only temporary. During my childhood we faced a serious lack of food resources, and sugar was luxurious. Normal citizens barely obtained necessities like rice through the government's rationing system, but my father had a way of obtaining a bag of sugar during his business trips to the international port of Yokohama city. He gave my mother the bag of sugar, which she cooked with red beans. Then she cooked sticky rice and made over one hundred rice balls wrapped in sweet red beans, called Ohagi. She made them twice a year after my father's trips to Yokohama in spring and fall. I was always amazed that a small bag of sugar could produce over one hundred Ohagi. My father took half of them to share with his employees. Shinya, Ume, and I could have only one Ohagi a day for three days. For those three days, I went to sleep thinking about Ohagi, dreamed about the sweet red beans, and got up to eat Ohagi. On the third day, eating the last Ohagi, Ume and I chewed forever until it didn't have any flavor left. Perhaps that was our first lesson of instant gratification as fulfillment, which disappeared quickly and left us with emptiness.

People from my generation would remember how the sweetness felt in our mouth and to this day, they talk about it fondly. Chiyo said she didn't know the taste of sugar until she went to Manchuria. Chiyo's father, the military officer, always followed the rationing system, so Chiyo only knew the taste of sweetness from her toothpaste. She said when her father first left Japan for Manchuria, he wrote her a letter and described a delicious sweet Chinese cake called Yuanxiao, made out of sticky rice, sesame seeds, nuts, and milk, sold all over the streets in Fengtian, Manchuria. When Chiyo's family followed her father to Manchuria a few weeks later, Chiyo asked her mother many times if her father would come and wait for them with Yuanxiao at the port. Chiyo's father certainly brought Yuanxiao, and she ate it in the car on the way to her new house. She told me how she thought it was the most delicious cake ever made. Several times, she tried to make it herself from memory, but it never turned out the way it tasted and melted in her mouth the first time.

Ume once told me that she worked as a comfort woman because of the slice of sweet potato she was served for lunch at Komachi-en. When she was dying in my apartment, my helplessness and desperation turned into weighty guilt, and I had terrible thoughts: how my ignorance and cruelty during the war had caused Ume to work as a comfort woman as a punishment to me. Taking care of Ume, I hadn't slept for days, and I thought about how I was going to be all alone after she died because of my bad deeds. One night, I wept and begged for her forgiveness.

While she watched me in amazement, I confessed how I had felt about comfort women in Indonesia, and how once, to punish them, I withheld food from them. Ume sat up and shook her head: *Do you know why I decided to work at Komachi-en? I was so hungry. If you don't know how to steal food, if you never learned how to provide for yourself, you'll even work at a place like that. Don't think of me like those poor women in Indonesia. I went there to work because they gave me a black bento box, with bright white rice, beans, a slice of sweet potato, and a bright yellow baked egg. I forgot about what kind of work I had to do there and devoured my lunch. I saved the sweet potato, and when I tasted its sweetness, I was happy. I was glad to taste it. When the box was empty, it was time for me to work. The work was awful and made me want to die, but for some reason, I couldn't regret eating all the food. How else would I feed myself? Father taught us to die before stealing food from others, remember?*

Ume never gave any other explanation other than the slice of sweet potato for working at Komachi-en. Much later, from Chiyo, whose job it was to interview Ume at the Home Guidance Center to assist her with an arrangement for the Christian Home for Children, I found out more. Ume, along with her classmates, worked at the munitions factory throughout the war, but as soon as the war ended, all the female students who lived in the dorm were ordered to go to Komachi-en. They went there, not knowing what sort of place it was. Ume said a government official, a young man, sweating from his forehead, obviously uncomfortable with his new job, held a piece of paper and read the details with his hands shaking: Women from eighteen to twenty-five years old could serve the new nation and the emperor, to protect the goodness and innocence of Japanese girls and women. He showed a picture of American Marines landing at Yokohama port and said that four hours after their arrival, the gang rape of a mother and daughter was reported. The man wiped off more sweat from his forehead and said that hundreds of rapes had been reported

in the Tokyo and Yokohama area. He stressed that the innocence and goodness of Japanese girls and women were depend-
ing on Ume's and her classmates' willingness to sacrifice. As
soon as they discovered the identity of Komachi-en, most of
them ran away, but Ume and two other women stayed. *I lost my
family and home, and I thought I was all alone in the world. Then why
shouldn't I sacrifice, to help someone's innocence? Of all the people, I probably deserved to sacrifice the most. I was unlucky because I was there when
they asked me to do this in the name of the emperor. My mother died for
him and I thought my brothers and father had also died for him. To deny
the emperor would mean denying everything my family believed in.* Chiyo
said Ume looked both proud and miserable when she described
her intention.

Chiyo explained to me how the system worked—the government ordered the head of the Japanese police force to create
a Recreation and Amusement Association. They were called RAA
and operated the comfort houses for the allied forces, which
arrived shortly after the surrender of Japan. RAA specifically
gathered civilians like my sister, so as to separate the comfort
house from lewd brothels with professional prostitutes whose
focus was making money. RAA promoted it as an honorable and
professional job offered by the police, which attracted many
women looking for jobs, not knowing what they were supposed
to do. Ume worked with various people—former typists, librar-
ians, cooks, farmer's wives, and many students from factories.

I turn on the light and wash my face with cold water. My
feet against the ice-cold floor feel painful. I wipe off my face and
look for Ume in the mirror.

"Ume, don't you think it's strange that you are a grandmother now?" She is still twenty-one behind the mirror.

"Your granddaughter is fearless, just the way you hoped your
daughter would be. She wouldn't hesitate to eat her strawberry
cake. I don't think she would hesitate to cry either." I'm relieved
that Helen loves candy, that she looks troubled when she is

afraid. I turn off the light and close the window. I breathe in and out slowly, then go back downstairs.

In the living room, Steve sits on the couch alone, reading a guidebook about Japan. I look around for Helen and Chiyo, and Steve tells me that Chiyo just took Helen to the guest room. I should have come down earlier to greet her before she went to sleep. On the coffee table, there are two cups of tea that Chiyo must have placed for us. I sit down by one. Steve constantly smiled when he was with Helen, but now, his entire body looks disheartened, with his shoulders drooping and his face exhausted.

"Thank you for having us. We are very grateful." Steve speaks properly with a hint of nervousness. I imagine that he hasn't traveled very much, certainly not as far as Japan, but he came here for his brother's daughter. His willingness and generosity amaze and puzzle me at the same time.

"It's very kind of you to take care of your brother's children." I light a cigarette and offer one to Steve.

"It's nothing."

"Nothing? Raising children is a lot of work."

"How many children do you have?" Steve smiles warmly.

"We don't have any children." I respond casually, but I see Steve's face quickly changing into apology and embarrassment. I'm used to people responding with such mortified looks, and even worse, with pity.

"Please don't worry. Not having a child really isn't something that has upset us." And this is true. While not being able to have children would be a tragedy for most families and even shameful for many women, for us, it was simply the way it was. After we were married for five years and Chiyo never became pregnant, I began to consider the possibility that we wouldn't be able to have children. That concept was both a bit lonely and a huge relief at the same time. Having someone that we'd care for more than ourselves was frightening to us. I imagine that Chiyo had thought about this, perhaps much more so than I did, but strangely, we never talked about it together. We just sensed that we understood each other.

"Will you tell me about Shizuka? I mean . . . Anna." I change the subject to save Steve from his ashamed look, but I feel his energy diminished even more by my questions.

"Before leaving for Japan, I was permitted to see her. The doctor was worried that my visit might be too stressful for her, but I thought it was important that she knew we were going to see you." Steve's words make my entire body tense and nervous. Sensing my discomfort, he speaks warmly to me. "I wanted to know if there was anything she wanted me to say to you, but she just looked surprised and didn't say anything. Nothing at all. I think she didn't know where to begin."

I don't know if I should be relieved or disappointed. I have always hoped and perhaps believed that Anna carried a deep indescribable sense of connection with her mother, but perhaps I was too hopeful.

"Anna told me that her doctor called her condition 'learned hopelessness.' She chuckled when she said this. Her doctor told her that she learned from her daily life to be helpless, and that she is extremely passive and perceives any task as uncontrollable. It's sort of like she found herself in the middle of the storm, thinking there was nothing she could do. Anna thought it was outrageous for anyone to say that helplessness is something we learn." Steve shrugs his shoulders and looks at me a bit uneasily.

"It's a little ironic that she was incredibly tough when James was in Vietnam, but now, she seems so lost."

"Anna's husband fought in Vietnam?" My voice must have included a bit of resentment, as Steve's body tightens. I'm just surprised, and I'm starting to understand why Steve is here instead of James.

"Yes, James was drafted and served for two years." Steve's voice gets smaller and smaller.

I remember when I was drafted. When the *red paper*—the draft notice—came to me, deep sorrow overtook me and I felt the presence of death in the most concrete way. The war in Vietnam and its gruesomeness were widely reported through the media in Japan.

"You must think James is terrible," Steve says, ashamed.

"Coming home could be just as hard as the war itself."

"How could that be?" Steve looks at me in bafflement. "James wanted to come home. That's all he could think of. That's what he said in his letters when he was away. But now that he's home, he doesn't want to be understood. He cuts everyone off. He wants to be in an unreachable place. He says 'no one in this clean America wants to know the dirty truth.'"

Steve's tone isn't resentment, but anguish. He leans over and rests his face on his hands, fingers crossed as if praying, and sits quietly lost in his thoughts. In a strange sense, I feel as though Steve came here to look for his brother. He is living his brother's life by doing everything that his brother would have done if he were well. When I returned home from the war, I felt that people really knew what suffering meant in their bones, since most people in Japan had experienced the war by being under fire or losing family members. But for James, I imagine that he feels isolated from his community that has no war experience. When I see young people today, I also isolate myself from them. Listening to my students at the college, I sense that they perceive my generation as uninformed, foolishly measuring the level of courage by our sacrifices. The truth is that many of us participated in the war because we recognized ourselves as a part of a community and accepted our possible deaths as a price of belonging. James's involvement in violence is ultimately the price of belonging to a community that participated in the war. Besides, people can be cruel to those who experience war. When we do everything we can to survive, people judge us coldly, suggesting that we should have died instead of living with shame. For some like Ume, their own fathers wish them dead. Maybe war experience is like a code that can only be understood by people who have lived through it. The pain James feels coming home to "clean America" is understandable to me.

I reach for the tea that Chiyo left for me. The cold tea tastes especially bitter in my mouth. Looking at Steve's anguished gaze reminds me of a man I met a few years ago when my colleague and I attended a charity gathering to help Japanese refugees and orphans left behind in Manchuria. The main speaker was a former farmer who immigrated to Manchuria with his family, and he spoke of his experience. The story was rather disturbing: he took his wife and their young son from a northern village to the south while the war was ending, and they were captured by Soviet troops and taken to a refugee camp where they had to spend the winter with very limited amounts of heat, food, or medical attention. Winter in Manchuria is cold enough to freeze a river. As they watched many adults and children die at the camp, the man and the wife decided to be sold to a Chinese farmer. The wife and the husband pretended to be brother and sister, and their son was introduced as their youngest sibling. The wife was sold to a poor Chinese kuli, a manual laborer, and became his wife, and the Japanese husband and child were hired as servants to the family. The wife had two more children with the Chinese husband during the eight years they lived there. All those years, the wife lived with both her husbands. When Japan provided a ship to return from Manchuria in 1953, for the last time, the husband came back alone. His son and his wife didn't get permission to return because the Chinese husband wouldn't allow them to. His wife and son are still in China today.

After his speech, my colleague walked to him and expressed his sympathy; how painful it must have been to live with his wife and her Chinese husband under the same roof. Then my colleague asked if he resented his wife in some ways, but he shook his head and said, "How could you ask such a thing? I don't know if you can understand what it was like for us.

Everything was a matter of life or death. My wife saved us all. I don't know if anybody could understand that." Then the man stormed out of the room, leaving my colleague in confusion over what he had done to offend him. *How could you ask such a thing?* Perhaps the man appeared overly sensitive and unreasonable to my colleague, but every question reveals our judgment, even if we are offering kind words.

What should I say to Steve, sitting in front of me, distressed and lost as to how to help his brother, who won't allow anyone to come close to him? Do you know that your older brother will never be the same? War memories are like a terminal illness growing inside our brains. But why should I say such a thing to Steve, who will never stop reaching out to his brother, just as I would never have stopped looking for Ume in the burnt land of Tokyo?

"You and James must have been very close," I say, breaking the heavy silence between us.

Steve pulls out his wallet from his back pocket, takes out a thin yellow paper with ripped edges and unfolds it carefully.

"This is the last letter James wrote to me the night before one of his patrols turned into a combat mission. I've been carrying it with me since I received it. It's a reminder of his old voice." Steve hands the letter to me. Small words in blue ink are all packed into this paper, and it's hard to read, as if all the words were thrown onto the paper in a hurry.

> James William Johnson
> RA22567221
> 4th Infantry Division
> APO SF 75216
> Feb 13, 1967

> Dear Steve,
> This letter is going to be short. We're leaving from the base again tomorrow, and I'm out of paper. I got this

bad feeling about tomorrow. Actually I get bad feelings all the time nowadays. So I thought I better write this letter before I leave tomorrow, but keep it to yourself. Don't talk to Anna about this letter. Definitely don't tell Mother about it either. But no worries. It's not like anything new has happened. I keep thinking that I could be killed anytime anywhere. One of the guys in my squad got shot during our patrol and his kneecap flew out and hit me in the face. I guess I can't shake off these bad feelings since then. Things got worse this month and it's been a struggle here every day just to keep my sanity. Oh, that guy survived. He's one of the lucky ones, probably on a plane right now to a hospital back home. Anyway, the main reason I'm writing to you is to ask you a favor. I wanted you to help Anna with Helen in case I don't come home. I know it's a lot to ask, but Mother and Father don't want anything to do with Anna. I know you don't care for her either, but I wanted to make sure that she has got someone to be there for her. Anna sent me some pictures of Helen, and boy, is she the most precious thing in the world! I didn't carry her pictures with me up until now because I didn't want them to get wet, but I got a plastic bag through my source! I'll take her with me everywhere I go. When Helen gets older, maybe you could take her out to dinner on my birthday every year, not just to any restaurant, but a really nice one, like the Harriet Hotel in San Francisco kinda place. You get the idea. I came up with this idea today. Maybe because it's Helen's birthday today. There're a bunch of pigs and jerks out there and I don't want her to get stuck with one of them. I want you to treat her really nice and then she'll know that she better get herself a really nice man. You're a good man and I know I can trust you. Anyway, just a thought. I'll appreciate it if you could do that for me. All kinds of thoughts just pop up in my head all the time nowadays, and sorry to dump it off on you. I guess I'm too serious. I said to this guy Tom in my unit that knowing how we could be dead right now felt like walking on water. Tom looked at me like I was crazy and asked what planet I was from. He laughed and said that I'd forget to dodge bullets if I kept thinking like that. I better go Steve. I'm running out of space. Write me again. Send me more pictures, too. Thank Mother for the sweatshirt she sent me for my birthday. (I guess it's winter at home. It's too hot to wear a sweater in Vietnam.) You're a good brother Steve and I sure love you a lot.

Your brother,
James

A reminder of James's old voice—I see what Steve is searching for and why his brother's change is breaking his heart. His voice is filled with his love and longing for his family. I return the letter to Steve, and he folds it gently.

"James told me that the last mission was one of those awful ones where you get pinned down to the ground. 'Your head lifted up, you get dead,' James said. He remembers the gunfire everywhere and thinking that it would be a miracle if he didn't get shot. A bomb blew him away and knocked him out. He thinks a U.S. helicopter came to lift his unit out while he was unconscious. They left him behind. What happened after that, I'm not sure. He doesn't tell me. He just said he was captured by Vietcong and dragged everywhere in the jungle for six months, until one day he escaped and ran to a U.S. helicopter, descending from patrol. James was shot in the shoulder because the commander thought he was Vietcong. It was actually a miracle that they didn't kill him, but instead decided to capture him, which was when they found out that he was American." Steve closes his eyes for a moment.

Walt Whitman's words are ringing in my head, thinking of James. *The dead there are not to be pitied as much as some of the living that have come from there.* When I first read those words in his essay, its truth gave me chills. I thought of Chiyo in Manchuria first, then Yukio's melted face in Hiroshima thirty years ago. How awful that Whitman's perception of the prisoners at Belle Isle during the Civil War could be so appropriate for us. And once again, his words are appropriate for James, who hasn't been able to shake off his bad feelings from the war.

"I'll take good care of Helen and Ken. I'll do anything for my brother, Mr. Takagawa. James was always there for me, growing up. He was very protective. If some kids gave me a hard time, he'd make sure that they'd leave me alone." Steve smiles nostalgically. "Once, James saw some older kids pushing me around at school. He came over, went to the biggest kid in the group, and whispered something into his ear. I saw this kid's face turning pale, and that was it. They left me alone and never gave me a hard time again."

"What did he say to the boy?"

"I asked him the same question later, and he just grinned in a funny way, but he never told me what he said." Steve chuckles. The gloomy image of James is so strong in my mind that I can hardly imagine what he was like before changing so drastically.

"I was so clumsy and curious about everything that I always got in trouble. James always watched over me and made sure that I didn't fall out of a tree or drop a hot pot on my feet." Steve holds the teacup and looks inside for a moment, and with a most serious gaze, he looks at me. "I just know Anna is devastated by how James has changed."

"You can't blame your brother for Anna's struggle."

"No, I didn't mean to sound like that. It's just that I remember Anna as such a fierce and strong person. I just know in my heart that she's going to figure it out and pull herself through this."

Fierce and strong? Ever since I received Helen's letter, I imagined that Anna had had an unhappy childhood and suffered a great deal. Instead, Steve tells me how Anna graduated from high school as a top student and had a full scholarship to attend college, how she used to work at a used bookstore near the campus and spent her money on books, how James and Anna went to see all kinds of artistic films that no one else really watched.

"For a while, I didn't care for Anna, since my family didn't approve of James dating a Japanese girl. But more than that, I thought she was making my brother do and see things that were weird. When I went to James's room in college, he had this poster of a Japanese film, *Rashomon*—with the face of a woman in heavy makeup and a man that looked like a samurai. It was exotic and scary. He passionately told me about the film, and I couldn't believe how much he had changed. I panicked and thought that she was a bad influence. I mean, my brother would have never gone to see *Rashomon* if it wasn't for Anna. Have you seen it?"

"Oh, yes, it's a quite striking film, indeed." I imagine Anna and James sitting in the darkness of a theater looking at the face of the main female character in her heavy makeup. She almost looks like a ghost. An intense and disturbing film is what I thought at first, but then, there was something very comical about it. All the main characters would take the blame for the murder for the sake of their pride, as if that were better than the shame of being a coward.

"But you seem to adore Anna now."

Steve laughs a little. "It's not that I have come to some kind of realization about her. They moved on without any approval, and I had to catch up, because they weren't going to stop for us. That was Anna. She was determined to walk through heated situations. I think James didn't feel scared as long as he was with her.

"When James first introduced me to Anna, I was intimidated by her. I thought she was mysterious. I don't know how to explain, but she had such thoughtful eyes, and she gazed at me deeply. She gazed at everyone like that, and we all felt like she was pinning us down. I was a bit uncomfortable at first, but James used to say that her gaze was one of the things he loved about her, how she really looked at him. He told me never to marry a woman unless I loved her as much as he loved Anna."

I close my eyes. On the night of Shizuka's birth, I borrowed my neighbor's wagon in the middle of the night to take Ume to the hospital. For the next several hours, I heard her moaning in the delivery room, and I walked back and forth in the hallway as if I were the nervous father. When I finally heard the cry of a newborn, a nurse came out, her arms scratched with fingernail marks. Ume held the nurse's arm as if she were drowning in the river and hanging onto a branch for her life. When the nurse took me inside, there was a small red baby next to pale Ume. The child looked barely human to me, though at the same time, she was a full person. Her large black eyes gazed up in the air with absolute intensity even though she couldn't see anything yet, and I held her tiny body, acutely sensing the room, the air, and my arms. I couldn't believe how difficult it was for her to be born, to arrive in my arms that were unable to help her. But in that moment, I didn't think about what might happen to her. Our senses are truer than our words, and Shizuka's eyes absorbed something very true about me. Such sensitivity would exhaust her someday if she grew up with that force always in her eyes. As I held her, she began to fuss and cry loudly. I had no idea what to do with a baby and tried walking around the room, but she wouldn't stop crying. But then Ume called to her daughter: *What's the matter, little Shizuka?* Immediately she stopped crying and turned toward Ume as if she was very surprised that the voice she had heard for the last nine months was no longer a part of her, yet was relieved that it was still close by.

"And her black hair," Steve smiles, "James loved her black hair and called it 'wild black.' Maybe because it was so long. He was always touching her hair. To this day, my parents don't really care for Anna, and my mother would say stupid things like, 'if only Anna could put her hair up into a ponytail, she wouldn't look so Asian . . .' Anna usually has her hair up, but when she sees my parents, she always lets her hair loose. I think she is quietly rebellious." Steve smiles.

My hands are suddenly covered with a mixture of sensations—Ume's thin hair while she was dying, and the warmth of little Shizuka in my arms. All these senses are unsettling and I am shocked by how much I physically remember them. I make fists and cross my arms before these memories overtake my body.

"After all, perhaps Anna and James will get through. There's no place like home, as the famous Sophocles poem says, 'Nothing is so sweet as to return from sea and listen to the raindrops on the rooftops of home.' When James is ready, he'll eventually come back to Anna and to you." I tell Steve what I want to tell myself.

"Return from sea and listen to the raindrops on the rooftops of home . . ." Steve mumbles. Home was where Ume listened to the rain fall and remembered the sound of thousands of silkworms biting the leaves. Home was where Ume imagined that the ocean waves were in the room. Home is sweet, even if it breaks our hearts sometimes. While Steve waits for his brother to heal, he has to trust that the sweetness of home is a solid memory somewhere deep inside James's heart.

JANUARY 1976

I don't know how to use the bathroom at Uncle Hideo's house. There is no shower, and inside the bathtub, they have orange peels! It's not really an orange, but I don't remember the name of the fruit. Aunt Chiyo told me how to use the bathroom. She said I can't use the soap inside the bathtub because everyone will use the same water. She told me lots of other things and left me alone, but I don't know what to do. I don't want to use the water with orange peels inside, and I think using the same water is yucky. I take a bucket and fill it with hot and cold water from the faucet. I wash my body with soap really fast and rinse it with the water. I get another bucket of water and rinse it again, but the water is warm this time. I go out of the bathroom, put on my pajamas, and run quickly to the warm dining room.

Aunt Chiyo is washing dishes in the kitchen. For dinner, she made many things, and I liked the rice, soup, and almost everything else except for the fried chicken that was too heavy with grease. Aunt Chiyo and Uncle Hideo were surprised that I didn't like it. I told them what Mom said about eating meat and sugar. They looked surprised, but not mad. There were so many different plates that I got confused about how to use them. It'll take Aunt Chiyo a long time to wash them all. I don't see Uncle Hideo anywhere in the room. He is like Shaky Hector because sometimes his eyes stop in front of my face and stare at me. I pretend that I don't notice him looking at me, but from the corner of my eye, I see him. I know why everyone looks at me hard. They all think I look like Mom when she was little.

"You're out of the bath already? Did you warm up in the bathtub?" Aunt Chiyo comes from the kitchen, wiping off her wet hands with her apron. I look down and shake my head. I don't want to tell her that I don't like her bathroom.

"Japanese bathrooms are very strange, aren't they? Poor thing, you look cold. Come along. You sit in front of the heater and let your hair dry!" She takes me to the living room, and I follow her. In front of the heater, my hands are warming up. Their house is so much colder than Uncle Steve's. Uncle Hideo said they only heat the room that they're in. The bathroom is as cold as outside.

I look through my bag but can't find my comb. I take everything out—my toothbrush, toothpaste, shampoo, soap, but no comb! I forgot to bring it. My hair is messy, but I don't have a comb. What do I do now, and tomorrow morning when I wake up? My hair is always messy in the morning. I look around for Uncle Steve, but I only hear his voice from the hallway.

"Your uncle is on the phone with your aunt." Aunt Chiyo points at the door.

"Aunt Mary?" I get up and run to the hallway. It's freezing cold!

"Can I say hello to Aunt Mary?" I whisper to Uncle Steve.

"Just a quick hello, O.K.?" He gives me the phone.

"Hello?" I don't hear anything, so I call her name, but her voice comes a little bit later, like an echo.

"This phone is weird. It's slow."

"That's because you're calling across the ocean," Uncle Steve says.

"Helen, sweetheart, how are you? I heard that you liked flying!" I love hearing Aunt Mary's voice. She sounds the same even though her voice goes through the ocean.

"I forgot to bring my comb, and my hair is wet," I tell her quickly.

"Oh, did you ask Mrs. Takagawa if you could borrow her comb?"

"No."

"I'm sure she'll let you."

"What about tomorrow?"

"She will let you use it again." I want to ask Aunt Mary if she could bring my comb, but I know she'll say no because it's too far away. Uncle Steve says that I have to say good-bye.

"I love you! I love you!" Aunt Mary's voice jumps in my head.

"I love you, too," I say, but I don't know what to do about my comb. I give the phone back to Uncle Steve.

"Go inside and ask Chiyo for a comb." Uncle Steve opens the door and pulls my hand. He is icy cold! I think Aunt Chiyo and Uncle Hideo should keep their phone inside the room.

I walk and sit in front of the heater again. I go over my hair to straighten it with my fingers, but they don't work as well as a comb. Aunt Chiyo is still in the kitchen washing dishes. I should ask her to let me use her comb, but when I think about asking her, my throat gets tight.

"Would you like a cup of hot tea?" Aunt Chiyo comes from the kitchen with four cups on the tray and puts them on the table. "You'll get cold if you don't dry your hair, Helen." She goes to the bathroom and comes back with a towel, hand mirror, hair dryer, and comb. I think she can hear my voice inside my head! Aunt Chiyo's comb is very pretty, made out of a tree. I can see the lines of the wood. Uncle Steve told me that a tree gets a line every year. I wonder how old this tree was. I try combing my hair, but this tree comb doesn't slide down like my plastic one at home. My hair is tangled all over after washing it.

"May I comb your hair?" Aunt Chiyo's hands are small like mine. I give her the comb.

I hold up the hand mirror to see her fingers move quickly. They feel like bees walking all over my head. The comb feels much softer on my head now. Mom was really good at untangling my hair, too.

"You have beautiful hair," Aunt Chiyo says.

"I'm trying to let it grow. Mom cut it short."

"When I was young, my mother told me that I had to cut my hair, too. But she cut it so short that I looked like a boy!"

"Why did your mom cut your hair?" I ask.

"Sometimes, girls were taken away during the war, so we all tried to look less like girls."

"You mean your mom was scared that the ghost Shizuka would come and take you away?"

"Ghost Shizuka?" Her hands stop moving, and she sits next to me. "Did you know that Shizuka is your mother's Japanese name?"

I nod. "But I'm talking about the ghost Shizuka, the one that finds girls with long black hair and takes them back to the ocean behind the wall in the closet."

Aunt Chiyo's eyes get big. I thought she'd know about the ghost Shizuka.

"Your mother told you all this? And she cut your hair?" Her voice gets soft, like how older people say hello to Ken at grocery stores. I hope I didn't say anything bad. Her face is serious. Maybe Shizuka is really scary, and I wasn't supposed to say her name.

"Shizuka is a brave dancer. Did your mother tell you about that? She was a well-known dancer here in Kamakura over seven hundred years ago," Aunt Chiyo says. Mom has never said anything about Shizuka dancing before.

"Didn't she jump in the ocean? If she died, isn't she a ghost?" Mom said ghosts were real and angry because they were once alive and they wanted to live.

"Well," Aunt Chiyo looks up like she is thinking, and says, "I suppose some ghosts are scary, but not every one. Ghost Shizuka isn't a scary kind."

"There are not-scary kinds of ghosts?"

"Yes, of course. For example, my mother is a ghost and comes and visits me all the time."

I have never met anyone that has a ghost mother. Something like that never happens in America. "Does she live behind the wall in the closet?"

"No, she lives above the ceiling." Aunt Chiyo points at the ceiling. "She just flies down and sits by me. When the moon is full, she even brings rice cakes filled with sweet red beans and eats them one by one."

"I didn't know ghosts eat cakes!"

"Only when the moon is full. Rabbits are inside the moon, pounding sticky rice to make rice cakes."

Now I think Chiyo is making up a story. I have never seen rabbits inside the full moon.

"You have never seen rabbits in the moon, have you?" Aunt Chiyo says. She knows everything I say in my head! I think she has special ears to hear what I'm thinking.

"Have you seen gray shapes and lines in the middle of the moon before? They are the rabbits. It's hard to tell from here on earth. The moon is so far away."

"And they make rice cakes?"

"Yes," Aunt Chiyo smiles.

"What do they taste like?" I don't know if she's telling me the real story. How can rabbits really live inside the moon? When I was up in the sky in the airplane, I should have looked for the moon. I was closer to the moon then, and maybe I could have seen the rabbits from there. But I don't remember seeing the moon at all.

"The moon rice cakes are just for the ghosts, so I have never eaten them before and don't know what they taste like. I just watch my mother eat them. They smell so good! Sometimes, I reach out and try to touch them, but my hand goes right through them. Then my mother says 'Not yet, you have to live for a while, but someday we'll have rice cakes together.'"

"That's mean!" I would be angry if Mom ate strawberry cake in front of me and said that I couldn't have any.

"Oh, but she looks happy. Her mouth is full and her eyes are calm. Sometimes she even sheds tears because the cakes taste so good. After eating, she's satisfied, wipes off her mouth, and flies back to China."

"She came from China? I thought she lives behind the ceiling." I don't know about China. Do ghosts fly from country to country?

"The ceiling is like a door. That's where she opens and enters the house. My mother died in China, so she will always be there, but it doesn't matter where she is. She's a ghost and can go anywhere anytime. She could come down from the ceiling right now."

I look up. Chiyo said her mother isn't scary, but I still don't want her to come from China. What if she comes down from the ceiling while I'm sleeping? I'll be scared if she sits by me and eats rice cakes.

"Is it a full moon tonight?" I ask Aunt Chiyo.

She bursts into laughter. "Don't worry. My mother won't be visiting here. I told her that you are visiting. She won't bother us."

"She wouldn't come if you told her not to?"

"No, ghosts won't come without an invitation. Have you seen the ghost Shizuka?"

"No."

"You see, that's because you don't want her to come."

But Mom said Shizuka would just come and take me away. Now, Aunt Chiyo says ghosts aren't scary and they don't come if we don't want them to. Maybe Mom didn't know that Shizuka wasn't a scary ghost. Maybe Shizuka doesn't even live behind the wall of our closet. She probably flies everywhere to visit people like Aunt Chiyo's mother.

"Tomorrow, maybe I'll take you to the Hachiman Shrine. There's a large beautiful stage where Shizuka danced." Aunt Chiyo claps her hands. "And, I will take you to Mr. Kawaguchi's bakery! You see, after my mother's visit, I always go to the bakery and buy lots of rice cakes, the biggest I can find. Mr. Kawaguchi makes wonderful rice cakes called Moon Cakes. They look like what my mother eats. Mr. Kawaguchi usually has it all boxed up before I arrive. He says, 'I thought you would be coming today because it was a full moon last night.' When I come home, I pour myself a cup of green tea like this," Aunt Chiyo points at her pink teacup, "then I start eating them all. Later, when Hideo comes home from work and sees an empty box of rice cakes, he asks me how I can eat so many!" Aunt Chiyo covers her mouth and starts laughing.

"How many cakes do you eat?"

"Let's see . . . last time I ate fifteen." She laughs again, and I laugh with her. Aunt Chiyo is so small. Can she really eat fifteen rice cakes? Where do they go inside her?

"Can I try a Moon Cake tomorrow?"

"Yes, yes," Aunt Chiyo is still laughing. Then she gets up to plug in the hair dryer, then starts drying my hair. All I can think about are Moon Cakes. I wonder what they taste like. Maybe they're made out of yellow fluffy stuff, and inside is custard. Aunt Chiyo said they have sweet red beans inside. I don't know what they are. All the beans that Mom makes are heavy and not sweet. They are really heavy. For food with a name like Moon Cake, red beans don't really match. I think whipped cream should be inside the yellow fluffy cake.

I look around the room and see Uncle Steve sleeping. The curtain is closed, but bright light is coming through the cracks. I don't know what time it is, but I have to go to the bathroom. I touch Uncle Steve's shoulder and whisper his name, but he's sleeping hard. I don't want to shake him to wake him up. I should just go out to the hallway and find the bathroom. I went there before going to bed, but I don't remember how to get there from this room. I get up from my futon. Last night, I slept on the floor. There are no beds. There are many things that Uncle Hideo and Aunt Chiyo don't have, like showers, heaters for all the rooms, beds, or even a car! Uncle Hideo said they just use trains and buses to go everywhere.

I slide the door slowly and go out into the hallway. I hear the sound of water from the kitchen. The hallway is still cold. This house is a little confusing because every room has a door. There are so many doors that I don't remember which one is the bathroom. I open the first one, but it's a closet. There are so many books and papers piled up inside, it's like a bookshelf with a door. I have never seen so many books!

"Helen? You're up. I thought I heard someone." Uncle Hideo opens the living room door. I close the closet quickly.

"You must be looking for the bathroom?" Uncle Hideo opens the door next to the closet. Can he hear my voice in my head, too?

"Goodness, you aren't wearing slippers. It's too cold to walk with bare feet." Uncle Hideo opens another door, takes out a pair of fuzzy brown slippers.

"Thank you." Uncle Hideo helps me put on the slippers. They are really warm and big.

"After using the bathroom, come to the living room, and we'll have breakfast together." Uncle Hideo doesn't look at me the way he stared at me last night. He smiles and walks back to the living room.

I open the bathroom, and there's another pair of slippers. What do I do with them? Maybe Aunt Chiyo heard me say in my head that I had to go to the bathroom, and she put them there for me. But these blue plastic slippers won't be warm like the ones Uncle Hideo gave me. I just push the blue slippers to the side and walk into the bathroom. It's cold inside because the window is open. From the window, all I see is the street and some houses, but the bathroom smells like the ocean. Sometimes on windy days, my house on the hill in San Francisco smelled like this.

After I use the bathroom, I walk over to the living room and knock on the door, which Aunt Chiyo opens. She's wearing a yellow apron with lots of flowers. She looks like spring. The room is bright with sunshine.

"Are you hungry? Your uncle told me that you like blueberry pancakes. I haven't made pancakes in years." Aunt Chiyo takes me to the dining table. There is only one plate and a glass of orange juice. Uncle Hideo is sitting with his newspaper and a cup of tea. Aunt Chiyo brings three blueberry pancakes from the kitchen and puts them on my plate.

"Aren't you eating breakfast?" I don't want to be the only one eating.

"We actually ate lunch already," Uncle Hideo says.

I look at the clock above the window, and it says one-thirty! Was I sleeping all morning? And Uncle Steve is still sleeping!

"You have jet lag. California is still yesterday, around the time you go to bed." Aunt Chiyo smiles at me, pouring more tea for Uncle Hideo.

Her blueberry pancakes are different from Aunt Mary's. These are thicker and fluffy, almost like cake.

"Do you like school, Helen?" Uncle Hideo asks.

"Yes."

"Do you have many friends? Are they nice?"

"They're o.k." Uncle Hideo has lots of questions. He wants to know everything, what I like to eat, where I go on the weekends, what classes I like, what we did last summer, what Ken looks like.

Aunt Chiyo says something to him in Japanese and his face gets red a little.

"I'll let you eat first. Meanwhile, I will get some pictures." Uncle Hideo scratches his head.

That reminds me that I brought this special picture of me, Ken, Uncle Steve, and Aunt Mary that we took before coming here. Aunt Mary said that we had to have a family picture to show Uncle Hideo and Aunt Chiyo. I get up and run back to my room to get the picture. I walk carefully around Uncle Steve who is still sleeping. I wanted Uncle Hideo and Aunt Chiyo to see Ken because he was too little to come here with me, but he is still another stick, holding Mom's empty tree. I also grab all the pictures that Mrs. Hogan gave me.

When I get back to the living room, Uncle Hideo is wiping his book with a white cloth. Then he opens it and points at the first picture.

"This is the only photo that survived the war. My neighbor kept it safe for me." Uncle Hideo takes out a brown picture with five people standing, looking all serious. The old man in the center looks angry. The woman next to him looks really bored or sad. They are all standing straight like trees.

"This is my family. This is my brother Shinya, my father, my mother, me, and this is your grandmother, Ume." He points at each person, and his finger stops at Grandma Ume. She is a little girl in the picture, wearing a kimono like the one the origami artist, Kyoko, wore at camp. When Mom talked about Grandma Ume, I always thought she'd be an old person. Looking at this little girl doesn't feel like seeing Grandma Ume. Even Uncle Hideo in the picture looks different.

"Is this really you?"

"Yes," he nods with a smile. Then he's staring at me like he did before. "You remind me a lot of Ume when she was little."

I look at the picture again, but I don't look anything like Grandma Ume.

"I noticed when you smiled that your teeth are just like hers."

My teeth look like Grandma Ume's? I will have to see my teeth later in the bathroom. I don't remember what my teeth look like!

I put all of my pictures on the table, too. Uncle Hideo and Aunt Chiyo bring their faces so closely to each picture that their noses almost touch the paper. Then, to see the back, they touch the edge of each picture carefully, like holding eggshells. They don't say anything for a while, just staring.

"I heard that your father went to the Vietnam war." Uncle Hideo points at Mom and Dad's wedding picture. He is looking at Dad's brown uniform.

I nod.

"My father was a soldier, too. He went to a different war," Aunt Chiyo holds Dad's picture.

"Everyone says my dad changed a lot after the war. Did your dad change, too?" I don't think I asked a bad question, but Aunt Chiyo's face gets tight and looks sad.

"My father actually died in the war, but if he did come back, I think he'd have been a different man."

"Why?"

"Many people died and got hurt because of my father."

"Your dad was a bad person?"

Aunt Chiyo just smiles and doesn't say anything.

"Do you think my dad hurt a lot of people, too?"

"I don't know." Aunt Chiyo's voice gets smaller, and she puts the picture of Dad back on the table.

Uncle Hideo touches her sleeve and starts speaking in Japanese. He doesn't sound angry, but he says something fast. She just looks at him and doesn't say anything back. Then she turns to me.

"I think your father is a good man. I'm glad he came home safely. He might have changed, but he's always your father." Uncle Hideo's lips are shut tightly, and his face looks worried. Everyone says the same thing, that my dad is always going to be my dad, but I know that. I don't forget it. Dad is the one who forgets me all the time.

"And this must be Ken!" Aunt Chiyo looks at the last picture of me, Aunt Mary, Uncle Steve, and Ken. We took this picture in front of the Christmas tree. It was Aunt Mary's idea. Ken looks goofy in the picture, with a big smile, standing next to his new bike. We look like a real family. Uncle Steve and Aunt Mary look like they are our real mom and dad.

I hear footsteps from the hallway. The door slowly opens and Uncle Steve pops his head inside the room. Then he smiles and scratches his head like he's embarrassed.

"Goodness, it's almost two in the afternoon! I'm sorry. I overslept!" Uncle Steve covers his head with both hands. I run and hug him. I know he was in the house, just across the hallway, but I'm happy that he's awake now.

"Helen, how long have you been up? You could have woken me!" He kisses the top of my head. I had thought about waking him, but I wanted to do everything all by myself.

⌒

Before we left the house, Uncle Hideo said that there would be a lot of people at the Hachiman Shrine because it was the day after New Year's. He was right! All I see is people's heads with black hair in front of me. The Hachiman Shrine is way up many stairs; there must be more than a thousand steps! I hold Uncle Steve's hand tight. If I get lost, he'll never find me. I put on my red hat, too, but many people are wearing hats.

We take a step up, wait for a few seconds, and move up again. It'll take forever to go all the way up with so many people! In the middle of the stairs, Uncle Steve points at a huge tree with a rope and two posts next to it.

"Helen, look at the big tree over there!"

The tree looks like Uncle Steve's drawing of Mom and two sticks—me and Ken—except that the tree is so big like a solid house, definitely not empty inside like Mom.

"That's a Byakushin tree, a city natural monument because it's about eight hundred years old," Uncle Hideo says.

"Are there eight hundred circles inside it?" I had no idea that a tree could live for hundreds of years!

"Do you like trees, Helen?" Uncle Hideo sounds excited. We are moving up and forward, but Uncle Steve and I keep looking back at the old tree. The more I look at it, the more it looks like an old man, sitting with his elbow on the ground. When he was on the way to the shrine, he sat down in the middle of the stairs and rested, but he never got up because he was too heavy. So he stayed there for eight hundred years, all grumpy, and became a tree! I like my story. Uncle Steve's picture had a thin tree in the middle of two short sticks holding it, but this old tree looks like he is holding the sticks.

When we finally get to the top, in front of the altar, I copy what Aunt Chiyo does—throwing some money into a wooden box, clapping hands twice, closing our eyes, putting our hands together in front of our faces, then bowing to the altar. I see Uncle Hideo praying with his eyes closed for a long time. We move away from the line because there are so many people behind us. We wait for Uncle Hideo, but his eyes are still closed; his face is serious, and he doesn't move at all. There is a small line of people behind him, waiting.

When Uncle Hideo finally opens his eyes, he looks around to find us.

"Maybe I was greedy to wish so many things," he says with a smile, but his eyes look sad. His sad smile reminds me of Mrs. Hogan, who always looked like she was going to cry.

I thought the stage for Shizuka's dance would look pretty, with something like a red velvet curtain, shiny floor, big lights, and chairs around it, but it's just a big empty house without windows. The dark wood floor has four thick legs that hold a green roof on top, and nothing inside. Uncle Hideo comes back from the gift shop and gives me a postcard that has the picture of Shizuka dancing. I thought she would look scary and mean, but she looks bright. She has a white kimono top with long sleeves and a red bottom. Her face is painted white, and her red lips and black eyes are drawn sharp. Her long hair goes all the way down to the floor and is tied into one ponytail.

A long gold hat is on her head, and she is carrying a folding fan. She looks serious, but her thick makeup looks a little bit like a clown.

"Shizuka sings as she dances like this." Aunt Chiyo takes one step at a time. It doesn't look like she is dancing, just walking slowly and moving her arms.

"Did you know that your mother is named after Shizuka, the brave dancer?" Uncle Hideo asks.

I nod.

"When you go home, will you tell your mother that your grandmother wanted her to be brave enough to cry out loud when she's sad? Can you remember to tell this to her? It's very important to me."

"Crying is brave?"

"Yes, it is!" Uncle Hideo smiles big. "When Ume and I were little, our father said that if we cried, everyone would know that we were sad. He told us to control our sorrow by tightening our stomach and holding tears. That's what my mother did, and so did Ume. She always endured her sorrow. She didn't want her daughter to do the same."

I remember Uncle Hideo's letter. He said that Grandma Ume wanted Mom to cry. That's so weird. If crying is brave, then Ken would be the bravest person in the world. I don't think anyone could teach me or Ken to tighten our stomach and hold our tears. We cry all the time.

Uncle Hideo wants to show us some other old tree at the Hachiman Shrine, but Aunt Chiyo says that she wants to take me to the Moon Cake shop before they close. So Uncle Hideo and Uncle Steve go to the garden, and Aunt Chiyo and I walk to the Moon Cake shop. Before, everyone was looking at Uncle Steve, but now, everyone stares at me instead. Maybe my red hat is too bright. I take it off and put it in my pocket.

"Won't you be cold without your hat?" Aunt Chiyo says.

"Everyone is looking at it. It's too bright."

"Oh." Aunt Chiyo looks around and walks closer to me. "I'm sorry, Helen."

Even without my hat, everyone's eyes follow me. Aunt Chiyo isn't tall like Uncle Steve, so I can't really hide behind her. I keep walking, looking down at the road.

Aunt Chiyo stops at a tiny shop with an old wooden door and says that this is the Moon Cake shop. This shop doesn't look like a place that makes Moon Cakes. Aunt Chiyo says something in Japanese as she opens the door. An old man and a young man come out from inside and they both say something as they bow. Aunt Chiyo bows back, saying something as she smiles.

"Helen, this is Mr. Kawaguchi, and his son, Tomio san."

"Hello." I bow to them, too, because they are bowing to me. When Mr. Kawaguchi's head is up, I see that his teeth are all gold! He speaks in his soft voice.

"He said what a lovely girl you are!" Aunt Chiyo says something back to them and they all nod. Can they really understand all the words they are saying?

Aunt Chiyo walks to the glass counter, where many colorful round cakes are placed.

"They are so pretty!" I point at the pink round cakes in a flower-shape with one leaf on each side.

"The pink one is Cherry Blossom, the white one is Cherry Flowers, and this yellow one is Chestnut." All the cakes are shiny and colorful. I want to take a bite from each one!

Aunt Chiyo talks to Mr. Kawaguchi, and his son brings a white box from the kitchen. That must be the Moon Cakes!

Aunt Chiyo opens the box. There are six white round cakes in two rows. But they aren't decorated like the other flower cakes. I thought the Moon Cakes would be prettier and special, but they look so plain and boring. If I were a ghost, I would visit earth with Cherry Blossom cakes instead of Moon Cakes. But maybe rabbits don't make Cherry Blossom cakes in the moon. Mr. Kawaguchi wraps the box, puts on a gold ribbon, and gives it to me.

"Thank you," I say, but I want Cherry Blossom cakes instead.

Mr. Kawaguchi's son comes from the kitchen holding a plate with two Moon Cakes and gives it to Aunt Chiyo. She bows and says something in her high tone of voice.

"Mr. Kawaguchi is sharing their freshly made Moon Cakes with us because you are a special guest! Please," Aunt Chiyo puts the plate in front of me. I put the box on the counter and hold a Moon Cake with both hands because it's so soft. I take a big bite of it and chew it twice. Then I stop because it feels weird in my mouth. I look inside the Moon Cake, and it's not red beans. It looks like black mud! I think they made a mistake on mine.

"What's wrong?" Aunt Chiyo says, covering her mouth. I look at her cake, and she has the same thing inside. I don't know what to do. The sweet mud is in my mouth.

"Here, you can spit it out." Aunt Chiyo quickly takes a tissue from her purse and gives it to me. I don't want to spit it out in front of Mr. Kawaguchi. But I don't want to swallow this mud. I stand there, and tears come to my eyes. I don't know what to do.

"Helen, it's fine to spit it out." Aunt Chiyo takes me to the corner of the store. So I take the tissue, spit out the muddy Moon Cake, and wrap the tissue around it.

"I'm sorry. I should have thought that you may not like red bean pastry. It's a little different, isn't it?" Aunt Chiyo touches my back. Mr. Kawaguchi's son comes out running with a glass of water and hands it to me. Then he puts out his hand in front of me.

"Rice cake?" he says. So I give back the half-eaten cake, but he is still holding out his hand, looking at my other hand. The bite that I spit out is getting wet inside the tissue, but he's waiting for it. I put it in his hand, and he walks back to the kitchen like nothing happened. I want to run away from this store. My face feels like it's on fire.

I take a sip of water fast, but it goes down the wrong pipe, making me cough. Aunt Chiyo gives me another tissue and pats my back a little. They are all looking at me. Mr. Kawaguchi has a really sad face and he says something to Aunt Chiyo.

"Mr. Kawaguchi says that the red bean was probably extra thick today, so he's sorry."

When I look up, Mr. Kawaguchi smiles with his gold teeth. My eyes are all hot so I close them tight, but it's too late. I can't stop my tears. They run down all over my cheeks and into my mouth. The salty and sweet tastes get mixed up in my mouth.

Uncle Steve isn't home yet when we get back from the Moon Cake bakery. I don't feel good, so I sit on the living room couch and try not to move. Though I didn't swallow the muddy red bean pastry at the bakery, my mouth still tastes the heavy sweet mud. My head hurts, and my chest is tight. I close my eyes and breathe a little faster to make the yucky feelings in my chest go away. Mom said sugar was poison. Maybe she was talking about red bean pastry. When I eat other sweet things, I don't get sick. I feel bad for spitting it out in front of Mr. Kawaguchi. Because I started crying, I didn't get to say sorry to him.

"Helen, are you all right?"

I don't know how long I've been sitting on the couch with my eyes closed, but Uncle Steve is sitting in front of me now.

"You don't feel well?"

"My head hurts."

"You should lie down for a while." Aunt Chiyo quickly goes to our room and makes my futon. I want to say thank you and I'm sorry about the Moon Cake, but I don't want to move my mouth. I put on my pajamas, get inside the futon, and close my eyes.

I wake up and stare at the ceiling for a long time. Outside is still dark, so I know I should still be sleeping. Uncle Steve is sleeping next to me, so I try not to make any noise. Since I've been in Japan, I'm sleeping a lot. I don't even have any dreams. Uncle Steve sleeps a lot, too. This place makes everyone sleepy. But I am wide awake now. After staring at the black room for a long time, it changes to purple. I think about getting up to go to the bathroom, but I don't want to leave my warm spot in the futon.

My headache is gone. I get up quietly and step out to the hallway. Outside the door, I see my warm slippers. I wish I didn't have to pee, since the bathroom is cold with the window open. I pee quickly and run out of the bathroom to get back to my futon. There is a light through the glass door to the living room, and I hear Uncle Hideo's voice, so I open the door and peep inside. He's sitting alone on the couch, reading something out loud in Japanese. His voice is going up and down, like he's singing, or just making soft sounds. I want to go and sit by the heater, but I don't know if I should come in. I stand by the half-open door until Uncle Hideo looks up and sees me.

"Helen, how long have you been standing there? Come inside and warm up." Uncle Hideo stands up quickly. He's still wearing his pajamas and bathrobe. He moves and lets me sit in the spot where he was sitting in front of the heater. The clock above the window says 4:55. He's up so early.

"Were you reading a book?" His book looks old, with all the edges ripped, and the brown cover is faded. He opens and shows me the book, which smells wet. Every other page has a picture or a drawing, and the opposite side has writing. Some pages only have three or four lines.

"This is a book about Kamakura. It has many stories and poems about the Hachiman Shrine. Many years ago, I found it at a used bookstore. Actually, this book became your grandmother's favorite." He flips the pages to get to the drawing of Shizuka.

"Were you singing Shizuka's song?"

"Singing?" Uncle Hideo's face gets a little pink. "I was reading some Japanese poems about trees at the Hachiman Shrine."

He flips more pages and goes to the end of the book. "This tree is called Nagi. Nagi's spirit is for safe traveling on the ocean."

A tree has a spirit? Everything is alive in Japan! I point at the short lines on the next page.

"Is this the poem for Nagi tree?"

"Yes."

"Will you read it?"

His cheeks get a little red again, but he sits up straight and reads the poem slowly.

> mikumano no
> nagi no ha shidari
> furu yuki ha
> kami no kaketaru
> shite nizo arurashi.

I love Uncle Hideo's reading. I have no idea what he's saying, but I love the sound. I want him to read it again. I flip to the next page.

"What about this tree? Does it have a spirit, too?" The tree is thin and has lots of white flowers all over it.

"That's Enju tree, with the spirit for delivering a baby safely."

"A tree can help deliver a baby?"

"It's really for good luck. When we go through things that are out of our control, we're helpless. That's probably how all this worshiping started."

"So spirits don't really work?"

"I don't know. Before your grandmother Ume gave birth to your mother, she came to the Hachiman Shrine and touched this tree."

"Did it work?"

"Well, she delivered your mother safely."

Now I have an idea. Inside the book, there are more pictures of trees and poems. I should look for a tree that will help Mom.

"Is there a tree with the spirit for a sad person, for someone who gets nervous and breaks all the time?" Uncle

Hideo opens his eyes wide, looking at me how he did on the first day.

"You're looking for a healing tree for your mother?" He touches his chin and looks up for a moment, then says, "Byakushin tree, the eight-hundred-year-old tree that you saw yesterday, will be a good one."

The fat tree that looked like an old man? I don't know if he would hear me from outside his eight hundred circles. My voice would have to pass through all the skin to his core, to his ears.

"What happens if I go and talk to the big tree about Mom? Can he make her better?"

"It's just for good wishes."

"But Grandma Ume had a baby safely?"

"Indeed, she did."

Even just for good wishes, I want to go and touch the tree. A tree's spirit helped Grandma Ume. So maybe an old-man-tree could help Mom and take away all the sad feelings.

"Can we go to see the tree now?" I get up quickly.

"Right now?" He looks up at the clock that says 5:30, then he looks at me and nods his head.

No one is on the street on the way to the shrine. I think Uncle Hideo and I are the only people awake in this town. It is so silent now.

"Where is everybody?" I look around.

"It's before six; too early and cold to be out," Uncle Hideo says, breathing fast. I'm warm because we walked so fast getting here. The Hachiman Shrine looks so much bigger without so many people, and I can see that Shizuka's stage is really right in the middle of the yard. We head to the stairs, but before going up, Uncle Hideo stops at the side.

"That's Nagi tree, the one that I was singing about this morning." Uncle Hideo turns to me. "When you heard me read the poem, you didn't ask me what it was about. Do you want to know?"

"It sounded nice." I shrug my shoulder. It's a tree song. I didn't understand what he read, but I thought it was supposed to be like that.

"I see," Uncle Hideo nods with smile.

We go up the stairs to the middle and stand by the old-man-tree. He looks just as crabby as yesterday, looking at me like he is tired and heavy. *Not again! I'm too heavy to get up! Don't make any wishes on me!*—that's what he would say if he had a mouth.

I step out of the stone stairs to go and touch the tree.

"Oh, you aren't supposed to touch the tree. It's a national monument." Uncle Hideo says.

"But I want him to really hear my wish."

Uncle Hideo looks around and says in a low voice, "O.K., but you have to do it quickly."

I touch the old-man-tree. His skin is so rough and hard! But there are many cracks on his body, so I bring my mouth close to the tree and whisper as loud as I can.

"I know you're old and tired. But will you help my Mom? She gets nervous all the time. Uncle Hideo said that you're a healing tree. Another tree helped Grandma Ume, so it's your turn to help my mom. I came all the way from America."

I think I said everything I wanted to say. I step back and look at the old-man-tree. He doesn't say anything back or do anything. I thought maybe he would give me a signal by dropping a leaf or something, but nothing.

"Shall we go home?" Uncle Hideo says.

"Do you think he heard me?"

"Yes."

"He's old. He might have bad ears."

"He doesn't use ears to listen. You didn't even have to speak. He just knows why you came to see him just because you're here."

Before leaving the shrine, I turn around and look back at the old-man-tree one more time. Maybe he got so thick because people kept coming to him with so many wishes that he had to carry them all, piled up inside him. Old-man-tree, I'm sorry that you're always being asked to do things. I promise I won't ask any more favors, but just this one is really important. If you help Mom, I promise I'll be good. I promise I'll never forget you!

COLOR

At the altar, before the spirit of Hachiman, I bring my hands together and close my eyes to pray for Anna—*may you favor Anna and her family with good wishes.* After all these years of dismissing the practice of worshiping, such a prayer sounds rather counterfeit in my mind, and I imagine the spirit rolling his eyes at me. Of all the people who have come here year after year faithfully to pay respect with gratitude, I am most undeserving of receiving good wishes.

Even while Ume was dying, I didn't think to pray for her, not even to wish for her peaceful departure from this world. As long as Ume was breathing, I focused on the fact that she was still alive, and I avoided thinking about her death. Immediately after her death, the overwhelming anguish consumed me, and I was too restless to stay in my apartment on my days off. Almost every weekend, I traveled from Tokyo to Kamakura with Ume in the ash box. Without asking my father, I knew I would be forbidden to place her in the family grave. Until I found another place for her, she was on top of my bookshelf with the rice and water that I placed next to her. Instead of sorrow, anger burned inside me because her life and death seemed so unfair, and even after death, since she had no place to be buried. Not knowing what to do, I took Ume to the place that she adored. Every time I was on the train with her, people with sympathetic gazes bowed to me respectfully. They assumed that I was on my way home from cremating a family member, so I bowed back to them, feeling guilty for causing their sympathy.

I think it was my fifth trip to the Hachiman Shrine when an old monk suddenly appeared and sat next to me.

"Losing a sister is such a hardship," he said in a dry voice, looking at me through his straw hat. I was startled by his mention of my sister. How did he know that my sister had died? I was too stunned to ask any questions and just absentmindedly looked at his wrinkly face.

"You go home with your sister now and have just one more trip to Hachiman next week. Then we shall take your sister to rest." He spoke with a weight of certainty. He waited for my response, but since I was speechless, he slowly got up, bowed to me, and walked away.

That entire week, I was restless and felt lonely with the thought of putting Ume to rest. I even felt angry at the monk for appearing so certain and trustworthy. I had no reason to do what he told me to, but deep inside me, I felt that my longing for Ume was changing into grief. Longing was an unresolved and alive feeling inside me, but grief was stillness. I felt tightly grounded to this life and watched the world pass by me while no one noticed that Ume was once alive and now was dead. With every day came added pressure, and I lived with a dull ache spreading over my skull. On Sunday when I woke up, I felt lethargic and sat with Ume's ash box all morning. *Ume, I'm not ready to treat you like the dead.* I didn't want to face the reality that would come to me at the last step of burial, that I had become all alone. *Don't be selfish, Hideo.* If I didn't take care of Ume's ashes that day with the help from the monk, I wouldn't be able to do it alone. Still, I cleaned the windows and wiped off the tatami floor in my apartment, delaying going to the Hachiman Shrine. By the time I finally made myself get up, wrapped Ume into a white cloth, and took a train to Kamakura, it was already evening. I don't know how long the monk had been waiting for me, but he, in a formal black and white robe, was standing with two other monks who seemed to be his followers. They all bowed to me slowly, and as I bowed back to them, the monk approached me. He stood in front of me, and before I could lift my head fully, my chest was filled with pressure. I could see the dark wrinkly hands of the monk above my head, waiting for me to give up Ume. When I faced him, all the pressure dissolved into tears, and I began to cry. I lifted the ash box, and the monk took it with both hands, bowing to me deeply. One of the followers said that I could follow them to Ume's grave. They walked slowly as they chanted a sutra, and I followed them to the small graveyard up on the hill. I sobbed like a young boy who had become lost on the way home. The monk said the soil there was as sweet as sugar because many children's ashes were buried there. They placed Ume under a small old tombstone, and quietly left me alone at the site. I sat there for a long time alone, which was when I realized that from this graveyard, I couldn't see the ocean, but could hear the waves.

I open my eyes and realize that I have been standing in front of the altar for too long, and people behind me have been going around me to get there. For hundreds of years, people have come to this shrine, closed their eyes, and bowed to the altar as they prayed for something that they couldn't control. There is a line behind me and I move away from the center and look for Chiyo, Steve, and Helen. They are waiting for me on the side, and Chiyo especially seems worried. I run to them and apologize for making them wait.

"All the years of not coming to a shrine on New Year's Day have caught up with you. Your wishes have accumulated!" Chiyo teasingly says, pinching my elbow hard. Chiyo appears cheerful, but I think I sense something fierce from her. Before I can face her, she is already walking down the stairs with Helen, pointing at the wooden stage in the middle of the courtyard. Together, they walk down the stairs like mother and daughter.

〜

At first, I thought Steve would be impressed by the tall Enju tree, but instead, he's on the ground, looking at the weeds around the tree and examining their shapes and colors.

"Weeds are my specialty." He speaks without facing me, studying the weeds as if he were a little boy fascinated by a rare insect. The appearance of Caucasians, especially of Steve's tall stature, has been receiving attention. On the train, people stood by Steve and Helen and just stared at them. Although I became frustrated by the many eyes looking at them, I also understood that people didn't mean to stare and didn't even realize how rude it seemed, but they couldn't help looking at someone with light skin, brown hair, and blue eyes. Steve maintained his sense of humor and said he now understood what it was like to be a movie star, though Helen, shy of the attention, often stayed behind Steve. Now that he is on his knees embracing weeds, people are again stopping to look at him.

Looking at Steve under the Enju tree, whose spirit was said to protect the birth of a baby, I remember how I brought Ume to this tree before she gave birth. As soon as we found the tree that grew straight, its branches spreading out to the sky with hundreds of white flowers and green leaves, we understood why people believed this tree's spirit would protect a baby's safe delivery. It was so full and celebratory, and all the white flowers appeared like the tiny hands of infants up in the sky. Ume walked around the tree and placed the side of her face against it, as if it had a heartbeat she could listen to.

The tree is without any flowers now, though a sense of fullness must have captivated Steve. He finally gets up from the ground and walks around the tree. While everything else seems to change, this place always holds a certain quietness, as if time is unmoving here. The Hachiman Shrine is said to be the house of the gods for warriors and wars, but I have always felt calmness and stillness from this place. I remember feeling this way as a child, and suddenly, I am filled with a nostalgic sensation.

Kamakura is the only place that makes me feel like this. I have wondered if certain sensations of home have stayed with Anna over the years. We think children can't remember their early experiences, but what we feel through our skin is the soil of our memories, and although we may not have the concrete memory, we remember certain sensations. I have always been afraid that Ume's hardships somehow seeped through her skin to Anna's body. I wondered if Anna would feel everything that Ume felt— her anxiousness during pregnancy, her shivering with fear while holding Anna because our neighbors banged on the door, yelling at Ume to quiet the baby.

After the hard labor, Ume wasn't well. I asked the landlady to care for Ume during the day while I was at work, but she refused as soon as she found out that Ume had a mixed-blood child. Soon, our entire apartment building talked about us, how we were raising a mixed-blood child. The medical students from downstairs complained that they couldn't study because the baby cried all the time. They said that if we didn't move out soon, they would ask the landlady to evict us. I expected a knock on our door in the middle of the night by the landlady, telling us to move out before dawn, but she never did. Everyone in the building gave us cold stares of disapproval of my sister's improper involvement with a foreign soldier. Once I found Ume and her baby in the closet when I came home from work. She thought sitting in the closet with the crying baby would help muffle the sound and stop the screams from spreading throughout the apartment building. It was the middle of hot and humid August, and she sat in the closet all afternoon with the baby.

Or Anna's skin may remember the sharp pains of hunger she constantly felt because of Ume's trouble breast-feeding. Anna was so hungry and she wouldn't stop crying. One night, when she became too weak to scream, Ume began to panic. I went out in the middle of the night, to all the markets, looking for powdered milk, which was very rare. All the markets owned by Japanese just sold whatever they had or found, which wouldn't include powdered milk. After running for an hour, I went to Professor Kudo's house and told him about Ume and the baby. He was shocked, mostly because I hadn't said anything to him about Ume's pregnancy. He got up right away and took me to the house of an American military officer a few blocks away. Professor Kudo worked with many officers from GHQ, discussing and negotiating the Japanese educational system, so he was comfortable associating with his American neighbors. It was almost midnight, an outrageous time to visit a stranger, especially an American military officer, but I couldn't afford to be hesitant about it as the sound of Anna's weak crying followed me and pushed me to go get help.

The officer was in his nightrobe when we arrived. Professor Kudo explained the situation to him, and the officer was very kind and made some phone calls. He told us to wait with him for half an hour; he made an arrangement for the milk and a nursing bottle to be brought to him. I had been so focused on getting the milk that I never even thought about getting a bottle! I thanked him many times, and he looked at me sympathetically again. I was all sweaty from running around and must have looked awfully nervous. The wife of this officer addressed him as "Colonel" instead of by his name and brought us cold drinks while we waited in his living room.

Exactly a half hour later, two men in military uniforms came with a box full of canned milk, powdered milk, two nursing bottles, as well as some other canned food. I was tasting what it meant to be powerful and to have authority. I was just a helpless citizen who couldn't find a single bag of powdered milk, but this officer could get anything delivered to him just by making a phone call. I was lucky that he decided to help me. The two soldiers saluted the officer and reported the order, its completion, and the time. The officer also told the soldiers to give me a ride home. I thanked him, but said that it was unnecessary since my apartment was very close. If an American jeep were to stop in front of my apartment to drop me off, my neighbors would be outraged even more.

I hurried back home with the heavy box, running all the way. When I came to the outside of the apartment and didn't hear Anna's crying, I was afraid that I might be too late. I was nervous and ran up the stairs quickly. There, I could not believe what I saw. The landlady was holding Anna as she breast-fed her, and Ume sat beside them. I placed the box on the floor and sat down in amazement. The landlady asked me if I had found powdered milk, and I nodded. She said that she was breast-feeding her youngest, and when she heard Anna crying for hours, the other residents yelling at our door, and the baby's weakening cries, she wanted to help.

I felt ashamed. I was ashamed that I envied the American officer's power. I knew that there were some young mothers who could share their breast milk in our building, but I didn't ask them, not because I was afraid, but because I didn't want to ask those who clearly despised us. A part of me refused to beg for help from them, but if they were asked to help a child who was hungry to the point of death, how could they refuse? I felt sick to my stomach, feeling that I was just like my father, who would rather die than beg for help. The price of my arrogance and pride was going to be the suffering of Anna, and now, I'm afraid that the sharp pain of hunger from that night has been engraved inside her, permanently.

Or the warmth Ume left on Anna's skin before saying good-bye—does she remember it? Ume held Anna so tightly until the last moment when she handed her to the nurse at the Christian Home for Children. Anna was sleeping, but Ume imagined that when she woke up, her tiny head would look around for the mother's warmth that she was used to. Ume could hardly eat the next day, and soon, her illness worsened. *I hope Shizuka will forget me as soon as possible,* Ume said weakly, lying on the futon: *I don't want to be her absence. Little Shizuka, forget me as soon as possible.*

Steve finally stops walking around the tree and comes to sit next to me on the bench. There is only a small space between our arms—we are strangers and close friends at the same time.

"Hideo?" Steve says gently, startling me because I sense that he is going to ask what I do not want to discuss.

"Did Anna ever meet her father?" Steve hesitantly asks me. "Or did he leave before she was born?"

For a moment, my mind is filled with blank shapes. I have thought about this, yet I just don't know how to talk about my sister, because no one has ever asked about her. And no one has ever asked me about Anna's father. I see that Steve is coming from a completely different understanding about my sister. Most people won't even say the words, *comfort women.* When we went to eastern Asia, we left everything there, including the language for our offensive acts. It's quite clever how we erase the language that describes our offense first, so that we have no way of describing it, which is why comfort women are so unfamiliar to most people in Japan. I assume the same for Steve. So how do I talk about this to Steve, who won't even know the meaning?

"If you can't talk about it, I understand. I'm sorry," Steve says.

"No, I just haven't talked about Ume for a long time." I try to sound as willing as possible. "Yes, Anna's father left Japan before Anna was born."

"Ume must have been devastated when he left. Did they know each other for a long time?"

"I don't believe so." My hands are sweaty, and my heart beats as if it's trying to run away.

"Was he an American soldier?"

"Yes."

"What was he like? Do you know where he's from?"

"I don't know much about him." I open and close my sweaty hands. I want to flee from all these questions.

"Will you tell me what you know about him?"

"About him?"

"Yes, the soldier."

If you want me to tell you what Ume told me about the man, I won't lie to you, but why do you want to know? It will be awful for you to hear it. Long ago, Chiyo gave me this warning, but I insisted.

"Ume said the soldier was a teacher back in the United States," I say.

It was the seventh man on the second night. He couldn't wait and protection wasn't used, just that once, Ume told me.

"She never told me his name."

The seventh man on the second night, she didn't even know his name, but she said he had smooth skin, narrow gray eyes, and thick dark eyebrows.

"They met at a café."

Most of her guests were polite, but this seventh man on the second day, he was angry and in a hurry.

"They became friends first."

When Ume asked him for a ticket, sold at the counter, he said he didn't have it. It couldn't have been true because otherwise he couldn't get in.

"He left before he knew about Ume's pregnancy."

When Ume presented the protection, he laughed and said he didn't have time for something like that.

"And Ume never looked for him."

That's everything Ume told me. Is this what you really wanted to know? Does anything change now? You have the rest of your life to live with what you know.

I begin walking and command my feet to move forward, but I can barely feel my toes. Steve follows me without saying a word. My mother told me that a lie would come back to a liar in an awful way. But a life without lying is a simple and luxurious life, and I have never had such a luxury, not in my lifetime. Have I just created something that will come back to me in an awful way? When I'm not sure if it's my lie or the truth that will hurt Anna more, does it matter? I close my eyes for a moment and wish I could walk away from Steve to the end of this street to get to the shore. There, if the waves were to swallow me alive, no one would think that I didn't deserved to be taken.

⌒

The gift shops in the airport sell keychains with wooden Japanese dolls attached, displayed in the windows. Helen has been standing in front of one store, unable to decide. She looks at each keychain seriously and tries to decide on the color of kimono for her doll, and Chiyo is helping her. When she finally picks out a doll with a green kimono, Steve pays for it quickly before she changes her mind.

"This is so pretty." Helen walks to the section where folded cloths are displayed.

"This is called Furoshiki. It's like a large handkerchief. We use it to wrap gifts." Chiyo takes one and places it on Helen's hand.

"It's so soft."

"Because it's silk. Did you know that your grandmother's family used to raise silkworms?" I say.

"Silkworms? This is made out of worms?" Helen looks down at the colorful cloth.

"Worms produce silk threads. When I was young, my family and I worked days and nights raising thousands of silkworms, so that young girls like you can have a silk cloth like this!" I smile at Helen.

"You had thousands of worms?" Helen's large eyes gaze at me in amazement.

"Yes, the silkworm house was always packed."

"The worms lived in a house?"

Chiyo and I laugh a little watching Helen's shocked expression. "They're very delicate, so we cleaned their house and fed them mulberry leaves. It was a lot of work."

"Did Grandma Ume work, too?"

"Sometimes. When we had to stay up overnight to feed them, I took her to the house because she loved the sound of worms eating the leaves. We used to say the sound is like rain hitting the roof, but Ume thought it was more like ocean waves."

Helen seems a bit puzzled. "So how do they make silk?"

"When they stop eating the leaves after the fifth molting, we pick up each worm gently and place it in a spinning nest."

"You pick up thousands of worms by hand?" Her mouth is open and she looks down at my hands.

"The silkworms spin as they release the silk threads, and in two days, they surround themselves in silk cocoons. After that, we gather all the cocoons and put them into boiling water to make them soft for reeling the silk threads."

"What happens to the worms?"

"They die in the hot water."

"Oh," Helen looks down at the silk cloth in her hand again. "Did Grandma Ume wear silk?"

"All the time. She wore many silk kimonos as a little girl."

Helen stands by the Furoshiki section and unfolds some of them. Each one has a different print of flowers, small and large.

"Would you help me select silk cloths for your family back home?" Chiyo smiles at Helen. "Many parents used to prepare silk kimonos for their young daughters. I think we should all have something silk, even Ken. He's going to be a fine young man who deserves a nice silk cloth."

"Really?" Helen's face brightens with excitement and begins unfolding almost all the cloths on the display counter. Chiyo and Helen start talking about colors, flowers, lines, and shapes in cheerful voices.

When Steve returns from the cashier, he looks at Helen frantically going through one Furoshiki at a time, smiles, and says that they'll never make it to the plane on time now. For a moment, I wish that were true, but unlike with the keychain, Helen makes her decisions rather quickly now.

"This is for Aunt Mary." She pulls out a white silk cloth with a print of purple and blue hydrangeas and light green leaves on the edge.

"And this one is for Mom." A pink silk cloth with the print of cherry blossom petals spread all over. The color of the petals and the background are unified by using different tones of pink.

"This one is for Ken." Helen pulls out a simple blue cloth.

"Ken gets one, too? He's a boy." Steve smiles.

"I know, but he's going to be a fine young man."

At this, we all laugh. While I'm laughing, the bottom of my stomach feels tight; they are going to depart soon.

"And this one," Helen holds a deep red cloth with a print of small white camellias in the corner, "is mine!"

"It's the same red as your hat." Steve takes the hat from his bag and puts it on her head gently.

I follow them to the cashier with the Furoshiki. Everything happens quickly—Chiyo asks the cashier to wrap each cloth, Steve is thanking Chiyo, all the wrapped cloths are put in a bag and handed to Helen. Hearing Helen's laughter, I feel anxious for the upcoming separation. This anticipation—heavy rocks rolling all over my stomach—is familiar to me. Right before good-byes, I always doubt my ability to endure the overwhelming loneliness, thinking maybe this time, I will be washed away by it. Soon, wearing her red hat, her red silk cloth in her hand, Helen will walk away from me to cross the sky again. I think she'll always cherish this silk that was made by the sacrifice of thousands of silkworms, and she'll remember her strength for the task that was given to her long before she was born.

FEBRUARY 1976

Uncle Steve came home with a color TV yesterday. He said he decided to finally be like everyone else and get a new one, even though his old one still works. I'm happy because we'll watch *Wild Kingdom* in color for the first time tonight, and it's much more fun in color. Ken is so excited that he can't sit still on the floor. He pretends to be a guide and shouts, "Look at this snake!" but then he lies flat on the floor and pretends to be like a snake. He even slithers to my foot and pretends to bite my toe like an evil snake, so I tell him that I'll kick his nose if he tries it again. Uncle Steve says he'll turn off the TV if we don't calm down, but I'm calm. Ken's being annoying.

As soon as the show is over, Ken runs to the bathroom to brush his teeth. Lately, he makes everything into a race, like whoever eats dinner first is the winner, or gets to the car first, that sort of thing. But I don't play his game. I don't want him to think that I take him seriously. Aunt Mary pulls my hand to get me up for bed. I go upstairs and see Ken in the bathroom. He smirks at me, and I know he's going to say that he's the winner.

"I win! I'm almost done!" Ken jumps up and down with toothpaste in his mouth.

"Don't talk when you're brushing your teeth! You're so gross."

"Is your bag all packed for school tomorrow?" Ken asks again.

"No."

"I win! Mine is all packed!"

"How about this? Do you know three hundred divided by five?"

"No."

"Sixty. I win!"

"That's not fair. We didn't study stuff like that yet."

"Doesn't matter."

"That doesn't count!"

"Yes it does."

"No it doesn't!" Ken shouts, but I just ignore him and start brushing my teeth.

"When you're done, why don't you two come to our room?" Uncle Steve pops his head in the bathroom. Before he finishes talking, Ken runs into their bedroom.

"I win! I'm here first!"

I just ignore him and keep brushing my teeth. Aunt Mary started this whole race thing when Uncle Steve and I were in Japan. Aunt Mary said Ken wasn't listening to her, so she made everything into a race. Then he wanted to do everything first, even his homework. Aunt Mary thought it was good at first, but now, he's annoying. My gums are starting to burn from the toothpaste, but I keep brushing so that Ken won't think I care about him being first.

When I go to the bedroom, Ken is diving into their bed and pretends that he's swimming with his arms and legs. He's still hyper from watching *Wild Kingdom*. Aunt Mary usually says something when he jumps on the bed, but now she just looks at him. Both Aunt Mary and Uncle Steve are still in their clothes, not ready for bed yet.

"We wanted to tell you something very important." Uncle Steve's deep voice stops Ken from wiggling on the bed. I sit on the bed and Ken sits right by me.

"I saw your dad this afternoon. We had lunch together." The word *dad* makes me straighten my back and sit still. Uncle Steve looks tired.

"He came to tell me that he and your mom are going to be separated for a little while." Uncle Steve's serious face looks at me first and then at Ken.

"Separated?" Ken doesn't get it. Aunt Mary sits near us and rubs our heads, but I don't want to be touched. My chest is in a knot, being pulled in opposite directions.

"It means they're getting divorced, Ken," I say.

"No, they're separated, just for a little while. Just until he gets better."

"Is he sick, too?" Ken asks.

"No, but things are complicated for your dad. He wants to figure out his life."

"What about Mom?" I ask Uncle Steve. Mom always stayed up late and waited for Dad. Now he wasn't coming home at all.

"She also thinks it's best for everyone." Uncle Steve nods. I don't understand why being separated would be best for me or Ken. Someone has to take care of Mom, but if Dad's gone, who's going to take care of her?

"What's going to happen to us now?" I turn to Uncle Steve.

"Your dad wanted us to take care of you, like the way we are now."

"Forever? Are we going to be your kids now?" Ken looks at Uncle Steve and Aunt Mary.

"Until your mom and dad get back together. We'll take care of you, and you can always count on us. We'll always be here for you as long as you need us." Uncle Steve puts his hand on Ken's head.

I look down. I don't know how to look at Uncle Steve. I like Uncle Steve and Aunt Mary, but I always thought Dad was going to come and pick us up because that's what he said he was going to do when he first dropped us off. It's not that I want him to come and get us, but he said he was going to. My face is getting hot.

"And one more thing," Uncle Steve sighs. "Your dad is actually leaving for Vermont tomorrow."

"Where's that?" Ken's eyes get bigger.

"Far away, on the other side of the country. We'll never see him again," I say.

"That's not true," Aunt Mary says, but I don't look at her.

"He's moving there? He's getting a new house? He's not coming back?" Ken's voice gets loud.

"No, no, this is just a temporary arrangement. It's hard to explain, but guess what? Your dad is going to come here tomorrow morning to see you both, so that he can explain. You don't have to go to school tomorrow."

"Why is he going so far away?" Ken mumbles.

"Because Dad wants to run away. He's a loser. I don't want a loser as a dad. I'm glad he's leaving. He hated us anyway. I never ever want to see him again!" I yell at everyone and run to my room. I shut the door, turn off the lights, and get into my bed.

Under the covers, I can't stop crying. Dad's always tired, and I know he doesn't like me. He thinks I made Mom sick. But I'm not home anymore. Why does he have to go so far away? If we go home and Mom puts us in the closet, no one will let us out. My face feels hot and tears keep coming from my eyes. My pillow is all wet, and my nose is running.

"Helen?" Uncle Steve knocks on the door.

I don't answer him.

"Helen, can I come in?" Uncle Steve opens the door a little.

"I don't want to talk," I yell back. I've never yelled at Uncle Steve like this. I stay under the blanket and hide my face. I don't want him to think that I'm sad, because I'm not sad. I'm just angry. Uncle Steve comes in my room anyway and sits on the end of my bed. I rub my nose and eyes against the blanket.

"I'm sorry, Helen."

"Why didn't you take me to see Dad today?" I say from inside my blanket.

"Your dad called from the diner. He said that he wanted me to come alone. He said it was urgent." Uncle Steve's voice sounds muffled from under my blanket. "But I'm sorry."

"I don't want to see Dad tomorrow," I yell. Sometimes, my mouth says something by itself. Tonight, I can't stop yelling. "I'm going to school tomorrow. I'm not going to see Dad."

"O.K.," Uncle Steve pats my head. "I'll take you to school tomorrow. You don't have to see your dad if you don't want to. Now, will you come out of the blanket, Helen?"

"No." My body is like a snail in its shell now. Under the blanket, it's all dark, but Uncle Steve's sad face is in my head. He pats my head again and leaves the room. I want tomorrow to come very soon. *I'm going to school tomorrow, I'm going to school tomorrow.*

The house is so quiet, and my room is dark. I'm still awake. I lie on the bed and stare at the dark ceiling. Rain is hitting the house and making a lot of noise. It's been raining all week, but tonight the rain is coming down especially hard. I get up to get Mom's pink silk and my red silk cloth from the drawer. I wanted to go and see Mom so that I could tell her about my trip to Japan, but Mrs. Hogan said Mom wasn't doing well enough. But I thought that's why I went to Japan, to tell Mom about it so that she could get better. I keep her pink silk cloth in my drawer next to my red one. I open it every night before going to sleep so that I won't forget everything that I have to tell her. Sometimes, I can't believe that I really crossed the ocean, but then I think about Uncle Hideo and Aunt Chiyo. Then I know that I was really there. I get back in my bed and put the silk cloths on my cheeks. Uncle Hideo told me that the rain hitting the roof sounds like thousands of silkworms eating leaves. I close my eyes, hold the silk in my hand and pretend that I'm not here, I'm not Helen, I'm not here at all.

〜

Uncle Steve's already in his truck waiting for me, so I put my coat on, get my schoolbag, and put my red silk cloth in my pocket. Aunt Mary comes after me, and before I go out the door, she holds my face with both of her hands and kisses both of my cheeks. She says she'll come and pick me up after school. I feel bad that I yelled at everyone last night. It's still raining hard outside. I run and jump into Uncle Steve's truck. I can see Ken, still in his pajamas, standing by the window watching me leave.

I don't know what to say to Uncle Steve this morning, so I just look outside the window. He usually has the radio on, but today, all I hear is rain, hitting the roof of the truck. We are driving down the hill, and all the water runs down the street, as if we are driving down a river. The rain is coming down so hard that it's hard to see the road.

"Helen, have you ever gotten scared of your own shadow?" Uncle Steve suddenly says. I look at him.

That's a weird question. I don't usually notice a shadow behind me.

"When the black shadow of your body is under the sun. Have you?"

"No." I shake my head.

"Your dad gets terrified of his own shadow since he returned from the war. He keeps thinking that someone's right behind him." Uncle Steve's face is all serious, holding the wheel, looking straight ahead at the rain hitting the front window. I remember Dad's young face, smiling at the camera in his brown army uniform on his wedding day. That's how he used to smile before I was born, but I have never seen him happy like that.

"I don't blame you for getting angry at your mom and dad. But they're doing all they can, even though it's not good enough." Uncle Steve's voice is quiet, but I feel like he's yelling at me. I look away from Uncle Steve. I don't think Dad is doing all he can.

He didn't keep his promise. I put my hand in my pocket and hold my red silk cloth. I don't say anything to Uncle Steve.

"You'll be with me and Mary for a little longer, and that's O.K., right?" Uncle Steve's voice is soft, but it makes me mad.

"I don't know," I say to the window. "What if you and Aunt Mary get separated, too?" I'm being mean now, but I'm angry at Uncle Steve.

"That'll never happen."

"How do you know?" I turn around and glare at him. "Dad said he'll come and get us. Dad said Mom will get better soon. Everyone keeps saying that I'll see Mom soon. But no one keeps their promises. Maybe you'll take me and Ken to the orphanage next!" I'm yelling now. Uncle Steve's blue eyes look darker, and his face is turning gray. His head is facing the road, with the saddest gaze. My heartbeat is ringing in my head. I want to run away to my room, to hide under the blanket again and never come out. I know that Uncle Steve and Aunt Mary won't be separated. I don't know why I said that. The truck slows down and stops in front of the school. I don't look at Uncle Steve. I'm afraid that his eyes might have tears. I open the door and run out into the rain, all the way to my classroom.

During recess, Sister Margaret comes up to me, and says that Dad is here for me and that he's waiting in the principal's office. I'm so surprised that I just stare at her face. Then I tell her that Uncle Steve said I didn't have to see Dad if I didn't want to.

"Don't be silly, dear. Come along." Sister Margaret quickly turns around and starts walking away from me, but I don't move. When she turns around, she walks quickly back toward me.

"Now!" Her voice is louder. I jump a little and follow her to the office. I feel nervous as I get closer to the principal's office.

Sister Margaret opens the door and lets me through first, then closes it. The principal, Father Patrick, and Dad stand up when they see me. Father Patrick smiles at me and says take your time, and leaves the office with Sister Margaret.

Dad's wearing jeans and a shirt. His face still looks tired, but he smiles a little at me.

"Would you come over here and sit down, Helen?" His voice sounds so familiar in my head. I don't move. I just stand by the door. He sits down where Father Patrick was sitting.

"I know you didn't want to see me today, but I had to see you before I leave for Vermont."

I don't say anything; I just stand by the door. Sister Margaret didn't understand that I didn't have to be here. I can walk away from Dad.

"Helen, I've been in touch with this man that I met in Vietnam. He was in my unit, and he is starting a new business in his hometown. It's a small glass company, and he asked me if I wanted to come and help him for a little while. So that's why I'm going there." Dad is really talking to me.

"But you already work at a bank."

"I quit my job while you were in Japan."

"You did? You mean you don't go to your office anymore?"

"Not since Christmas," Dad says firmly.

"Where do you go every day?"

"I've been home with your mother. I've been taking care of her."

I walk to the chair and sit across from Dad. I look at his face closely. I think he's lying to me.

"Then why are you leaving Mom?" I ask.

"I'm not leaving your mother. I'm just going away to help my friend for a little while, but I'll be back by fall, I promise, Helen."

"You always say you promise, but you don't keep your promises!"

"There isn't a promise that I didn't keep, Helen," Dad says calmly. "I promised that your mother will get better, and she is getting better. I promised that you'll see your mother soon, and you will. I will come and get you and Ken in the fall. That's a promise."

"What if you don't?"

"Haven't I always come home?" Dad looks at me for a long time. He was always late, but he always came home. There was never a day that he didn't come home from work.

"Why are you scared of your shadow?" When I ask him, I see his eyes move from behind his glasses. He has the same sad gaze that Uncle Steve had this morning. I put my hand in my pocket and feel the soft silk in my hand. I pull it out and walk to Dad. I hand it to him, and he looks down at the silk.

"What's this?" He touches it with both hands.

"It's silk."

"Silk . . ."

"Did you know that thousands of silkworms die in hot water when we take silk threads from the cocoons?" I speak fast. I don't know why I'm telling him about silkworms. I get up and walk to the door to go back to the classroom. My face is all hot.

"Helen," Dad calls, holding up my red silk cloth.

"You can have it," I say. I see a shadow right behind Dad. He should keep this silk cloth in his pocket and hold it when he's scared of looking back. He should always look back even though he's scared because then, he would know that it's just his own reflection right behind him. No one is coming to get him.

It's still raining after school. At the entrance door, I am looking for Aunt Mary's car, but instead, Uncle Steve's red truck drives up. I was all ready to see Aunt Mary. I was going to tell her that I was sorry for yelling. But now I see that both Aunt Mary and Uncle Steve are in the truck. The truck slows down and stops in front of the door. I push the heavy door and walk to the truck.

"Get in, quick!" Aunt Mary opens the door with a big smile. I get up in the front seat next to Aunt Mary. My hair and face are a little wet.

"How are you?" Uncle Steve smiles, but looks sad at the same time.

"O.K." I look down. My mouth is a stone today. I can't break it to say I'm sorry.

Uncle Steve starts driving, and Aunt Mary says we have to go back to the dentist to pick up Ken. I nod to everything that Aunt Mary says, but now, my entire body is becoming a stone, so stiff. I don't look at them. I can feel Aunt Mary gazing at me. I want to say I'm sorry, but if I open my mouth, I think I'm going to start crying. In my head, I tell myself to keep looking at the wet road in front of me.

"Did you see your dad at school?" Uncle Steve asks.

I nod, looking straight ahead.

"Are you all right?"

"Yes," I breathe in and out slowly. "I gave him my red silk cloth from Japan."

"The silk that Chiyo bought for you?" Uncle Steve looks surprised, but quickly smiles. "He must have been thrilled."

I shouldn't have opened my mouth. Now my body is all water. My eyes are getting blurry. I blink my eyes so that the tears might go away. If I open my mouth to say I'm sorry or thank you, the stone will turn into a river. I put my fist in my empty pocket and tell myself to keep sitting still like a stone.

MARCH 1976

On Sundays, Aunt Mary makes a big breakfast. When I wake up, I smell the frying eggs, bacon, and pancakes from downstairs. I get up and go downstairs in my pajamas. I can eat breakfast before changing my clothes because it's Sunday. Ken's already at the table cutting his blueberry pancakes. I sit next to him.

"I'm up first!" Ken says, smirking with his blueberry teeth.

"Yes, you are." I let him be the first so that he'll stop his stupid race.

"I'm eating the first pancake!"

"Don't talk when you have food in your mouth."

Uncle Steve is reading the newspaper, but looks up and gives Ken a look. Aunt Mary comes to the table with seven more pancakes and syrup. She puts one on my plate and three on Uncle Steve's, who puts away his paper and dishes eggs onto his plate.

"It'll be a busy busy day today," Aunt Mary says, like she's singing. On Sundays, we all go to the grocery store and have to help carry bags from the store to Aunt Mary's car, and then to the kitchen. I like going to the grocery store.

"Listen, we're making a garden in the backyard of your house in San Francisco next Sunday, so we'll go shopping for all the seeds today," Uncle Steve says, taking more eggs.

"A garden at our house? No one lives there." I stop eating. Dad has moved to Vermont, Mom is living with Mrs. Hogan, and Ken and I are in Tiburon with Uncle Steve and Aunt Mary.

Aunt Mary has a big smile. "We've been talking to Mrs. Hogan, and we came up with the idea of Sunday Gardening."

"What's Sunday Gardening?" Ken's mouth is full of pancakes.

"We'll make a garden next Sunday in your yard. Then we'll go to your house every Sunday to take care of it. Your mom and Mrs. Hogan will join us there. We'll work the garden together every Sunday." Her red hair moves as she turns her head toward me and Ken. Ken stops eating and looks at me. I put down my fork, too.

"You mean we get to see Mom now?" I ask.

"It'll be more like working with her," Uncle Steve says.

"Why are we making a garden with Mom?"

"Do you like flowers, Helen?"

I nod.

"What kind of flowers do you like?"

"Umm . . . hydrangeas." I look at Aunt Mary. I know they are her favorite, too. The hydrangea has so many little flowers that make one big flower.

"How about you?" Uncle Steve turns to Ken.

"Big sunflowers." Ken shrugs his shoulders.

"Do you think your mom likes flowers, too?" Uncle Steve looks at me first and then Ken. Mom used to buy white and pink roses at Polovick's store and put them in a clear vase with cold water.

"I think so," I say.

"Every Sunday, if you and your mom take care of the flowers that you both like, you'll have a wonderful garden by summer." Uncle Steve's blue eyes get big.

I have wanted to see Mom for so long, but now that Uncle Steve and Aunt Mary say that we're really going to see her every Sunday, it's a little scary. I want to see her, but I don't want her to get scared of us again.

"Is she better now? She won't be scared of us?" I ask Uncle Steve.

"I don't know how she'll be each Sunday. She has good days and bad days. But your mom said she wants to see you. I think we just have to be open and patient." Uncle Steve reaches over across the table, takes my hand, and holds it tight for a second.

Uncle Steve's always like that. He won't say that Mom will get better soon, or that it'll be o.k. like Dad used to say. He says it may be good or bad, but we still have to do it. Like going to Japan, we were scared of going there, but he said we had to do it for Mom. Even when I was mad at Dad for leaving us, Uncle Steve said Dad had to go to Vermont. He says if we know what to do even though we don't know why, we still have to do it.

After breakfast, Aunt Mary says we all have to get ready to go to the nursery. Ken takes his plate to the kitchen and runs upstairs because he'll have to be the first one to get into the car. I go to my room and change, too. I stand in front of the mirror and look at my face like the way Mom used to do. I get a little nervous thinking about seeing her. What if her face changes to pale white when she sees me and Ken and she says not to come to her? I open my drawer and see Mom's pink silk cloth. I can finally bring it to her. But then, I won't have a silk cloth anymore because I gave mine to Dad. Mom, Dad, and Ken will all have a cloth but not me. But I guess that's o.k. because I picked them all. I can remember what each one looked like.

At Anderson's Nursery, Ken steps on the bottom of the cart and holds on to the handle, and Uncle Steve pushes him down the aisles. This place is like a grocery store, but I don't know most of the things on the shelves. Aunt Mary is by the fountain outside, looking at birdhouses. Uncle Steve has been loading up the cart—many pots of pansies and marigolds, hydrangeas, and many more flowers, but I don't know their names. He smiles at me and says that we'll work hard next Sunday. I try to smile, too. These flowers are really going to be planted in the backyard of our house. We have never had any flowers in our backyard before. I don't know if they will even grow there.

"What do you think about these?" Aunt Mary says, holding both a wooden and a white birdhouse.

"I think a birdfeeder is better. Birds don't come to look for a house, they come for food. We can put it in the tree." Uncle Steve points at the birdfeeder section outside.

"That's a better idea. I'll go look." Aunt Mary turns to me and signals that I should come with her. I take the wooden birdhouse and follow Aunt Mary. She's excited about this Sunday Gardening. I know it'll be fun planting all these flowers and putting a birdfeeder up in the tree, but the bottom of my stomach is pulling me down.

"Which one do you like?" Aunt Mary asks, taking each bird-feeder from the shelf. She grabs one with a clear cover and yellow edges and asks me if I like it. I nod. She grabs a big bag of birdseed, too, and we walk back to Uncle Steve, who is standing by the cashier.

The cashier lady takes everything from our cart and says each thing out loud—ten tulip bulbs, eleven lilies, four narcissus, thirty pots of pansies, thirty marigolds, five pots of hydrangea flowers, ten packs of seeds, dirt, fertilizer, stones, shovels, watering cans, hoses, wire, sticks, a birdfeeder, and birdseed. Uncle Steve pushes his cart all the way to his red truck that is already half full with his own work tools. He carefully loads everything in his truck. When he's done, the truck is so full that there isn't room for anything else.

～～

The king of wanna-be-first won't get up, so Uncle Steve pulls Ken's blanket off of him.

"Right now. I mean it. Let's go!" Uncle Steve says as he leaves the room. He looks busy getting everything together for our first Sunday Gardening day. But Ken is still curled up in the middle of his bed. I'm all ready. I'm wearing my garden clothes—a T-shirt with a big purple flower on it and dark pants and tennis shoes. Aunt Mary and I picked them out last night. Ken has his garden clothes out, too, but he's pretending that he's asleep. But I know he's scared.

"Come on, I'll race you, Ken." I shake him a little, but he turns the other way.

"Where's your silk?"

"What?" Ken lifts his head.

"The cloth that I gave you." I look around.

"In my top drawer. You told me to keep it there," Ken mumbles, still curling up like a snake. I go to his drawer, but don't see it anywhere.

"I can't find it!" I open every single drawer and find the cloth mixed in with his socks! It's all wrinkly. I fold it into a square shape and put it in the pocket of his pants.

"What are you doing?" Ken slowly gets up.

"I put this in your pocket. If you get scared, put your hand inside your pocket to touch it, O.K.?"

"Why?"

"I don't know. It's for good luck." Having silk is a good thing. I help Ken get dressed. He's moving slow, but I don't yell at him. When he gets scared, his tummy sometime starts hurting.

"Why is it for good luck?" Ken pulls his silk out from his pocket.

"It's made out of silkworms. Thousands of them."

"Worms?" He looks down at the cloth. "Wow!" He puts it back and starts running downstairs, saying that he's the first to get into the truck.

Uncle Steve drives down the hill a little slower today because all the flowers and plants are in the back. Once he takes the entrance to the highway, the ride is smoother. Uncle Steve turns on the radio.

"Oh, Neil Diamond!" Uncle Steve sings along with the radio. Ken giggles because Uncle Steve makes funny faces as he sings. I laugh, too, but my stomach feels weird when I laugh.

"Are you all right?" Aunt Mary asks me.

"My stomach hurts a little."

Aunt Mary touches my forehead and neck with her cool hand. From her wrist, her soft perfume covers my face.

"Steve's singing always makes my stomach upset, too." She winks at me.

Uncle Steve gives Aunt Mary a look, but still smiles.

I put my hand in my pocket and feel the smooth silk. I push my hand all the way into my pocket to hold it. I try not to touch it too often because I don't want it to get wrinkly, but when my heart starts beating fast, I just put my hand in my pocket and look for the smooth silk. Today, I can give it to her. What should I say to her first? What if she doesn't want to see me? Uncle Steve told me that Mom has both good and bad days. What if she's having a bad day today?

His hand reaches out and touches my head, and he says not to worry.

"Uncle Steve! It's Sunday, but you're working today," Ken says with excitement. Uncle Steve's a gardener Monday through Friday. Now he has to work on Sunday, too.

"No," he shakes his head. "Today, I'm a supervisor. I don't get to be a supervisor usually." He smiles.

The truck keeps going, taking us to our house, where we haven't been for months. The truck keeps moving forward, we're carried by it, and there is nothing I can do to stop it.

The truck slows down and takes the exit. Suddenly, the view of the road becomes familiar. Ken stops talking, and we both look around. Uncle Steve takes a left turn and drives up the hill. I am nervous. I hold the silk in my pocket. We pass Polovick's store.

"That's the grocery store!" Ken yells. We keep going, passing Joan's Bakery, Green Village Park, a hill, the big trees by the post office, and I'm out of breath. I have to catch up with the truck moving toward our house, which is slowly coming closer to me.

Ken puts his head outside the window. We drive up to our house and stop. I'm holding the silk cloth tight in my pocket. The house looks just the same, white and plain. The mailbox still has our name, "Johnson." No one moves for a moment.

Uncle Steve is the first one to open the door. I tell myself to move and get out of the truck, but my arms are heavy. We all walk to the back of the truck, and Uncle Steve begins unloading everything. Aunt Mary and Ken take some flowers and start walking toward the back of the house. My stomach feels weird again, but I keep moving. Once I stop, I worry I won't be able to start. Uncle Steve gives me a pot of hydrangeas, and I pull my hand out of my pocket. The silk in my hand is all wrinkled because I was holding it so tight. I put it back into my pocket again.

"Are you O.K.?" Uncle Steve looks into my face. I nod and tell him that I'm just nervous. Instead of giving me another pot of hydrangeas, he takes my empty hand, and walks with me to the back of the house.

Ken and Aunt Mary are walking ahead of us. The backyard looks much smaller than I remember. In the corner, Mrs. Hogan stands next to Mom, who is wearing a straw hat. My heart jumps when I see her pale face under the hat. I keep my eyes open to see her and tell myself *I'm seeing Mom right now.* The hydrangea touches my chin as I walk on the bumpy part of the yard. Uncle Steve's hand has wrapped around my entire hand and keeps pulling and pulling. Mom's eyes open wide for a moment, and I think she's scared of me. But she doesn't scream or step back. Like the way she used to stand in front of the mirror, her eyes are fixed on me. Uncle Steve keeps walking forward, so I get closer and closer to her dark eyes until I stop right in front of her, and there's nothing between us except for small tears in her eyes and the hydrangeas tickling my chin.

All morning, we work hard on different tasks. Uncle Steve plants marigolds by the back door and hydrangeas by the fence.

Mom and Aunt Mary plant the pansies in large wooden pots. Mrs. Hogan and I are putting tulip bulbs in the flower bed in the backyard. Ken's with me, but he isn't really working; he's just playing with worms.

I watch Mom from a distance as I plant the tulip bulbs. Her pale face and long black hair make her look like the dancer Shizuka. Her skinny fingers slowly pull each pansy out from the black pot and place it in the wooden pots. Once in a while, she nods and even smiles a little at Aunt Mary. They're talking about something. I haven't really said anything to Mom yet. When I first saw her this morning, she asked me if I was well and I just nodded. Then she looked at Ken and asked the same question. Ken mumbled something. We both stood and stared at her. I completely forgot about the pink silk cloth in my pocket. I want to go and give it to her.

Uncle Steve says that it's time to take a lunch break. Aunt Mary made sandwiches this morning before we left. He says to finish up what we are doing and go inside the house.

"Worm spaghetti for lunch!" Ken holds lots of worms with both hands.

Uncle Steve smiles. "Don't leave them on the ground, Ken. They'll dry out and die." But Ken just stands there, playing with the worms. Uncle Steve tells me to take Ken in the house and help him wash his hands.

"Put the worms away," I say to Ken.

He holds one up. "Did you know that worms are see-through in the light?"

I walk closer and look at the worm. Worms look dark brown on the ground, but under the light, it looks as though it were made out of brown water.

"What's inside a worm?" Ken asks.

"That must be his stomach." I point at a line inside its body. "Put it away. You have to wash your hands."

Ken isn't really listening to me. He holds up each worm in the light with his fingers, watching it move up and down. They must be hot under the sun. I get down and grab a shovel to make a small hole.

"Put them in the hole," I tell Ken.

"But I found them."

"Just do it!" I grab his hand. He gives me a stupid look and puts the worms in the hole. I know they like cool dark places under the ground. In the sun, the brown water inside their thin skin will be burned away, and they'll be just skin. I've seen many worms' skins on the road in summer. Ken's so mean sometimes.

We walk to the house. The inside looks both familiar and new. The house is clean and open, but it feels smaller. Ken walks around and I follow him. The smell of the house—the smell of the wall, the old dusty smell, covers my nose.

Aunt Mary is putting sandwiches and chips on the table in the dining room. I forgot how empty and white our house was. The walls at Uncle Steve's house have all kinds of colors, like yellow and green, but our house looks so plain. I follow Ken to the bathroom. Mom's standing in front of the sink, washing her hands. Ken and I look at each other. His eyes get narrow like he's a little scared. I know he wants to run downstairs, but I hold his dirty hand and we stand behind Mom. Then Ken steps back and stands right behind me.

"Hello," Mom looks back and says in a small voice, then steps aside and lets us get to the sink.

"Wash your hands, Ken." I turn on the water for him and give him a bar of soap. Ken glances at Mom and starts washing his hands. We can smell the soap. Mom doesn't leave. She watches Ken's bubbly hands as she holds her towel to her chest. I hope she's not getting upset or scared. When Ken finishes washing his hands, Mom wraps his hands with the towel. He looks down at the floor, suddenly shy. He dries his hands forever, not knowing what to do next.

"You can go downstairs," I tell Ken. He runs to the dining room. Mom's still standing by the sink; she turns the water on for me. She doesn't look sad or happy. I wash my hands with cold water.

"Steve told me that you went to Japan to visit my uncle," Mom says. I have wanted to tell her everything about my visit to Japan all morning, but I have no idea where to start. I don't know which story will cure her from getting nervous all the time.

"What was he like?" she asks.

"Uncle Hideo was really nice." I turn off the water and think about more to say about Uncle Hideo. He wasn't just nice. He had so many stories to tell. Mom wraps my hands with the towel as she did for Ken. Her fingers are long and bony.

"He said you were a tiny baby," I say, drying my hands. Mom's eyes are fixed on me now.

I pull out my pink silk cloth from my pocket and hand it to her. "This is for you from Aunt Chiyo. I picked the color." Mom feels the cloth with her fingers.

"Isn't it soft? It's silk." I get closer to Mom. "Did you know that Grandma Ume's family used to make silk?"

"No." Her eyes are now fixed on the cloth.

"Did you know that silk comes from silkworms?"

"No."

"I gave a red one to Dad."

"You did?" Mom's face brightens a little, and she holds it up and looks at the pretty cherry blossom petals all over the cloth.

"And Shizuka isn't a ghost. She's a dancer." I want Mom to know that her Japanese name isn't the ghost's name.

"Yes, I know."

"You do? But you said Shizuka was a ghost because she drowned in the ocean."

She touches my cheek lightly. "I'm sorry that ghost Shizuka was scary to you. She isn't scary to me. When I was at the Christian Home for Children, a very kind English teacher told me the tale of Shizuka. Back then, I didn't know that he was my uncle and I felt so special that he told me the story about my name. In the story, he said, there was a myth that Shizuka walked to the ocean one day and never returned. I didn't understand the story then, but now I know that she drowned herself because her child was thrown into the ocean."

Mom holds my hand and takes me to her bedroom. My chest suddenly gets tight. I'm afraid that she is going to put me into her closet again. She's waiting for me by her door. If Mom wants me to go into the closet, I know I'll have to go. But she doesn't put me into the closet. She goes to her drawer and takes out a piece of paper, a poster. There's an Asian man with a sword, and a woman with strange makeup. Her eyebrows are very black and short in the middle of her white face. Her eyes are large and black, looking up at the man. She's grabbing the man's sleeve, and she looks like she's going to start screaming. It says *Rashomon* on the top of the poster.

"I found this movie poster when I was in college. Your dad and I went to see it many times. I thought this must be what Shizuka looks like." Mom points at the scary woman's face. She's wearing a pink kimono, and her face is all white. "The poster was up at the used bookstore where I used to work, and the owner said the poster wasn't for sale, but I begged him." Mom starts taking out two more posters and a book. The first one is a picture of an Asian man. "This man is Yukio Mishima. He is a Japanese writer. He wrote this book." Mom opens an old brown book. "And I think this is a Japanese ship. I used to collect Japanese things." Mom points at the other poster, the picture of a ship, and a flag.

"Shizuka doesn't look like this at all," I say. "I saw her picture in Japan. She danced on the big stage inside the empty house. I went to see it. Uncle Hideo said Shizuka was a brave dancer. He said Grandma Ume wanted you to cry when you are sad. That's why she picked Shizuka for your name." I try to repeat what Uncle Hideo wanted me to tell Mom, but I don't make sense. Mom's hands start to shake a little, and I wish I hadn't said anything. Her pink silk cloth is shaking in her fist, and her cheeks are turning red. She sits on her bed, looking down at her fists. She breathes in and out slowly like she's holding her anger. I don't know what to do. I don't want her to break apart. But Mom holds up the wrinkled silk cloth that looks whiter in the light, leans her head back, facing the ceiling, and places the silk cloth on her face. She sits like that for a while.

"Mom?"

She doesn't say anything. Her face is still covered, and the middle part of the cloth moves up and down as she breathes. I don't know what's happening to her.

"Mom? What're you doing?" I want to run downstairs to go get Uncle Steve.

Mom takes the cloth away from her face, folds it neatly, and puts it in her pocket. She looks at me. My heart beats fast seeing her eyes so close. Aunt Mary calls our names from downstairs.

"We better go now." Mom slowly stands up. Her skinny body walks down the stairs, and I follow her. I see a corner of the pink silk sticking out of her pocket.

LETTER

March 14, 1976

Dear Helen and Steve,

Spring is finally arriving in Kamakura. Looking at our cherry tree that will bloom soon, I imagine how our yard will be covered by pink petals, like the silk cloth you brought back for Anna.

I greatly appreciate your letter sharing news of your family and the photographs. Chiyo and I think Helen has grown taller since we saw her in January. Chiyo said to me, "Every bone must be growing inside Helen's body!" You must think we are strange to say such a thing, but for elderly people like us, even a simple and obvious sight of a young girl's growth is surprising. We placed the picture of you and your wife embracing Helen and Ken on the table in our living room. We could almost hear your laughter from the picture.

Thank you for sharing James's progress with us. Steve, there is something to be said about friendship among the veterans, as you said in your letter. Strangely, when I heard about James's work cutting glasses at his friend's small company, out in the country in Vermont, it gave me a solid sense of joy. As for Anna, she is quite brave to be home alone. You mentioned that Mrs. Hogan is nearby, which makes me feel at ease. I understand that at some point, she would have to get back to her life.

Years ago, Ume wished that Anna would forget her mother as soon as possible, and I believed that she truly wished this until she was close to her death. She said that she wasn't afraid, but I think her fear grew as her death became more real and closer to her. She asked me to hold her hand and watch her all night in case she fell asleep. Ume always had my promise to always remember her as the mother of a small baby. But now, Helen will grow up with the memory of Ume, and I hope that this is ultimately what Ume wanted after all.

Chiyo is playing her double bass right now, and the entire house is vibrating as I write this letter. I wish I could enclose Chiyo's music inside this envelope, but for now, you can hear the dark sound of double bass from the smeared ink in this letter.

Perhaps someday, we will have a chance to share this music with you in person. We hope so. Until then, please take care of yourself and your family.

Sincerely,

Hideo Takagawa

APRIL 1976

Since Uncle Steve found scary weeds called nutsedge in the backyard this morning, he's trying to get rid of them. Uncle Steve said that nutsedge has strong roots, and a part of the roots always stays under the ground and grows back even if we pull it. They don't die even after putting poison on them. I'm pulling dandelions, and it's mean work. I have to use a big fork-looking tool to dig them out. Uncle Steve calls me Weed Queen, but I think a queen has many maids that do all the work for her. Once we clean up this space, we're going to make it into a summer tomato garden. Ken's digging dandelions with me, but he's also finding worms and putting them into a pile. Uncle Steve tells him to go and plant sunflower seeds with Mrs. Hogan instead.

Our Sunday Garden has many flowers planted now. Some of the tulips are ready to bloom. We put pansies along the brick sidewalk that we made last week. We made five flower beds last month, and we are making more today. Uncle Steve wasn't kidding when he said he was going to be a supervisor. He tells everyone where to go, what to dig, and how to plant flowers. He's a very good supervisor because he never gets mad at anyone. My favorite white hydrangeas are growing by the fence. I notice that the stem of the hydrangea has extra work because one stem has to hold many small flowers.

Mom's standing on a chair, placing the yellow birdfeeder up in the tree. She always wears the pink silk cloth around her head for Sunday Gardening. I want to tell Mom that in Japan, the silk cloth is for wrapping a present, not a head, but I'm so excited to see her with the cloth that I don't say anything to her. Aunt Mary tells Mom to place the birdfeeder more to the right. She almost dropped the birdfeeder once, but she hung on to the metal string, and it didn't fall.

Ken comes running to Uncle Steve with sunflower seeds in his hands.

"We have extra seeds. Can we plant them somewhere else?"

Uncle Steve looks around and points at the empty flower bed by the window where he and I cleared the weeds this morning.

"Is this sunflower going to be tall?" Ken asks.

"Very tall."

"How tall is it going to be?"

"You see your mom standing on the chair there?" Uncle Steve points at Mom. "The sunflower will grow above your mom's head." I imagine thick stems growing by Mom on the chair and big sunflowers blooming just above her head, smiling with yellow teeth by the birdfeeder.

"That's tall," Ken says, looking up.

"That's really tall," I say in amazement.

Ken and I go by the window. We make small holes in the ground and put a couple seeds into each hole and cover them with dirt.

"Please grow soon," Ken says to the sunflower garden. Then he sits down on the grass, still looking at the garden seriously. I sit next to Ken. The grass feels warm on my legs.

"I want the sunflowers to grow now." He touches his face with his dirty hand, getting his nose muddy.

"We just planted the seeds."

"When is it going to have flowers?" Ken looks at me.

"Not till summer."

Ken gets up and goes to Uncle Steve. He comes back with the full watering can, dragging it. I help him. It's heavy. We lift the can as high as we can to water the sunflower seeds, making a small rainstorm over the garden. We walk around the edge of the garden to make sure that all the seeds have been watered.

"There! The sunflowers will grow faster. It'll be like a jungle soon!" Ken jumps around like a monkey living in the jungle that he saw on *Wild Kingdom*, but I don't think it'll be like a jungle. It's going to be more like a small forest of flowers, all colorful.

Mom's still standing on the chair, tying the birdfeeder to the branch. Her face looks dead serious. It's fun to have a bird restaurant up on the tree! There'll be so many birds that will come and go this summer, and I want to count each one of them. My head is going to be full of birds! I imagine Mom walking through all the colorful flowers in our garden to go and fill the seeds of the birdfeeder. And I will water our garden so that Mom will always have many many flowers around her.

ACKNOWLEDGMENTS

The following works were invaluable
in the writing of this book:

The Least of These: Miki Sawada and Her Children by Elizabeth Anne Hemphill (Weatherhill, 1980); *Hidden Horrors: Japanese War Crimes in World War II* by Yuki Tanaka (Westview Press, 1996); *Masan Jiken—the Incident of Masan* by Yukiko Nakamura (Soushi-sha, 1983); *Boku no Manshu-My Manchuria* (Aki Shobo, 1995); *Wasure-rareta Onnatachi—Forgotten Women* by Kazuyoshi Nishizawa, Ed. Nakazima Tami and NHK (Nihon Housou Shuppan Kyo-kai, 1990); *Kodomotachi wa Nanatsu no Umi wo Koeta: Elizabeth Sanders Home—Children Crossed the Seven Ocean: Elizabeth Sanders Home* by Kazuhiro Ikeda (Nippon Telebi, 1981); "Disappeared Sisters in the Field of Manchuria" in *Asahi Shinbun's* "Voice—the series of historical memories" (Asahi Shinbun, Oct. 22, 2003); Documentary Program, *Kodomotachi wa Nanatsu no Umi wo Koeta: Elizabeth Sanders Home—Children Crossed the Seven Ocean: Sanders Home's 1600 Children* (Nippon Telebi, 1978); Documentary Program, *Kodomotachi wa Nanatsu no Umi wo Koeta: Elizabeth Sanders Home—Children Crossed the Seven Ocean: The record of Sanders Home's Mothers and Children* (Nippon Telebi, 1978); Documentary Program, *Wasurerareta Onnatachi—Forgotten Women* (NHK, 1990); Documentary Program, *Manshu ni Kieta Nihon-jin: Disappeared Japanese in Manchuria* (Nagoya Terebi Housou, Oct. 29, 1978); *Tsuruoka Hachimangu; The Record of Showa: The Dream to the Conquest of the Continent of Asia, Vol. 4* by Katsumasa Harada (Shuei-sha, 1980); *The Record of Showa: The Era of Occupation, Vol. 9* by Rinjirou Sodei (Shuei-sha, 1980); *Genpei Souran-Ki no Josei* by Fumiko Enchi (Shuei-sha, 1977); "War Stress and Trauma: The Vietnam Veteran Experience" by Robert S. Laufer from *Journal of Health and Social Behavior* (Mar. 1984), *Maboroshikoku-Manshu, Photo essays* by Tsuneo Enari (Shinshou-sha, Tokyo 1995).

A special thank you to Broadcast Library: The Broadcast Programming Center of Japan in Yokohama-shi. Thank you to Fan Shen for translating Chinese. To Tony Wenzel and Steve Wenzel for sharing their memories. I am especially grateful for Chuck Cosgrove for sharing his experiences and photographs from his time in Vietnam.

⌒

The poem by Sappho is from *Sappho*, tran. Mary Barnard (University of California Press, 1986).

The Japanese Tanka poem for Nagi tree is from *Chusei Waka-shu Kamakyra-hen* (Iwanami Press).

⌒

Thank you to Chris Fischbach, Allan Kornblum, Molly Mikolowski, Lauren Snyder, Linda Koutsky at Coffee House Press. Also to Sister Mara Faulkner and Jim Moore, Julie Schumacher, Virginia Wright-Peterson, Gretchen Potter, Sandy and Paul Schaumleffel, and Sara Crowe. A very special thank you to Jennifer Ramp for her talent and generosity. I am indebted to Peter Wenzel for his deepest and most enduring support.

COLOPHON

The Ocean in the Closet was designed at Coffee House Press, in
the historic warehouse district of downtown Minneapolis.
Fonts include Village and Viva.

FUNDER ACKNOWLEDGMENTS

Coffee House Press is an independent nonprofit literary publisher. Our
books are made possible through the generous support of grants and
gifts from many foundations, corporate giving programs, individuals,
and through state and federal support. This book has received special
project support from the Jerome Foundation. Coffee House Press
receives general operating support from the Minnesota State Arts Board,
through an appropriation by the Minnesota State Legislature and from
the National Endowment for the Arts, a federal agency, and major general operating support from the McKnight Foundation, and from the
Target Foundation. Coffee House also receives support from: an anony-
mous donor; the Elmer and Eleanor Andersen Foundation; the Buuck
Family Foundation; the Patrick and Aimee Butler Family Foundation;
Gary Fink; Stephen and Isabel Keating; Seymour Kornblum and Gerry
Lauter; Allan and Cinda Kornblum; Kathryn and Dean Koutsky; the
Lenfesty Family Foundation; Rebecca Rand; the law firm of
Schwegman, Lundberg, Woessner & Kluth, P.A.; the James R. Thorpe
Foundation; the Archie D. and Bertha H. Walker Foundation; the
Woessner Freeman Foundation; the Wood-Rill Foundation; and many
other generous individual donors.

*This activity is made possible
in part by a grant from the
Minnesota State Arts Board,
through an appropriation by the
Minnesota State Legislature
and a grant from the National
Endowment for the Arts.*

To you and our many readers across the country,
we send our thanks for your continuing support.

Good books are brewing at coffeehousepress.org